DAY BEGINS AT DAWN

THE DRAYMAN'S DAUGHTER

"Rise before Dawn" Psalm 119 v147

By

GWENYTH CLARE LYNES

BPH

The Blackcurrant
Publishing House

Front Cover Photograph is of the Author's Great Grandfather and Grandfather
Back Cover Photograph is the wildflower meadow, Clumber Park, Nottinghamshire

This book is published by
The Blackcurrant Publishing House
Suffolk, England

B
PH

All Scripture quotations are taken from the Holy Bible, King James Authorised Version.

ISBN 978-1-0369-0276-6

The Newton Westerby Chronicles

***

Because of You
Out of my Depth
Broken and Lost
Barbados Joy

***

A Godly Heritage – Love Letters 1939-1943
Collated by Gwenyth Clare Lynes
(Written by her father A.D. Butler to her mother)

ACKNOWLEDGEMENTS

This book has taken a long while to come to fruition. The setting and some incidents emerged from research my husband, Trevor, and I undertook in relation to family history of the era covered in Day Begins at Dawn. Over the years we received assistance from numerous people in record offices throughout East Anglia for which I am grateful.

Once again my heartfelt thanks to Jon for thoroughly checking the manuscript, to Andi for technical help and to Isabelle and Oliver for cover design and meticulous I.T. input.

The encouragement and support of my writing friends at the Pen to Paper group has proved invaluable.

My very grateful thanks to you all for making the publication of Day Begins at Dawn possible.

DEDICATION

Day Begins at Dawn tells the story of happenings in the lives of the ancestors of some of the Newton Westerby families during the mid nineteenth century and is the first novel in the Newton Westerby Historical series.

Events recorded in the author's family history are reflected in incidents in the lives of Newton Westerby residents. "Why should such interesting occurrences remain hidden in archives and record offices?"

In Memory of my Great Grandparents
Daniel and Sarah Templeman
And
Joseph and Rebekah Carr

Also

My Husband's Forebears
James Housego and Mary Ann Clarke
And
Francis and Ann Todd

Giving thanks to God for their faith and fortitude
which sustained them through difficult and changing times.

GLOSSARY

Inspired by the bustling anchorage of Newtown mentioned in Gillingwater's Mediaeval History of East Anglia, Newtown-West-by-the-Sea, referred to colloquially as Newton Westerby, has been placed somewhere south of the Norfolk/Suffolk coastal border. Once two communities divided by a river the majority of this fishing port has long disappeared so only exists in the imagination of the author and reader. The local inhabitants speak with a Suffolk/Norfolk accent and tend to use double negatives i.e. woan't be no more/ not no more.

They also pronounce some 'ing' endings as en, i.e. keepen, comen etc and leave off d's i.e. an' for and.

Frequently an 'a' is added to words i.e. a'sayen.

T's are left out in speech – more a guttural sound i.e. in'erestin', boo'iful.

'Be' is the commonly used form of the verb 'to be', regardless of tense – i.e. she be a'comen; thass be cold.

Ow/ou pronounced ew i.e. you-yew, snow-snew, show-shew while do sounds like too.

O pronounced oo i.e. so-soo, go-goo no-noo.

A'cide - decide
Acrorst – across
Afeard/afrit – afraid
Afore - before
Agin – again
Aloan – alone
Allus – always
Arter/arternoon – after/afternoon
Bin – been
Bor – boy
Brung - brought

Doan’t – don’t
E/ee - it/him/he/her/them
Fer/fergit – for/forgot/ forgotten
Foine - fine
Frackus – noisy disturbance
Gal – girl
Geart - gate
Git/gits – get/gets
Gorn - gone
Hev/ha’nt – have/haven’t/hasn’t
Hin - hen
Hum/hus – home/house
Hoss – horse
Hurrit - hurry
Int/ent – isn’t/ haven’t
Juss – just
Larn – learn
Loike - like
Lorst – lost
M’/ma/ moine – my/mine
Maak - make
Mardle/mardling – to chat/chatting/gossip
Moite – might
Muss /mussn’t- must/must not
Nivver – never
Noicely - oi/she/he be doin’ noicely – well/I am well/she/he is well
Noite – night
Nuthen - nothing
Oi/oi’ll/oi’m – I/I’ll/I’m
Ole/owd – old
Orf - off

Ow’n – our
Riddy - ready
Roite – right
Rud – road
Sel’ – self
Sooner/yew ole sooner – cadger/you old cadger
Squit – nonsense
Sup - drink
Suthen – something
Taters - potatoes
Thass – that
Uns - ones
Uvver – over
Wass – what
Woan’t – won’t/ will not
Worrit – worry
Wuz – was
Yew - you
Yow’n/yourn – your/yours
Yus/yup - yes

THE FARMER'S DAY

Home in the twilight they were walking,
Too tired for anything, not even talking.
Trudging up the pathway dreary,
They were tired and faint and weary.

Up early morning all in a hurry,
Bustling about, all flustered and flurry.
But soon they are ready and off they go,
Leaving the women to knead the dough.

One works the horses, and one tills the soil,
And one mends the fences for his daily toil.
The others between them mind the farm,
And see the animals come to no harm.

And when the night begins to fall
They hear the shepherd dog's rounding call.
So, they leave their work, steps homeward bound,
Knowing with God all is safe and sound.

Gwenyth Clare Lynes (nee Butler) 1959

CHAPTER ONE

"Home in the twilight they were walking..."

Plum stones pelted down through the air as a gentle breeze rustled leaves on the branches of fruit trees in the orchard.

"Moine's furthest," a girlish voice yelled triumphantly.

"Noo, oi won! oi won!" Caleb's exuberance shook the branch on which he was sitting with his sister. Two pairs of feet dangled precariously from one of the limbs of a tree that was laden with ripened plums as both children clung to overhanging branches to keep their balance. Caleb wobbled. Peggy's long, mousey hair fell across her face as an arm shot out to steady her wriggling brother. She automatically flicked back the straggly strands as she shuffled cautiously to gain a more secure position. Beneath them the setting sun of an early autumn evening cast dancing patterns through the branches onto the well-trodden path. Every so often well aimed plum stones pitted the earth as they joined in the dance of the game that was being played, each child trying to outdo the other in the distance they could spit out the stones. Muffled giggles interspersed the pitter-patter of the falling stones as they hit the ground.

"This be roite merry!"

The thud of plodding footsteps caught Peggy's ear.

"Shh! Someone be a'comen," she attempted to caution

her younger brother but with a mouth full of plum her muffled speech became a spluttered ejaculation, the plum kernels spurting out in front of her. Caleb shifted position the better to see who was approaching, then tossed his head disdainfully, "It only be Stan an' Fred."

"Doan't let them see us."

"Let's hev some fun. Here git some ammunition riddy." Caleb reached out to pull more of the luscious fruits from the tree. Eagerly he passed them to Peggy.

"Shh, then, or yew'll give us away." She bit into the juicy flesh, sticky little trickles meandering down her arm.

They held their breath as their older brothers came closer, stones at the ready in swollen cheeks. Unsuspecting, young Fred trudged wearily by the side of his elder brother, Stan, glad the day's work was done. Tussled heads hanging down and ingrained hands thrust into their pockets walking home in the twilight brought a satisfactory end to a good day's work. Neither was in the mood for talking. Both were in their own little world. Stan's thoughts were on his rumbling stomach. He hoped Ma would have prepared something for supper that would fill the aching gap that had gnawed inside him since his frugal dinner, but Fred's mind was on the horses.

He loved working with the horses from gentle Bessie to fiery Champion. Taking the burrs out of their manes and brushing their coats till they shone gave him such pleasure. His face lit up as he recalled the way they nuzzled his hands when he replenished their mangers with fodder and neighed as he greeted them first thing in the morning. He didn't even mind the smell when he was mucking out. *Hope I can work wi' them fer allus, loike Mister George.* George Kemp was the Squire's drayman and equine factotum and because of his natural skill at handling horses the late squire had appointed him head groom in charge of the stables. In recognition of his expertise Lord Ralph, the current squire, retained George in that position. George's great love was the Suffolk Punches and when he saw that Fred also had a genuine fondness for the large working horses offered him a job in the stables. But Fred's father wanted the boy to stay on at school.

Jeremiah regretted the decision to make his eldest son, Stan, work on the land, as soon as he was physically able to, yet remained unable to adequately read or write. He didn't want to make the same mistake with Fred, for he was a bright lad, already a fluent reader and gaining mastery over numbers and their associated problems. However, he had not reckoned on his wife's objection.

"Yew hold yow'n noise, Jeremiah Bemment. The bor be got all the larnin' he needs," declared Hester whose word was law in the home. "Yew'll larn more from doin', m'bor, than sittin' an' lis'nen', an' yew'll earn suthen fer yow'n keep," Hester told Fred.

Jeremiah knew when he was beaten. It was his job to provide for his family, Hester's to care for the children and organize the home. So, he went out in all weathers and did battle with the sea to bring in fish to be sold to pay the rent and put food on the table.

Hester's decision pleased Fred. Horses were all he cared about, apart from Annie, the drayman's daughter.

"One day oi'm a'goin' to git wed wi' Annie. She be my best friend an' the prettiest gal in all the world."

"Thass not loikely m'bor so's don't ye be settin' yow'n heart on ee," said Ma.

"We'll juss see," he replied sagely to Ma. For all his

twelve years he knew his own mind and heart. Despite what Ma said Fred was convinced that one day he and Annie would get married. As his best friend they regularly spent time together, especially as she lived so close to where he worked every day. Annie was fun but not silly and giggly like other girls and far more sensible than lads of his own age. He liked spending time with her more than anyone else he knew. She understood his empathy with the horses. Frequently he caught her watching him from the steps of her home as he washed down the horses in the stable yard, brushed their coats or trotted them to where they were needed for work across the estate. He was glad Annie never spoke or moved in such a way that would startle the horses. Her interest in nature and care for animals was something he shared. He also admired the way she applied herself to learning tasks about the home that Mrs Kemp was teaching Annie alongside his sister Peggy. Already, Fred had decided to give a farthing of his wages to Ma and save the other one till he had sufficient put by to pay the rent for a cottage, even if it took ten years. Then he would marry her.

As Stan and Fred drew closer to their hidden siblings, Peggy and Caleb prepared for the surprise attack. They had quickly picked and eaten as many plums as they could to satisfy their hunger. Now they gobbled sufficient to use as ammunition holding the inner kernels in their mouths ready to fire on their unsuspecting victims. Peggy looked so comical with both cheeks bulging that Caleb could not refrain from chortling. He lost control and his entire collection spewed out of his mouth and rained down on his brothers as they walked beneath their lofty position. Exasperated that his action had spoilt the prank they had planned Peggy opened her mouth to admonish him and, as a consequence, spurted her hoard all over Fred. Shaken so abruptly from their dream world Stan and Fred looked up in astonishment.

"Ouch! Pesky gulls!" Fred wiped the debris from the thick, wavy brown hair that covered his head. Stan ran a sleeve across the locks that hung across his forehead to clear away the sticky mess that clung to them.

"Nah! More like two-legged rascals." He had spotted the dangling feet as he glanced up. He reached out and tugged at an unshod foot. Peggy squealed as she was dislodged from her perch.

"Shh! Peggy," Caleb called out in an exaggerated whisper, a second too late, as Peggy sailed through the air into her big brother's arms snagging her skirts on a protruding twig. Her heart sank for she knew the resultant rip would gain her a resounding telling-off from Ma and a tedious evening learning to rectify the repair. Darning was not her favourite occupation.

"Aarrh! Now, what shall we do wi' two-legged varmints?" Stan teased as Peggy squirmed from his hold onto the ground before darting swift-footedly towards the row of cottages, where they lived, laughter following her footsteps.

Pretending not to know Caleb was still up in the tree Stan walked away saying to Fred in a loud voice, "We muss a'cide what punishment to give when we catch up wi' ow'n attacker."

"Go wi'out supper. We could hev their'n."

"Good idea, bor, 'cos oi be a'starven'."

Caleb's forehead wrinkled in a scowling frown at the thought of being abandoned up in the tree and left with nothing to eat.

"Stan! Stan, doan't leave me!" The momentum of his shriek knocked him off balance and he hurtled down from the branch. Stan turned immediately and automatically reached out his arms. His quick thinking broke Caleb's fall. When his brother squealed Stan recognized that the little boy was more frightened than hurt so gave him a quick hug then hoisted him onto his broad shoulders to carry him the rest of the way home.

“Yew woan’t really eat ma supper, will yew Stan, 'cos oi be roite hungry.”

"We...ell! Pranksters hev to be punished, yew know. What did yew hev fer dinner?"

"Nuthen, Ma be asleep, thass why we wuz eatin' plums."

"Asleep?"

"Yus!"

Stan's heart dropped like lead to his boots. Abruptly he swung Caleb to the ground.

"Race yew hum, bor. C'mon, Fred, race yew, too."

The boys ran as fast as their weary limbs would allow them and burst through the cottage door.

"Ma! Ma! Ma!" they yelled in unison. Stan's eyes swiftly appraised the scene before him. Anger surged up within him and involuntarily his fist clenched. He banged it hard against the bare kitchen table.

"No! Noo! Nooo!" he shouted in anguish. He stepped towards the dying embers of the fire and bent to lift a loose flagstone in the hearth. He drew out the leather pouch that nestled there. There was no need to look inside. His fingers could feel its emptiness. His ears could not hear the chink of coins that it should have held.

"Why, Ma, why?" Stan shouted at the prostrated figure sprawled in an unseemly manner across their late father's wooden armchair in a drunken stupor.

"Why be Ma still asleep?" Caleb asked in a bewildered tone.

Stan pretended not to have heard but turned hurriedly and pounded out of the cottage bumping into Peggy as she carried in a jug of water from the pump.

“What be yew a’doin’?” he demanded.

“Fillin’ the stew pot wi’ water,” her voice quivered at his fierceness.

"What fer?"

"Supper."

"What be there to goo in it?"

"Doan't know," she stammered tearfully, alarmed by Stan's ill temper. Stan never raised his voice, and his irate crossness frightened her.

Stan stomped back across the room and flung open the triangular-shaped door which opened onto a cupboard under the stairs which their mother grandly referred to as the pantry.

"Look! C'mon, Peggy, get closer an' look. What food do yew see?" he demanded.

Seeing his sister's tears Fred rushed alongside Peggy. Side by side they peered through the gloomy space at the barren shelves.

"Nuthen," they said in unison.

"Roite!" he barked. Stan slammed the door shut. An exasperated sigh escaped his lips.

"Doan't yew worrit, Peggs. Yew put the water on, an' oi’ll git us suthen to goo wi' it," Fred said confidently. "Maybe oi'll find a thrown away fish head down on the beach by the sheds an' yew can maak some soup."

Stan, more aware of the gravity of the situation than his

siblings, knew that their mother's actions had left them without a farthing; no money for food to eat or coal for heat; not a penny for rent; nothing left for candles or oil for light or thread to mend clothes for their backs. She had blown his hard-earned wages on a whole jugful of liquor for one brief moment of solace. Annoyed for allowing his own fears to scare his siblings Stan bent to riddle the embers in the grate, to revive the dying coals, to bring warmth into the chilly room as the cool evening air drew in. The scuttle set by the fireplace was empty save for a handful of sticks and one small piece of coal. In exasperation he shouted, "Where, oh where, be Beatie when we need her!"

"Yew know she be scullery maid up at the Manor Hus."

"O' course oi know 'cos oi walked her up to the Big Hus but she oughter be here helpin' us out," he snapped.

"She be best where she be. At least she'll get fed. We'll manage, Stan, juss yew see."

"Oi'm not soo sure," Stan stalked off to vent his feelings on the landlord of The Rising Sun for supplying his Ma with liquor paid for with money intended to keep the family from starving and a roof over their heads.

Fred, although a little more than six years his junior, kept a calm head, and soon followed Stan out of the door. With a hand on the knob he called back to his sister, "Dry yow'n tears, Peggy, or yew'll maak the water too salty. Juss keep it a'simmerin', oi'll be back soon wi suthen to put in it. Caleb, goo yew in the yard or down the beach an' see if yew can find some more driftwood or sticks fer the fire, then help set the table."

Caleb pulled a face and crossly stamped a foot.

“Oi doan’t wanna doo the horrid job!!!” he shouted petulantly.

"Cale...b!" Fred warned.

"Doan't yew boss me!!!"

Peggy wiped the tears from her face with the back of her hand while moving towards her youngest brother.

"Come yew on, m' bor," she spoke encouragingly taking hold of Caleb's arm, "oi'll leave this a'simmerin' to come an' help yew."

CHAPTER TWO

"Too tired for anything..."

The family crisis gave Fred an unexpected spurt of energy. He rushed out of the yard, stopped by the pump to rinse the plum debris from his hair then, changed his mind about looking for discarded fish heads by the drying nets behind the fish sheds and sped along a well-worn coastal path instead. As soon as he came to the score in the cliffs he made his way up the steep incline, paused at the summit to get his breath, then charged along the back lane. He ran across the field and up the track that led to the stables. There was one place where he knew his request for help would not be refused. His equine friends snickered as he ran past their stalls, but he did not stop. He was desperately hungry and guessed his brothers and sister also felt the same hollowness, so the sooner he fulfilled his task the better.

When he reached the last stable at the end of the block Fred ran up the stone steps constructed on the outside, two at a time, to arrive the front door of George's home. Without hesitation he clenched his fist and thumped hard on the solid wood.

Despite the lateness of the hour it was Edith who opened the door.

"Why, Fred, whatever brings yew here at this time o'

day, an' soo wet?"

Breathlessly he gasped, "Had to rinse out o' ma hair the plum stuff Peggy an' Caleb spat down on me an' Stan but, Mrs Kemp, can yew loan me a carrot an' some taters an' a smidgen o' drippin'?"

"Come yew in, bor, an' keep out the evenin' chill." Edith raised her eyebrows but refrained from asking questions, just grabbed a piece of towelling and tossed it to Fred.

The kindness of her welcome and the cosiness of the room wrapped him in warmth as he rubbed his hair dry as best as he could.

As he stepped over the threshold the sumptuous aroma emanating from the pan over the kitchen fire that greeted his nostrils set his ravenous stomach rumbling.

"Why, bor, hev ye not been hum fer yow'n supper?" George kindly inquired.

"Noo, um, oi mean yus, but Ma's prostrate an' we hev noo supper."

"Noo supper, whatever be yow'n Ma a'thinkin' on? An' what did yew hev in yow'n pail at dinner?"

"Me an' Stanley shared a crust wi' an' onion, Mrs Kemp, an' oi grabbed a handful o' hosses mess. Sorry Mister George, but oi be roite hungry, an' Peggy an' Caleb scrumped plums 'cos there be noo food at hum to maak supper."

"Oi see!" Edith laid her hands gently on the boy's shoulders and guided him towards the table which was spread in readiness for the Kemp's evening meal. Above Fred's head her eyes met those of her husband. Unspoken thoughts were communicated in that glance as Edith cocked her head towards the pan on the hearth and George nodded assent in reply.

Annie turned in her chair and beamed at the unexpected visitor. "Hello, Fred, oi be roite pleased to see yew. Come sit yew here by me," she offered. "Ma's made stew fer supper. Would yew like some?" Fred smiled at his friend, grateful for her generous gesture.

"Yus, do sit down Fred, an' catch yow'n breath. Edith will cut yew some bread an' drippin' while oi goo an' harness Bessie to the cart, then they'll slip on their outer garments." As he spoke George began putting one arm into his coat. "We'll come an' share supper at yow'n place."

Fred's dark brown eyes sparked open wide in astonishment. "But it be near dark outside," he spluttered. However, George was already making his way out of the door. Edith simply smiled kindly at the boy as she handed him a slice of bread and dripping then busied herself with necessary preparations for transporting supper to another location.

In no time at all the Kemp family and Fred were bundled into the wagon George had fetched and travelling along the lane in the deepening dusk. Edith carefully nursed the stew pan wrapped in a towel on her lap. Annie held an apple pie while Fred had been entrusted with loaves of bread and a crock of beef dripping. At his feet sat a sack of goodness knows what but his instincts told him these kind folks would make Peggy's heart glad by its contents.

By the time the travellers reached the Bemment cottage Stan had simmered down having got his grievance against the landlord off his chest and expended his energy chopping the driftwood that Caleb, with Peggy's help, had dragged home off the beach. Still unable to rouse his mother he had built up the fire and mixed a brew with the water Peggy had boiling, tossing in a handful of remaining cabbage and mint leaves he had plucked from the overgrown vegetable patch.

"Not very fillin' but at least it will warm yew up," he said as he handed cups to the children. "Better a dinner of herbs where love is than a stalled ox an' trouble it say somewhere in the Good Book." His heart churned at the sight of their pinched faces. *Dear God, how am oi goin' to fill their empty bellies?* The responsibility thrust so suddenly upon his eighteen-year-old shoulders seemed incredibly daunting.

A clatter at the door caused the youngsters to jerk up their heads as Fred burst excitedly through the door with arms full of bounty followed by George, Edith and Annie equally heavy laden.

"Look, Stan, look! Mister George an' Mrs Kemp an' Annie hev come to share supper wi' us." He tumbled the bread onto the table and turned to Peggy. "Oi told yew oi'd find us suthen fer supper, Peggs." Her eyes lit up in disbelief.

"Oi hope yew doan't mind Stanley, but Edith prepared extra today an' when we heard o' yow'n need we knew the reason why," George explained.

Peggy and Caleb stood gaping through the gloom at the largesse that so suddenly descended onto their bare kitchen table while Stan appeared to be struck dumb.

The two families had long been friends and were frequently in and out of each other's homes, but Edith sensed Stan's discomfort at this unexpected turn of events. She placed the still hot stew pan onto a trivet on the table and cast a quick eye around the badly lit room to locate her friend. Disturbed by the unkempt squalor of the cottage her heart sank at the unwomanly posture Hester presented. *Dear God, have mercy.* Shaken by what she saw Edith busied her hands with practical matters. She lit the candle she had brought with her and placed it in a holder on the table.

"Now, come yew on, Peggy, an' bring the dishes over here an’ help me serve. George, please slice the bread. Fred, put the pie Annie be still holdin' on the hearth. Stan, bring yew an extra chair an' sit by me. Doan't look soo woe-begott'n. If yow'n Ma wuz in her roite mind an' we wuz in a fix she would do the same fer us, as yew well know." Edith's forthrightness eased the scruples that were plaguing Stan's thoughts. He sat down and encouraged his siblings to do the same. Relieved of the pie Annie smiled at Peggy as she quickly moved towards her, slipped a friendly hand through her arm and guided her to the table. "Let's sit together."

"Would yew like George to ask the blessin'?" Edith asked Stan. She could see the lad was still struggling to find his voice. With the mixed emotions surging through his mind at that moment Stan knew that would be best so nodded his agreement.

"Father God, we bless Thee for Thy provision an' give thanks for wholesome food that will nourish ow'n bodies. Thou knowest ow'n need soo we pray for guidance in ow'n conversation an' actions. Come with comfort an' healin' to all in this hum, we pray, in the name of Jesus Christ, Thy Son, Amen!"

For some moments naught but the crackling wood burning on the fire broke the silence in the kitchen as hungry mouths tackled Edith's delicious stew and starving bellies were filled. George then kept the younger children occupied with snippets about his day's activities with the horses on the farm in order to give Edith opportunity to speak with Stan about the family's predicament and how he felt it could be resolved.

"Since Pa wuz lost at sea Ma ha'ent bin a'thinkin' straight. Her faith an' energy seems to hev deserted her. She be done noo washin' or cleanin' in the hus, there be noo food in the pantry, an' she be let the vegetables in the garden git all grown uvver. There be noo oil fer the lamp an' she seem not to care what happens to the young 'uns. Their clothes be tatty an' getting' threadbare an' they be a'runnin' round shoeless. Wi' Beatie up at the Big Hus now, Peggy's bin a'tryin' to cope but she hev run out o' provisions. Oi wuz a'savin' up to taak time orf work towards the end of the week to goo to market an' git what we needs."

"An' yow'n Ma be spent it all?"

Stan nodded.

"Last week she blew a week's wages on one meal," he added with a sigh.

"Yew'll hev to hide yow'n money in a different place, m'bor. As eldest yew'll hev to decide how yew be a'goin' to tackle this."

Again, Stan nodded. His shoulders slumped further towards the table.

"Jeremiah would be grieved that Hester is behavin' in this way but roite proud at how yew be handlin' the situation, m'bor. Now, yew'll hev to maak plans on how best to help out yow'n Ma."

Mention of his absent father brought an emptiness to his chest. A deep-seated longing to see that familiar rugged face once again and hear the deep resonance of his quiet voice giving words of wisdom and guidance, beset him. Stan closed his eyes, the picture of his father's arm raised, in what turned out to be his final farewell, overwhelmed him. Edith laid a motherly hand across his shoulders. Stan appreciated the unspoken understanding the kindly action conveyed. But it stirred up again the anger he felt at his mother's thoughtlessness. She should be the one dispensing care to her family.

"We'll leave the rest o' the stew fer yew, an' there be enough vegetables an' bread fer a couple more days but how yew a'goin' to manage arter that?" Edith asked quietly.

Stan shrugged his shoulders. "Oi doan't roitely know. The rent be due next week. Oi could use some advice," he pleaded.

"When there be circumstances such as yow'n word travels quick. Yow'n neighbours won't see yew goo hungry m'bor soo maybe yow'n next wages can goo towards the rent."

"Yus, oi be roite grateful for that. Pa valued yow'n friendship soo it would be remiss o' me not to turn to yew fer help an' guidance."

Edith patted his hand. "Think nuthen' of it m'bor. It wuz Jeremiah who taught us the Way of Salvation soo helpin' out his family is the least we can do fer soo foine a man."

The small gesture brought tears his eyes. To cover his embarrassment Stan lifted his to elbows to the table and dropped his head into his hands. *What a foine young man Hester an' Jeremiah hev raised. Dear God, give him courage fer the task ahead. Oi be a'thinkin' oi'll need to hev some straight talkin' wi' Hester when she comes to her senses.*

To distract the others from seeing Stan's momentary distress Edith stood up and cast her eyes around all those sat at the table. "Who would like some more?" She set to refilling the dishes the children eagerly held out. She was wise enough to know the young man needed time to make his own decisions about the family's future even if he might require help to carry them out.

When the last morsel of apple pie was gone Edith organized the younger children in the clean-up and preparations for bed giving George opportunity to chat more manly things through with Stan.

Hester still hadn't stirred by the time the Kemp family were ready to leave.

"Now, yew git yow'n sel' to bed, Stanley, yew hev work a'morrow, an' yew be too tired to maak decisions a'noite. Oi'll be over to see Hester in the mornin'."

Stan swallowed, words failed him, so he nodded in appreciation of Edith's kindness and care acknowledging he was too tired for anything more this night.

CHAPTER THREE

"...not even talking..."

George settled Bessie in her stall for the night and put away the wagon. With leaden feet and slumped shoulders he ascended the stone stairs to his home with a heavy heart. He found it difficult to accept a mother's slovenly disregard for her children's wellbeing.

Jeremiah had been a God-fearing man and a good friend, a hard-working fisherman, a conscientious husband and a strict but loving father. His loss at sea, along with the Skipper and crew of the Grayling, during one of the fiercest gales to hammer the east coast in decades, had devastated not only his family but also the close-knit coastal community of Newton Westerby. The storm had lasted for four days and as soon as it was known that the Grayling had gone down, George knew that Stan scoured the beach day after day in the hope of finding his father alive, washed ashore on flotsam from the broken vessel. But though he and his paternal grandfather, Jonas, along with some of the men of the village searched persistently it was not until two weeks later that remains were sighted on the shore some miles further south down the coast. One was identified as the skipper by the key on a cord around his neck and the other, found half a mile away from him, as Jeremiah because of the size of the body and the remnant of fisherman's jersey still attached to the upper part of the torso. To Mrs Catchpole's distress nothing was ever found of young Arthur, the cabin boy.

Jeremiah would have been shocked at Hester's reaction to his death, numbing her grief by drowning in liquor, obliterating her household obligations and neglecting the needs of the family. She was not naturally a feckless woman. What had happened to her trust in Almighty God?

As he entered his home with quiet reserve George elected to keep his thoughts to himself but the moment she saw him come through the door Edith vented her feelings concerning her friend's lackadaisical housekeeping.

"How can she not feed her children!"

George nodded shrewdly, fondled his daughter's blond locks as he walked by her and placed a calloused hand affectionately across his wife's shoulders.

"Oi be a'thinkin' life be hard enough wi'out addin' to the difficulties by dullin' yer sensibilities wi’ too much liquor."

"What do yew think Hester be done wi' Jeremiah's pay?"

"Obviously thoughtlessly frittered it away."

"Oi could hardly question Stan about how his Ma spent the huskeepin' money his Pa would hev given her afore he left on his last fishin' trip."

"Yew be roite, m'gal. Oi juss thank God fer a wife who wisely knows how to hold her tongue an' manages our meagre supplies wi' such efficiency we nivver goo hungry."

Edith shrugged her shoulders. "None of us in the village hev much but Hester's attitude doan't sit very well wi' me."

"Oi realize it be a blow to lose Jeremiah in such a manner an’ she misses him dreadfully, but it's not as if she be unused to managin’ on her own. He wuz away at sea fer weeks at a toime. Hev a quiet word wi’ her next toime yew see her, m'gal."

"Oi plan to call by a'morrow afore oi goo to Ma an' Pa's."

The next day after completing her early morning chores Edith encouraged Annie to speedily don her bonnet and shawl.

"Afore we goo, nip yew down to the hin hus, m'gal an' see if there be any eggs. We'll slip some in a basket an' taak them uvver to Hester's. If yew be quick we moite git there in toime fer yew to walk to school wi' Peggy." Annie beamed up at her mother, then eagerly bounced down the stairs to scout for eggs.

Edith's usual cheery countenance was absent as she contemplated seeing her friend. *Lord, bring her comfort an' relief from the grievin'. Open her eyes to see the needs o' Peggy an' the boys. Give her the strength to cope, an' me the wisdom to say the roite words.* Prayer ascended from her heart about what she felt was likely to be an uncomfortable meeting with her friend.

Edith negotiated the stone steps leading down from her home with care and once at the bottom turned the corner towards the vegetable patch. She could hear Annie's excited chatter coming from the chicken run as she searched for eggs.

"Look, Ma, there be seven."

"Hurrit m'gal, leave two by the geart an' put the others into the basket. Thass be sufficient fer a meal fer us, such as batter pudden or scrambled uvver bread toasted by the fire." Edith hustled her daughter. She wanted the painful visit ahead done with. Obediently Annie nestled two eggs in a tuft of grass by the gate post and placed the others into the basket.

“We’ll pick them up when we git hum.”

***

Stan had planned to be up first the next morning in order to have the fire roaring away before his siblings woke but as he rubbed the sleep from his bleary eyes a sumptuous aroma confused his semi-wakefulness. It seemed to waft from a distance, yet the more awake he became the closer it drifted towards him and assaulted his sense of smell and set his taste buds in motion. He flung on his clothes and took the stairs two at a time to reach the kitchen.

"Peggy! Dear Peggy. Yew be up already! God bless yew. We hev food." Joyfully he hugged his youngest sister's shoulders. She had a pan sizzling with the dripping that Edith had given them the evening before.

"Careful Stan."

"What be yew a'cookin'?"

"Bubble an' squeak wi' some o' last night's left-uvvers an' fried bread."

"Thass wonderful!"

He whizzed around and set the table before calling his younger brothers and shaking his mother who was still displaying an unwomanly posture, snoring in the chair the other side of the hearth, with her mouth wide open.

As he paused at the foot of the stairs Stan called up loudly, "Fred! Caleb! Come, yew on. See what be fer breakfast." He took a step back and shook Hester's arm again, "Ma, Ma, breakfast be riddy."

There was a loud rap on the door. The latch was lifted, and a head peeked through the opening.

"Mornin', Mrs Bemment, hev yew a jug? Farmer

Baldry's had me stop by wi' a gill of milk fer yew?"

"Why, Zeb, how kind. Step in," Stan greeted the cowman from Home farm.

"Would yew like a bite to eat?" Peggy offered.

"Noo, got to finish ma round. It doo smell boo'iful."

The noise at the door roused the boys. Inquisitiveness could not keep them in bed a moment longer. Within minutes they were dressed, bounding down the stairs, eyes eagerly scanning to see what the commotion was all about.

"Mornin', Zeb," they chorused in response to the cowman's wave and greeting before grabbing a seat at the table and tucking into the meal Peggy set before them.

Stan presented Zeb with a jug. The welcome, creamy liquid flowed right to the brim.

"Thanks."

The door banged behind Zeb as he left. Hester stirred.

Caleb saw the movement, got up and yelled excitedly, "Look, Ma, we got breakfast."

Hester held her head and moaned, "Quiet m'bor."

"Why did yew sleep, Ma, an' not maak supper?"

"Well, um, oi er...

"Nivver yew mind that now, Caleb, come eat up yow'n breakfast an' git yow'n jobs done afore yew hev to leave fer school." Caleb pouted. But at Stan's stern look he quickly took his seat at the table without further ado. Having issued instructions to his youngest brother Stan turned towards his mother. "Noo givin' us excuses, Ma, come to the table an' eat," he said firmly.

Hester shook her head.

"Ma, yew hev the breakfast Peggy's fixed fer yew. Fred an' oi be orf to work now. Oi've brung in some wood fer the fire an' there be stew ready to put on fer tea. Peggy an'

Caleb hev school this mornin' arter they be done chores an' Edith be a'comen by later. As we've prepared breakfast yew can hev the pleasure of cleanin' up while a'waitin' fer her to call in."

Hester sighed, shifted languidly to reposition herself in the chair. She had no desire to eat, speak or move ever again. All pleasure in duties about the home had been snatched from her; his eyes would never see it again. The window of anticipation she always experienced at his homecoming had been closed forever. Jeremiah's larger than life presence would no longer fill this homely space. His brawny arms never again be held out to embrace her with love and warmth.

Life had become meaningless. She felt so drained, with little energy to exert herself to do anything. Nor, despite Stan's urging, did she wish to allow another morsel of food to pass her lips. What was the point? Jeremiah was gone and not coming back. While he was missing there was still hope. But now, life no longer held significance for her. All she had left was a loneliness that turned her days into mechanical motion and her nights into sleepless longing. She wanted none of it. She could not abide either. The memory was too painful. Liquor obliterated it from her mind. But it was a short-lived remedy and necessitated frequent calls over the side wall to the landlord of The Rising Sun. She no longer believed God cared about her or had the remotest interest in her needs and feelings, actions or words. The here and now was irrelevant. She was too young to be widowed.

Tears spilled from her eyes and coursed unbidden down her cheeks.

With Jeremiah she had believed in eternity but now that

she was alone, and bereft, Hester no longer had the will or desire to pray. Faith seemed to have deserted her. God had let her down. There was no point trusting someone who was so unreliable. She would not go to church again. Stan and the others could please themselves. She didn't much care. The light of her life had gone out when she saw the battered remains, of what was a sorry trace of her strong man, on the beach. Her father-in-law tried to shield her from viewing what they had found, but Hester determinedly pushed her way through.

Now she simply did not have any reason to keep on living.

"Ma!" Stan called impatiently.

Hester moaned but made no attempt to budge from her position.

“Ma, yew need to stir yow'n sel', an' yew muss eat."

Hester gestured Stan away.

With a heavy heart Stan finished his meal, pulled on his boots, shrugged his arms into his coat and along with Fred made his way to the stables. He worried about his mother's lack of response. Even talking seemed too much of an effort for her, now, let alone tackling the necessary household chores that needed attention, inside and outside the home.

***

Breakfast pots still littered the kitchen table when Edith knocked and walked through the door of the Bemment's cottage. Hester remained inert by the hearth. Edith sighed, slipped off her shawl, put a kettle of water on the trivet near the fire to boil, pushed up her sleeves and prepared to tackle some of the chaos that pervaded her friend's home.

"Hester, m'friend, come yew on," she cajoled as she gathered the dirty breakfast pots to the sink and cleared the messy table. "Yew really need to get yow'n sel' together fer the sake of the boys an' Peggy."

"Noo, noo," Hester wafted a hand to push her friend away. "Leave me be."

Edith wiped over the tatty oil cloth that covered the table, then bent to put another piece of wood on the fire. "Ooh!" She exclaimed. As she straightened she kneaded the small of her back.

"Whether yew like it or not, Hester, life has to goo on. The children need yew."

There was no answer from the passive figure in the chair. Undeterred Edith picked up Hester's chilled hands in her own and rubbed them as though by so doing she could generate a reaction that would stimulate life and break the inertia that was gripping her friend.

"The Lord be a'taaken Jeremiah. He not be a'comen back but yew hev to carry on till yew be called Home. Hester, yew hev a responsibility to care for the family yew an' he made together. Doan't yew know yow'n children were a'starven'? What would Jeremiah think o' the way yew be neglectin' them?" Hester snatched her hands away and signalled for Edith to leave. However, Edith was not so easily fobbed off and poured the tea she had left to brew.

She placed a cup in Hester's hand. "While yew drink that oi'll finish these pots from breakfast then oi must be away to Ma an' Pa's afore the bell sounds fer gleanin' to begin."

Edith scurried around putting as much of the kitchen to rights as time allowed. She called Peggy and Annie, who were amusing themselves in the wilderness that once had been a productive garden and set them to dry up the cutlery before seeing them off to the schoolroom. She surreptitiously kept half an eye on Hester as she worked. The cup of tea hadn't fallen, nor had it been put down, so she hoped it would be drunk.

"Yew be a'goin' to hev to adjust yow'n huskeepin', Hester. The children be copin' roite well, but they'll require yow'n guidance now their Pa be a'gorn. If yew would loike, George will help the boys to dig an' riddy the vegetable patch fer next spring so yew hev greens to eat." She peered through the grubby window. "Surely, despite the weeds, there muss be suthen edible out there!" She turned and moved thoughtfully towards Hester. "Now that Beatie's up at the Big Hus maybe Peggy can come up to moine more frequently an' larn alongside Annie how to bake bread an' pies an' the loike. Yew know how they love to do things t'gether."

"We ent got noo flour," Hester blurted out. Edith delighted at drawing out such a response patted her friend's hand. "Not to worrit, oi hev sufficient in the bin, at present, to share wi yew. If yew give permission, George an' oi'll set things in motion. But yew doo need t' stir yow'n sel', Hester, an' come a'gleanin' or else yew be all a'goin' to starve come winter."

Had she not been closely watching her friend Edith would have missed the slight dip of Hester's head.

"Yew be blessed wi' good children, Hester, but they do need yow'n support."

"Naah! They'll manage. They doan't need me."

"O' course they do. They be yow'n family an' they need their Ma."

Hester roughly shoved Edith's hand away.

"Beatie'll run the hus an' Stan be bringin' in a man's

wage. They'll watch the li'tle 'uns. They'll fare well wi'out me."

"Hester, Beatie's not here an' Stan's not much more than a bor. They doo need yew."

Hester shot bolt upright in the chair.

"Where be Beatie? Why ent she here?" She raised her voice. "Beatie, come yew here. Beatrice, come now!" Hester commanded and banged her hands down on the arms of the chair.

Edith drew up a chair in front of her friend to sit in a more comfortable position. Quietly she addressed Hester with a calmness her racing heart contradicted.

"Beatie be at The Big Hus, now. Doan't yew remember? She be gorn to be scullery maid. Soo the others do need yew, Hester. God will see yew through."

"God? Doan't talk squit! He be a'gorn along wi' ma man."

She dismissed Edith with an angry flick of the wrist and slumped back down in the chair.

"Oh, ma friend, yew needs the dear Lord more than ever." But Hester's frame remained still and unresponsive so, Edith got up to finish the chores.

"Sorry to leave yew, Hester, but oi muss be orf to see Ma an' Pa then oi'll be a'gleanin'," she said a short while later. "All be riddy fer the children's supper. Doan't fergit to pull the pan acrorst the hearth." She bid farewell to Hester's motionless form and trudged along the overgrown pathway with a heavy heart.

CHAPTER FOUR

"Trudging up the pathway dreary..."

By the time Stan and Fred reached the stables the autumn haze of early morning was beginning to lift. George was in conversation with the estate manager but broke off when he saw the Bemment boys approaching. He had already acquainted Mr Jenner with their home situation. Stan's glum face encouraged George to immediately get down to business and apportion their jobs for the day.

"Mornin', lads. Fred, goo yew an' muck out Prince. His lordship requires him this mornin', soo yew be a'workin' alongside Wilf to git him ready."

"Yus, Mister George." Fred's spirits soared. He loved the handsome horse. Almost at once the world around him took on a golden hue. His stomach satisfied with the breakfast Peggy had placed in front of him meant he could concentrate on the job in hand without the discomfort of hunger pangs of previous days. He even noticed the glow of the early sun as it caught on a dewy spider's web strung across the lintel of the upper stable door. He all but skipped to pick up the shovel and bucket for his task. As he entered the stall the sharp sweet smell of horse filled his nostrils. He spoke in soft tones to Prince who responded by nuzzling his proffered hand. "Well, m'bor, be yew pleased t' see me?" The horse whinnied in response, stepped up to Fred and nudged his head into the boy's shoulder. "Come yew on, yew ole sooner, oi need to sort yow'n quarters out."

Meanwhile, George turned to Stan. "Stan, as yew know, we wants to cut North Acre field as the weather be set fair. Will yew prepare Bessie an' Ditton fer the wagon on to which the men will put the dried shocks. Blossom be thrown a shoe. Send one o' the lads wi' her to the smithy."

"Be good when they be finished the new forge an' the farrier be closer at hand. Shoeing will taak less toime."

George nodded in agreement. "Yus, Joseph Castleton an' his men be a'workin' flat out to accomplish that. Meanwhile, we'll hev to continue to taak the hosses down to the village. Oi'll taak Blossom along wi' Clover to swap over with the working hosses as soon as the lad gits back. Check yow'n scythe be sharp an' join ole Alf's team, bor. Be yow'n Ma a'comin' to glean?"

Stan shook, then hung his head. Without his Ma gleaning there would be no grain to mill into flour for the winter months. "How will we manage fer food wi'out the staple fer bread an' pies? She ha'ent bin out in the fields on gleanin' days since harvest began which be another reason why the pantry be bare." His heart sank lower as he disconsolately shuffled off to fulfil his allotted task.

Mr Jenner watched the interchange and raised his eyebrows questioningly at George. Stan's demeanour conveyed an abysmal message.

"Umph!" grunted George thoughtfully as Stan slouched away. He turned towards Mr Jenner. "Do yew think Cook could spare Beatrice fer a few hours to help wi' gleanin'?"

"I'll call in to the kitchen on my way up to see his lordship and enquire of Mrs Sands. Perhaps Beatrice's siblings could also miss lessons for a spell to give a hand?"

he suggested tentatively.

"Excellent idea, Mr Jenner. When Fred be finished wi' Prince oi'll send him up to the schoolroom afore he goes to the field. Hester be all o'pieces since Jeremiah be a'gorn."

***

Buxom Mrs Sands, whose bark was known to be worse than her bite, greeted Elias Jenner's appearance in her kitchen brusquely.

"Oi suppose yew be wantin' a sup o' coffee." She barely lifted her head to look at the man who had entered her domain but continued to beat the living daylights out of the mixture in the bowl she was holding.

With cap in hand he stood silently to one side watching her action.

"It be alroite fer some as can taak the master's toime fer his own pleasure." She continued to rail him. Undeterred by the cook's sarcastic reception the estate manager greeted Mrs Sands cordially.

"Good morning, Cook, what a pleasant morning it is and what a pleasing aroma is emanating from your oven."

"Yew can cease yow'n flattery, Mr Jenner. Soft talk woan't git the job finished. Whilst ye may hev the toime to idle the hours away wi' chatter oi hev to git a meal riddy to place on the Master's table." She stopped her beating to throw a handful of sultanas from a jar into the batter mix.

"Maggie, be that pudden basin greased, yet?" She called out sharply.

"Yus, Cook," responded the kitchen maid sheepishly scuttling to position the required receptacle within reach.

"I can see you are busy so I will not detain you longer

than necessary, Cook. I just called in on my way to his lordship's office to ask a favour of your generous nature."

"When did yew ever come in here wi'out wantin' suthen?" Mrs Sands retorted.

"A situation has arisen that requires your assistance."

"What happenstance on the estate can possibly require a cook's attention?"

"How is the new scullery maid shaping up?"

Surprised by his question Cook stopped her beating looked closely at her visitor, then cocked her head towards the scullery.

"Noicely, thank yew fer askin'." Mrs Sands snatched at the proffered bowl Maggie handed to her and proceeded to pour in the mixture.

"I am glad because I would like you to release her from duties for the rest of today."

Cook shook the wooden spoon aloft in her fist at Mr Jenner.

"Doan't yew come in here a'tellin' me what a'doo wi' ma staff."

"Nevertheless, Mrs Sands, her services are required elsewhere today. I will be here at 12 noon to escort her."

Cook flung the wooden spoon into the now empty bowl and thumped her fist on the kitchen table.

"Yew can't do this, Mr Jenner."

"Thank you for your cooperation, Cook. Ensure Beatrice is ready on time, dressed in her oldest clothes."

"She'll hev to forego her afternoon out," quipped Mrs Sands decisively."

"No, that is not possible. Her services are also required on that occasion."

"Noo! Noo! Noo! Mr Jenner, yew cannot interfere wi'

ma kitchen loike this!"

"Cook, I am sure with your expertise you can organise someone else to fill-in for her. Maggie, for instance," he said as his eyes lighted on the kitchen maid. "If Beatrice is as good a worker as you say she is I dare say she will more than make up for this time. She certainly will not be idle whilst away from her scullery chores but kept pretty busy."

"Wait till the mistress hears o' yow'n high-handedness!"

"My lady is fully aware of the situation and recognises the need for Beatrice to be engaged elsewhere at this time. Thank you for your understanding in this emergency, Mrs Sands. Will you speak with the young lady or shall I?"

Cook shrugged her shoulders and huffed in disgust as she nodded her assent. Elias Jenner was glad he had the foresight to mention the Bemment's plight to Lady Marion when their paths crossed on his return to the Manor House from the stables as her ladyship walked along the path which led to the formal gardens.

***

When the church bell rang to indicate the commencement of gleaning Beatie was there in the field working with Edith, her nimble fingers gathering fallen stalks rapidly to fill her folded apron. Alongside her were women from Newton Westerby village as well as outlying hamlets on the estate. The men scything the crop were more than halfway across North Acre field. Following close behind them were those forming the full heads of wheat into shocks to be forked onto wagon beds.

Soon massive hay carts and wagons piled high with sacks and sheaves, cut on previous days and left to dry, passed the busy women, as they swayed behind the teams of Suffolk Punches. With plodding hooves the heavy horses heaved their loads down dusty country lanes to the barn with the threshing floor. In coming days the corn would be flailed before being carted to Jenner's mill to be milled into flour.

George as head horseman, and appointed lord of the harvest, had given word to start the process at daybreak. With a chanting song the men moved together in rhythm till some of the women brought 'levenses at set times throughout the day. The breaks were welcome. Heat from the sun as it moved across the sky made the task thirsty work so liquid refreshment was guzzled with relish. George knew if he did not push the men too hard he would get the best work from them. On the other hand, all the labourers knew the importance of bringing the harvest home before the weather turned. A sit down under the shade of a clump of trees to the side of the field sipping a cool drink, mingled with rivalry and banter, refreshed the workers for the next phase. Yarrow was always gathered in large quantities from the hedgerows and gardens. Gallons of it were brewed into a beverage and the men would regularly take it to work in their tin cans. Jugs of it stood aside in most pantries ready for the women and children to drink it when they were thirsty and at harvest time it was always plentiful for the workers.

Lord Ralph insisted sufficient ears were left on the ground for the gleaners so that families in his employ had enough to be milled into flour for bread and pie crusts, Suffolk swimmers and their like, to tide them over the winter months. His neighbouring landowners did not hold with this view and vigorously opposed allowing those they referred to as peasants to follow the reapers believing they looked upon it as their right rather than a concession in the gift of the farmers. On one occasion his lordship's nearest neighbour even went so far as to take a poor, struggling tenant to court as an example to those who would dare to trespass on his land at harvest time to snatch even a single ear of corn. On the whole, residents on the Newton Manor estate were for ever indebted to their benefactor for his generosity and did not take his kindness lightly, but mostly repaid it with diligence and loyalty. There were the exceptions, but the Squire and his estate manager, did not have to step in because his tenants and workers dealt with slackers and scroungers amongst themselves.

Within twenty minutes of the clanging of the commencement bell children's voices could be heard shrieking and calling. Those engaged in the backbreaking work glanced up. They were amazed to see the school mistress, Miss Amy Peskett, accompanied by the school children running across the field.

"Well, thass the limit! This ent the place fer jollifications," grumbled Mrs Tuttle to her neighbour.

"Yew be roite. The schoolhuss be the place fer larnin'." Gertie Saunders did a second take and was astounded to see her own brood amongst the noisy crowd. "Rodney, Florrie, git yew back to the schoolhuss. Nellie this be noo place fer yew. Taak the li'tle uns back," she yelled.

Undeterred by the tittering, Miss Peskett led her exuberant troop of followers, like the Pied Piper of Hamlin, up to the group of gleaning women.

"We've come to help yew, Beatie." Peggy and Caleb danced gleefully around their older sister. She hugged them tight. "Annie's here too." Beatrice looked around at the eager faces.

"Oi be roite please to see yew all."

Glad to be free from the schoolroom the children chased each other, squealing with delight as they played tag. Frequent cries of "ouch" were heard as the cut corn stalks chaffed their bare ankles as they ran, till a look from the school mistress subdued their antics. They began gathering the fallen ears with gusto, laughter following in their wake. Miss Peskett encouraged diligence but kept a watchful eye on her pupils to ensure they mixed fun with profitable toil. "Oi'll git more than yew, Miss," challenged more than one voice.

When Miss Peskett received the message Fred conveyed she decided it would be of benefit if all the children spent an afternoon in the fresh air and looked upon it as an opportunity to teach them the importance of charitable acts of kindness. The majority came from impoverished homes and knew the pain of scrimping and empty bellies.

At the end of the day Stan was overwhelmed by the quantity of gleanings the children and others deposited on to a piece of sacking that had been placed on the ground by the door to their cottage. A lump rose in his throat at the kindness of their neighbours. *Dear God, Yourn provision be amazin'.* His many "thank yews" seemed inadequate for the generous spirit displayed by the repeated handfuls that were thrown onto the growing mound of grain.

Caleb dashed passed him. "Ma, Ma, juss look at all the wheat we collected fer yew," he called out as he burst through the door. "Yew soon be a'maakin' bread an' pies fer supper." But Hester lolled in a state of unconsciousness totally unaware of the largesse upon her doorstep.

Stan took off his cap and brushed a sleeve across

watering eyes. What a load he would have to cart to the miller. He bent down to tie the corners of the hessian across the bounty before him, then humped it on his back. He shoved the cottage door open with his shoulder and pushed passed his sisters busy by the fire. Sisters? His eyes did a double take. Beatie was there working on their evening meal alongside Peggy. He dumped his load on the floor by the pantry cupboard and rushed back to hug Beatrice.

"Oh, Beatie, oi be roite pleased to see yew. God's goodness juss keeps on givin'."

Beatie laughed. "Careful, bor Stan, or yew'll hev me spillin' ow'n supper all uvver the hearth."

Stan's joy was short lived and soon turned to dismay when he saw the drunken stupor that still encompassed their mother. He hadn't yet received his wages for the current week's work although he had given thought to where he would hide them as Edith had suggested.

"Then how?" Worried beyond measure he rubbed a hand across his brow as he queried his mother's ability to acquire more liquor.

As he escorted Beatrice back to the Big House following supper the two siblings discussed the situation at home, Beatie tearfully distressed by the state of their mother.

"Oi be roite worrit about Ma."

"Yew didn't gi' Ma yow'n wages, did yew?"

"Not this week. Oi don't git them till a'morrow."

"Keep them. We be a'managin' foine. Mr an' Mrs Kemp hev advised me how to budget the pennies, an' they soon be a'teachin' me an' Fred the gardenin', an' Peggy be larnin' bakin' along wi' Annie. Fred be good at findin' fish heads down at the sheds that Peggy maaks into soup, an' t'noite oi be a'showin' Caleb how to set snares on the common to catch rabbits. So doan't yew be a'feared about us. Dry yow'n tears m'gal, we be doin' juss foine."

"Yew be soo positive, Stan."

"Oi be a'larnen', but it taaks toime. Hev yew seen Grandpa Jonas lately?"

She nodded. "On m' arternoon out last week. Oi took him a pastie Cook allowed me to maak from left-uvvers. Oi think he still misses Pa, but he say a me he be doin' noicely."

"Thass good. We all miss Pa. Some days it be harder than others."

Not trusting herself to speak Beatie simply nodded in agreement.

At the back door of the Big House they said goodnight.

On his return to the cottage Stan called into The Rising Sun to remonstrate with the landlord, threatening to turn on the taps to empty his barrels if he passed another jug of liquor to his mother again.

"Truly, Stan, oi ent giv'n yow'n Ma liquor since yew last come in."

"Then how?"

Stan trudged up the pathway dreary with an uneasy heart and leaden feet mulling over how he was going to sort out this mess. He was no nearer to a solution to the dilemma as he wearily approached the last few yards home.

He pushed open the cottage door to find Fred in tears.

"Stan, ma savin's be a'gorn!"

CHAPTER FIVE

"They were tired..."

Burdened by his mother's reaction to grief Stan fretted over the enormity of the responsibility that had been thrust upon his youthful shoulders. He seemed unable to save Ma from herself. He traipsed to all the village hostelries and learned that his mother had frequented most of them to have her jug replenished putting the cost on the slate when cash was unavailable to her. Stan requested the landlords to cease supplying her. Her constant inebriation, lack of care and interaction in family life distressed his youngest siblings. They were fractious at home and one day he learned that this behaviour had spilled over to school for at the close of the school day, Miss Peskett called at the cottage to enquire what was causing Peggy and Caleb to be so distracted and quarrelsome that they were unable to pay attention in class. Miss Peskett sensed that there seemed to be more than their father's death giving rise to uncharacteristic misbehaviour. When she stepped across the threshold of the Bemment home her eyes were opened to the predicament facing the youngsters and she endeavoured to allay Stan's fears.

"I'll do all I can to assist Peggy and Caleb through this difficult time, Stan. I could come after school on a Wednesday and help them to catch up with their lessons if you thought that would help."

"Thank yew Miss Peskett fer yow'n kindness. I accept yow'n offer to help them."

“I’ll see you two tomorrow,” Miss Peskett said to Peggy and Caleb as she left. Peggy smiled sweetly but Caleb pouted. “Oi doan’t wan...” he began crossly but Stan silenced him with a stern look.

Whilst Fred was still upset about the loss of his savings Stan pointed out that in time he would soon be able to make up for the shortfall. "In fact, yew keep all yow'n wages ev’ry other sennoite..."

"But..." Fred's eyes widened in disbelief. Stan was well aware how hard Fred worked. "We'll manage till yew recoup what yew hev lorst but doan’t tell Ma o’ ow’n arrangement," Stan advised the next morning as they made their way to the stables. He patted his pocket. “Oi picked up ma pouch afore comin' out. Yew could do the same when yew gits paid this week.”

"Oi don't hev a pouch, an'..." Disconsolately Fred turned out the pockets of his jacket to reveal multiple holes, then proceeded to show the same ruinous state in his trouser pockets. They groaned in unison.

"Peggy could maak yew one."

"But Ma will see her sewing an' ask what she be a’doin’.”

"Umm! Perhaps Mrs Kemp will help us."

Fred nodded his head in agreement, his hunched shoulders relaxed, and his face brightened. “She be soo helpful.” Edith Kemp's sewing skills were well known. Having resolutely reached this decision to guard his wages and savings Fred's natural sunny disposition returned. The lift in his spirits eventually rubbed off onto the younger children so that on subsequent mornings they went off to school with a cheerful attitude to partake in the day's activities more positively and attend to their tasks at home in a better frame of mind on their return. They all missed their father's presence but Stan's efforts to make each of them feel valued encouraged a happier atmosphere to prevail amongst them despite Hester's continuing withdrawal from family and home involvement.

The last of the harvest had been gathered in before the weather broke. Top Field, which had been most affected by the earlier storm, was the final area to be harvested. Under George's direction hay was also scythed and forked into stacks that pointed majestically towards the sky.

"Come yew on, bors, put yourn best foot forward, it be imperative to git this stacked an' thatched afore the weather breaks."

Threshing was almost complete and grain ready to be carted down to Jenner's mill. The spirits of the men were heightened. This period of busyness guaranteed labour was plentiful for willing workers and for the thrifty it provided a buffer when work slackened after harvest.

Harry Jenner and his boys, clad in their dusty aprons, worked flat out shovelling the grain at the mill. The wheat passed through the cleaning machines, separating the precious kernels from the chaff, before it fell down a canvas tube into the hopper to supply the millstone. A jigging motion shook the corn into the trough over the stones in uniform quantities. The millstone grinding the grain into flour that poured down the shoot into waiting sacks was constantly in need of dressing. However, if the stone dresser was too busy elsewhere it put work at the mill behind.

Harry could be somewhat cantankerous and mean

spirited when this happened or things did not run as smoothly as he wished, but he was widely known to be most fair in his dealings with landowners and tenant farmers, as well as gleaners from the village. Most preferred dealing with him rather than other millers in the area. Milling required great skill gained through years of experience. It was arduous work and a miller's return was as dependent upon the success of the harvest as the farmer. His eldest and youngest sons learned from an early age that the efficiency of the mill depended on every member of the family pulling their weight and were keen to learn the trade and follow in his footsteps. Shy, quiet Colin shared his father's passion to produce the finest flour from the grain and the process of milling simply enthused and fascinated Danny, but burly Joe hated the mill and grudgingly carried out the tasks he was appointed to do. He didn't share his father and brothers' maxim that careful, hard work produced quality grade flour and subsequently brought in customers. Joe detested the floury particles that clung to his hair and clothes and clogged his lungs and grumbled on the rare occasions he had to assist his mother to weigh and bag the flour.

Jenner's Mill was one of only a few mills that was dual powered, but to Harry's chagrin the storm that had taken the Grayling had severely damaged one of the shafts on the Mill's sail. Once the wind died down he sent Colin and Danny up to fix it, but it took some while before they had it in good working order.

"Well done, m'bors," Harry said with relief as he clapped his sons on the shoulder. "Thankfully yew hev got it a'goin' agin afore the grain from Manor Farm an' the surroundin' farms arrives fer millin'."

The mill stream constantly had to be kept clear of debris so that the water wheel didn't get clogged up and jeopardize the smooth running of the mill. As Joe preferred working out of doors Harry appointed that responsibility to him, but he hated having to take orders and being under his father's thumb.

Many villagers relied on the flour, derived from their autumnal gleanings in the wheat fields, to last the family throughout the year. Harry set aside a day to grind gleaners corn which was paid for by him keeping the bran or alternatively a quart out of a bushel of wheat. This worked well except when the treatment of a gleaner was not scrupulously honest. His brother, Elias, the squire's estate manager, frequently called in during milling to keep an eye on proceedings. Despite the storm it had been a good year overall and yields were high, and he wanted to ensure the miller did not set aside more than the agreed toll and keep surplus for himself. It wasn't that Elias distrusted his brother, but it was a known fact that if anyone had the misfortune to call on a day when Joe was in charge proceedings were less than cordial, weights questioned, resulting in underpayment.

***

"Thass boo'iful, Peggy," Stan belched with satisfaction and wiped his mouth across the back of his hand. "Oi be a'goin' to the mill afore dark to find out which day Miller Harry be a'grindin' gleaner's corn." He pushed his chair back from the table and stood up. "Yew an' Caleb come wi' me, Fred, an' we'll check the snares on the way hum," he said to his brothers hoping it would give him opportunity to chat some family matters over with Fred.

"Noo, Stan," Peggy began to cry. "Doan't leave me," she pleaded.

"Oi'll stay wi'..." began Fred, but Peggy's sobs increased as she plunged her head upon folded arms set down on the table in front of her. Alarmed by this unexpected outburst Stan rushed to his sister's side, crouched down, grabbed her arm and with a finger gently lifted her head. Peggy flinched.

"Peggs, what be wrong?"

Tears flowed uncontrollably down her cheeks.

"Hev yew hurt yow'n sel'?"

Peggy nodded.

"Roll up yow'n sleeve," he instructed.

Reluctantly she bared her arms. The colour and pattern of bruises displayed suggested her injuries had been inflicted by another person rather than an accident or a fall.

"Who did this to yew?"

Peggy shook her head.

Stan lifted her chin higher and looked directly at her tear-stained face. The fear in her eyes caused him to radically alter his plan. He straightened up.

"Fred, pour water from the kettle into the sink, then stoke the fire. Caleb, clear the table an' grab the towel..."

"Ugh!!! Why me?" he moaned.

"We'll all help to get jobs done quicker. I will wash the pots. Peggy yew be best to put up the left-uvvers. We will all goo to Jenner's Mill."

The chores were completed with lightning speed. The boys slipped on their coats. Peggy gathered her shawl around her arms and Stan ushered his siblings through the door. "Ma, we be orf to the mill. Yow'n supper be on the hearth."

Hester stirred. "Not Joe. Doan't deal wi' Joe," she firmly called after them.

“Why, Ma?"

"Juss doan't speak wi' Joe."

Stan raised his eyebrows, but Hester would not impart further information.

Thoughtfully he closed the door.

"Yew be orf somewhere?" their neighbour called as he crossed the yard.

"We be a'goin' up to the mill, Elsie, to see about millin’ the gleanin's. Yew want oi should ask about yow'n?"

"Thass be roite good o' yew, Stan,"

"Ma be aloan."

"Oi'll keep an eye on her."

Stan raised his hand in acknowledgement then strode purposefully to catch up with his brothers and sister. It was a fair stretch to the mill from the row of cottages on the beach and dusk hovered uncertainly. The youngsters followed the course of the river, keeping to the well-worn path along the bank. Caleb was running ahead as Stan caught up with Fred and a tearful Peggy.

"Ma did that to Peggy," said Fred in a horrified whisper.

"Ma?" Stan was incredulous.

"Peggy say Ma pretends to be asleep till we goo out o' the hus, then she gits up an' grabs Peggy by the arms an' shakes her, an' demands where we hev hidden ow'n wages."

"Oi be soo sorry, Stan," Peggy sobbed. "Oi didn't tell her, truly oi didn't, but Ma soo hurt ma arms an' followed ma eyes. Once she found the coins she rushed out o' the hus.

"Dear Peggy, it not be yow’n fault. Oi juss be very sorry yew bin hurt," Stan bent to gently hug his little sister. "Doan't yew worrit. Oi’ll sort it out. Yew goo keep company wi' Caleb." Slowly she dragged her feet along the ground to catch up with her brother.

Fred and Stan continued to walk companionably in silence as so often they did at the end of a day's work. Though tired in body Stan began to put some resolution into the thoughts that were darting through his mind.

"We can't leave Peggy aloan wi' Ma agin," he said quietly.

"Perhaps Ethel could goo keep company wi' Peggy when we not be hum."

"Good idea. Oi'll speak wi' Elsie but we woan't say why."

Fred nodded. Though slightly younger their neighbour's girl would be good company for Peggy.

"Oi be a'thinkin' o' givin' ma wages to George fer safe keepin', Fred."

For a moment Fred pondered his brother's words.

"Oi'll do the same."

"Doan't mention it to Peggy or Caleb."

"Roite. Ma be soo different."

"Grief an' too much liquor change people."

As they walked, emerging evening sounds broke upon their silence, but they were largely ignored. Stan's sluggish brain accelerated as he reviewed activity and conversation of the last hour. So many unanswered questions tumbled relentlessly in his thoughts. *Why hev Ma suddenly taaken to drinkin' liquor? Who be still supplyin' her? Why won't she eat?* He cringed at the idea that Ma no longer cared about her children. *Surely she ha'ent stopped lovin' us because Pa be gone. Why mistreat her own daughter? How can I protect Peggy? An' stop Caleb bein' soo awkward an' argumentative.*

The evening was cloudless and still. Water lapped softly against the riverbank. Moored fishing boats rocked gently as they walked by. *Why had Pa's boat succumbed to the storm and disintegrated so close to shore?* There had been a multitude of speculations, but no one really knew the answer. *Dear God, can Yew make sense of it all? Why did Ma warn against speakin' with Joe Jenner about millin' the gleanin's*?

Lost in his musings Stan failed to notice Fred had gone ahead to join Peggy and Caleb who had stopped to scrump late blackberries from the brambles along the hedgerow. He quickened his pace and caught up with them.

"Come yew on, mussn't dawdle. Race yew to the lane." Spurred on by the challenge the youngsters scurried ahead so that by the time he reached them his siblings were chatting with Danny Jenner who had been drawn to the door of the mill house by the sound of their laughter.

"Evenin', Danny, when be yow'n Pa millin' gleaners' wheat?"

"Gleaners' wheat!" A voice shout contemptuously. "Yew ent gleaned nuthen." Joe Jenner's burly, unkempt body joined his surly voice as he ascended from the side of the mill pond. Pitchfork held menacingly in front of him he approached the group leering at them through a twisted mouth.

"Doan't deal wi' Joe." Ma's voice echoed in the recess of Stan's mind. Before he could reply, the door to the mill cottage opened and Colin stepped out to greet them. Uncomfortable with Joe's aggressive stance Stan turned and spoke to Colin.

"Good day to ye, Col. How be yer Ma an' Pa?"

"They be doin' noicely," Colin replied with a splutter,

his words interspersed with a sudden bout of coughing.

"Which day be ye millin' gleaners' grain?"

"Yew ent gleaned noo corn," Joe shouted spitefully, cruelty sliding out of his eyes.

"We did, we did," Caleb shouted, jumping up and down. "Me an' Peggy an' Beatie picked loads."

"Doan't talk squit, Squirt. Beatie ent hum," Joe jeered.

Colin's eyes lit up at the mention of Beatie. Soo thass how the land lies, thought Stan.

"Beatie be doin' noicely up at the Big Huss but came to help wi' gleanin' along wi' Miss Peskett an' the school children as Ma be sickly." Stan spoke kindly for Colin's ears alone.

Colin, of little words, inclined his head in acknowledgement.

"Tuesday sennoite. Bring ee early mornin'."

Stan nodded his thanks. "Elsie an' Jem Capps?"

"Same."

Stan called to his siblings. "Come yew on. Muss be hum afore dark."

They waved farewell to Danny, Joe's scathing remarks ringing in their ears. Peggy and Caleb scampered along the lane, crossing the bridge that spanned the river, that fed the stream, that filled the mill pond that powered the sails that worked the mill.

"Water be pretty useful," mused Fred as he looked back over the parapet at the roaring torrent.

"True, but also mighty powerful," replied Stan, "unpredictable an' deadly."

They knew to their cost the havoc uncontrollable water caused. They were living with the aftermath of such an occurrence.

“Yew can channel it, but yew can’t tame it. Keep to the lane," he called to Caleb. "We will call on Mister George an' Mrs Kemp as we pass by the stables."

If George and Edith were surprised by their unexpected evening visitors they did not show it but welcomed them in. Annie was delighted to have bedtime pushed back. The youngsters gathered round her by the hearth and through stifled yawns chatted together. Stan and Fred spoke briefly with their self-appointed mentors who readily agreed to be custodians of their wage pouches. George put his arm across Fred's shoulders to allay his youthful fears. A boy trying to take on a man's role, he thought. For Edith's ears alone Stan quietly spoke of the recent revelation concerning Hester's mistreatment of Peggy. Edith shocked beyond measure, stumbled to the table. Stan pulled out a chair for her.

Concerned, George stepped towards her. She lifted eyes to him and smiled and motioned for him to light the lamp.

Stan called to his tired siblings and in encroaching darkness they took their leave picking up a couple of snared rabbits on their way home. Peace settled around his heart. Several issues had been resolved that evening.

Thank Yew, God, fer blessin' us wi' such good neighbours.

CHAPTER SIX

"...and faint..."

Quite some months later, as the sun rose and early morning broke over the dwelling above the stables, the hiss of a boiling kettle accompanied the sweet lilting song that fell from Edith's lips. Bubbling gurgles of a Monday morning washday pan also joined in the cacophony of sound as Edith engaged with her routine at the start of a new week. She was a busy little body who tackled her chores with energy and sang to brighten the task. The white starched cross-over pinafore which enveloped her comely figure did little to hide her expanding waistline as she reached alternately between stirring a pot hanging over the fire and pushing the posser up and down in the wash tub.

"Oi do hope the Bemment children hev a crust to fill their stomachs afore they start the day. Stan do seem to be keepin' on top o' things, but Hester be still far from roite." The gruel for her family's breakfast was almost ready to serve and the simmering clothes which caused steam to rise into her face would be right for rinsing when George came in for his meal. Edith was an organized person and very saddened by her friend's continuing slovenly approach to homemaking. Most of their neighbours struggled to survive on the pittance they earned from their labours in the fields or on the sea but since the loss of her husband Hester appeared to have given up the struggle. No amount of cajoling by Edith or scolding from anyone else seemed to have any effect in lifting her spirits. Jeremiah would have been devastated at the state of his beloved Hester. His heart would have soared at the valiant way Stan was doing his utmost to hold the family together.

Edith sighed and paused to wipe the beads of perspiration from her brow. The early start and busyness caused her to feel tired and faint. She sat for a moment and pushed dampened wisps of hair from her eyes, eyes that George called cornflower blue. He said they sparkled and danced amidst her straw-coloured hair just like their counterparts in the ripened corn fields where he spent so much of his working time these days preparing the land for that anticipated harvest. Momentarily, she cupped her left cheek with the palm of her hand as she dreamily recalled the moments just before George had left to attend to the horses in preparation for the day's work. He had tenderly caressed the side of her face with a hand calloused by hours spent labouring in the field and the stables, kissed her forehead then the tip of her nose and finally his lips descended on to her rosebud mouth; their special ritual prior to his going out to perform early morning chores before breakfast.

Briefly, Edith glanced affectionately around her little domain then, as she turned back towards the tasks in hand, she patted her swollen abdomen. A sigh escaped her lips again as she arched her aching back. How she longed for the day when she had a proper washhouse, preferably one at ground level that would eliminate the frequent trawl up and down the outside stone staircase carrying buckets of water to fill the wash pan. It was necessary to repeat the process when she carried the washing down the steps to hang onto the washing line which George had erected for her across the lower end of their vegetable plot using discarded ship's masts. In her present condition she found it a tiring process. Some cottages had a water butt to catch the rainwater from the roof of the out-house which was used for washing and cleaning; a shared pump or well in a communal yard provided drinking water. Edith's home had neither. All water had to be fetched from the pump in the stable yard.

The precious washing water was used again for their weekly bath, Annie still delighting in the playful routine her parents created. The ritual took place in front of the hearth on Monday evenings in a zinc bath that usually hung on a nail fastened to the wall at the base of the outside steps which George humped up on his back. Edith's bath time followed once their daughter had settled for sleep, George adding a panful of hot water to the cooled water in the tub when it was his turn. Some of the water was used to swill down the outside steps on Tuesday morning after they had been scrubbed. In recent times George had taken it upon himself to carry the remainder down in bucket loads when he came home for his midday dinner and throw it across the vegetable plot, but only after some had been used to scrub out the privy at the far end of the garden.

Edith's father had spoken disparagingly of the dreary, ramshackle accommodation when the Squire, Lord de Vessey, first offered it to his drayman and his new bride.

"It be a disgrace. Only fit fer vermin to live in." But the young couple, having eyes only for each other, were thrilled at the opportunity to have a home to call their own even though it was a dilapidated roof space above the stabling where George's beloved Suffolk Punches were housed, and vermin were content to reside. The young couple could see its potential and were grateful to their employer for his benevolence for it meant they wouldn't have to live in cramped quarters with either his or her parents. They were not faint-hearted at the prospect of hard work ahead of them needed to make it a habitable space.

The stable lads and farm hands willingly offered helping hands to ready the space for occupation. They had bounded up the stone steps but the door at the top seemed to be wedged. When pushing would not open it they heaved their shoulders against the unyielding wooden obstacle. As it slowly budged ajar a distasteful, musty odour emanated from the gloomy interior.

"Yeow! What a stink!" George held his nose as he squeezed through the gap and clattered across unseen obstructions, tripping over galvanised buckets sending stagnant water sloshing in all directions. Clutter and grime pervaded the murky roof space. Undeterred George set to shifting items that were blocking the door so that he could open it to let air and light in.

His friends helped clear away the junk and rubble that had accumulated over the years and searched for fallen pantiles to make the roof watertight again. Panes of glass were obtained from elsewhere, cut to size and puttied into the solitary window frame which was, thankfully, still intact. Midst laughter, as tangled webs clung to their hair, the rafters were brushed clear of debris which was carted down the steps and added to the growing bonfire pile to the rear of the overgrown plot that had been optimistically designated the vegetable patch but not before George, being of a careful nature, rescued what could be salvaged or mended and put to good use.

George also set traps to catch the rats that had for so long been the only inhabitants of the neglected roof space because Edith couldn't 'abide the varmints'. With permission, floorboards from a derelict cottage on the de Vessey estate were dismantled and carted to the stables where George and his pals nailed them into the spaces between the beams and joists to create a ceiling to the dwelling. It was then lime washed by the lads, along with the walls, creating a light airy chamber for the newlyweds, chiefly Edith, to fashion into a home.

Following their marriage Edith continued to work as lady's maid to Lady Marion de Vessey in the Manor House. Against opposition from her father she and George pooled their meagre wages to pay the rent and buy food they were unable to grow.

"It be a husband's responsibility to provide for his family!" But his dogma did not bother George or Edith. They were quite content with their arrangement. They were a proud, hardworking couple, so that the struggles to make ends meet that they encountered in the early days of marriage remained within the confines of their loft home. They endeavoured to make the most of their limited resources, refused to grumble about their lot but just got on with the tedium of each day. They enjoyed one another's company, and the walls frequently echoed to the sound of laughter and joy.

They were both resourceful people growing as much produce as they could on their vegetable plot once it had been cleared of weeds and brambles. As Edith learnt to master the bread oven, which had been built into the side of the newly erected chimney over the fireplace and hearth the lads had fashioned with bricks hauled on a handcart from the derelict cottage, she also experimented with her cooking skills. Faithfully she tended to her hens, the egg money from sales at the weekly market was used to buy staples such as oil and coal, additional flour and oatmeal and occasionally meat or fish. Fish was not so plentiful since her father's accident aboard his fishing vessel. He was now permanently laid up and the boat was sold.

George longed for the day when he could afford a piglet to fatten up and provide them with their own meat. He sauntered down to Home Farm when a sow was due to farrow anxious to learn what might happen to the runt of the litter hoping the pennies he jangled in his pocket were enough to make it his. To date he had been unsuccessful.

If there were coppers left over from the egg money Edith saved up for additional extras such as material for curtains or cotton and needles to sew a patchwork quilt for their bed from scraps of leftovers from garments she had previously made. She was an enterprising, hardworking young woman; a facet both her husband and employer admired and appreciated. It was this quality that had enabled Lady Marion to argue her cause, quite against convention, to keep Edith on as her maid following her marriage. With Annie's arrival this arrangement radically changed but sewing, particularly fine embroidery work as well as occasional mending, was sent to the stable loft for Edith's accomplished hands to work on. Once Annie commenced school Edith spent a couple of mornings up at the Manor repairing household linen and attending to Lady Marion's personal wardrobe. She was also able to mend their own clothes and fashion something for Annie out of castoffs from the big house. Gradually, over the years, she made peg rugs for the floor using hessian sacks pegged with left-over scraps of material cut into strips so that they had something soft to walk on instead of the bare boards. She also pieced together oddments to make patchwork covers and quilts for the bed and chairs and sewn together larger strips to make linings for the curtains for both window and door to keep out the wintry draughts.

The multi-functional room where Edith was now working so cheerfully provided cooking, sleeping and living quarters for the family of three to whom this space was home. She pondered how they could rearrange the space to accommodate the anticipated new family member. George whitewashed the walls regularly to reflect as much light as possible from the one window which faced east and gave illumination to the cooking and eating areas. As the winter days receded daylight began to come earlier. The glow of the breaking dawn peeking through the window and the burst of the rising sun which heralded the start of each new day lifted Edith's spirits as she rose from her bed. George whistled as he performed his ablutions.

"Ain't this grand! 'Cos we be living near the most easterly point on the coast we sees the break o' day fust in all the land."

"Yus, it be soo good to be where morning wakens an' watch daylight push away the darkness o' night an' see the risin' sun dance an' glisten upon the tossin' waves," Edith agreed.

The hearth and open fireplace occupied the wall at one end of the room and sat beneath a resplendent hood taken from a disused labourer's cottage that Edith had thoroughly cleaned and polished. Above it George had erected a functional mantle shelf fitted with hooks of various sizes from which hung pans and implements needful for cooking and baking, its upper surface was graced by jugs, bowls and candle holders. Edith was so thankful George was handy with his hands. The sparse items of furniture scattered about the room were testament to his skill; mended spindles, re-formed chairbacks and split seats sanded, broken legs all put back together to make them serviceable.

In the middle of the floor space in front of the hearth a wooden kitchen table scrubbed to a brilliant whiteness dominated with a chair set under each side, one for each family member and a spare for any visitor who cared to call. The one at the far end was high-backed with scrolled and spindled arms, for use only by the man of the house till Annie clambered into it one day and with hands held aloft teased,

"It's moi chair. Oi be master today." Whereby her father took slow strides towards her declaring playfully,

"Is that roite? We shall see about that, m'gal." By the time George reached the chair Annie was out of it and darting around the table. A game of chase ensued. When caught George threatened to tickle his teasy torment of a daughter to death till a smiling Edith said it was time to eat, and the family settled down to enjoy their meal and discuss events of the day together.

"Trouble be a'brewen up at the Big Hus."

"How so?"

George tapped his nose. "Mark ma words, Master Quentin be a'treaden on shaky ground."

CHAPTER SEVEN

"...and weary."

George's gloomy prediction of possible trouble at the Manor caused Edith some concern but she wisely kept her thoughts to herself. *Oi juss thank Yew, Good Lord, fer Yow'n lovin' kindness an' the peace an' harmony we hev in ow'n hum.* In the quiet of her heart Edith also gave thanks for her hardworking, caring husband and was glad Annie had such a close relationship with her father. It was a delight to see them interact with each other. Joy bubbled in her heart as she watched the two play together as their little girl grew and developed. Even at the end of an exhausting day's work George still had endless patience with his mischievous and inquisitive daughter. He was never too weary to give attention to this young life who brought so much joy into their home. The new life Edith was carrying would only add to their family contentment. *Thank Yew, Lord, fer this kindly man.*

Edith's own memories of a father in her childhood were of brief encounters with a persistently absent, austere whiskered man who barely acknowledged her when he was home from sea, let alone speak or play with her. She also had a mother who spoke her mind and constantly admonished her about trivial misdemeanours. Edith would readily admit she had imbibed some of her mother's sharpness and at times struggled to curb her own unruly tongue. Yet there was a sparkle in her eye and a softness to her spirit that had captured George's heart and given him courage to approach her stern father to ask for her hand. From the moment of their marriage they endeavoured to build their union on mutual respect and godly values particularly after Jeremiah had shared the Gospel news of repentance and forgiveness. Each contributing their skills to create a home of love and warmth.

It perturbed Edith that George sensed upset at the Big House. Master Quentin's outbursts so frequently rippled into the lives of all who lived and worked on the estate. Lady Araminta, the former lady of the Manor, had thoroughly spoiled her younger son. His fun-loving antics amused her, and she could see no wrong in the tricks he played upon unsuspecting victims but since his father's death Quentin's irresponsible behaviour had become more outrageous particularly when he was in his cups. *Dear God, please give Lord Ralph wisdom when dealing with Master Quentin's despicable actions.*

Edith valued tranquillity and worked hard to make a calm, welcoming space for George to come home to each evening. Her nimble fingers were never still, and her lilting voice generally accompanied whatever task she might be doing. The lovingly restored loft space was testament to that. At the far end of the room that made up their home was a black metal bedstead, another throw-out from the big house. Adorned with intricate brass knobs it stood resplendent against George's pristine white wall. Edith had painstakingly worked a patchwork bedspread which was now thrown over a mattress stuffed with feathers plucked from their own cocks and hens prior to their entry into the roasting pan. It had taken some years to collect sufficient to make it firm, but comfortable. At the foot of the bed, alongside the wall, just inside the door stood a fine chest of drawers rescued from someone's upstairs attic meticulously repaired by George's skilful hands. Edith spread across it a table-runner she had embroidered on which was placed a porcelain pot holding a scented geranium; a slip of a cutting given by a well-wisher on their wedding day. On the floor by the side of the bed rested a brightly coloured peg rug the result of nightly labours sitting by the hearth on winter evenings when George would read from the Good Book before they shared family prayers together.

Towards the foot of the bed was a handmade low-sided-cot, little more than a large rectangular box without a lid, strewn with knitted blankets. A child-sized quilt nestled around a tousled haired sleeping child whose feet were dangling beyond the end.

"Well, that be a rum ole do! Yew be a growin' too quick, m'gal, soo oi muss chop orf those feet," George teased one day.

"Pa! Oi needs ma feet," was Annie's indignant response. To Edith, George winked and said, "Oi'll look fer timber to extend the bed."

"Come yew on, ma sleepy gal, it's toime yew wuz a'stirrin'. Pa will be hum shortly fer his breakfast an' we mussn't keep him a'waitin'."

Annie opened her eyes and smiled up at her mother.

"Oi'm just a'goin' to hang out the clothes. There be washin' water in the bowl. Yew be dressed by the toime oi git back."

The growing girl stretched an arm over her head, kicked her legs from under the covers, "Yus, Ma," and was out of her bed in a trice.

Edith had put the washing on to boil as day began to dawn, George having carried buckets of water up from the pump the previous evening and stoked up the fire before going down to the stables for early morning chores. The clothes were now rinsed and mangled, so she carried the full basket on her hip down the outside stone steps to hang them on the line behind the stable block to blow in the spring breeze. With abandon Edith flung the smaller items on the top of the hedge that bordered the vegetable patch. If the weather remained fine the clothes and linen would be dry by the time she returned from visiting her parents in the beach hamlet.

Each day prior to breakfast George tended his precious Suffolk Punches. As he prepared the horses for the day's work he chatted with Fred and Stan and the other stable lads to assign them their tasks for the day. In the meantime, Edith made gruel for breakfast in between running up and down the outside stone steps in all weathers carrying water from the pump and emptying slops each morning. She baked pies or bread for George's mid-morning pack-up, if he wasn't coming home at mid-day, and dinner for her parents who lived in Fishermen's Alms-houses down on the beach. Since she was very young Annie had climbed on to a chair to get alongside Edith, for she enjoyed nothing better than helping her mother to cook and bake vegetable or savoury pastries then deliver them along with the articles Edith had sewn, embroidered or mended for folks in the village or up at Newton Manor House. Whilst Annie was captivated by the awe and grandeur of the Big House she was drawn to the coziness of the snug terraced cottages of the beach hamlet. "They be friendlier."

After hanging the washing Edith scrubbed out the privy at the bottom of the garden with some of the washing water. She left the remainder for George to carry down the outdoor staircase to throw on to the emerging vegetables in the strip of land they had cultivated with Annie's help amongst much laughter and teasing. Throughout her developing years Annie's fascination at shoots appearing through the soil, her delight at bird song and collecting eggs from the chicken run, constantly intrigued both her parents. The sights, sounds and scents of the seasons interested Annie as she absorbed all she saw and heard. Her parents encouraged her interest in nature and from an early age involved her participation in all practical aspects of producing their own food. Grubby hands frequently accompanied muddy skirts, as the little girl learned the value of God's provision. "Look Ma taters."

Every Friday morning Annie had 'helped' Edith sell the eggs at the market until she started attending school. Her dimpled face with its infectious grin charmed even the most hesitant to purchase the wares the pair held in their baskets, so she was sometimes rewarded with a farthing. It was all hers. Sometimes she bought a ribbon for her hair or chose a piece of lace for her dress. On occasions she picked out some chewy toffee which Ole Mother Jenner made and sold from the doorway of her cottage. Teaching her daughter to be thrifty Edith suggested, on some days, that Annie save it. So, she took it home and placed it in the corner of the bottom drawer in the chest by the door which also housed her spare change of clothes.

Most days, after breakfast George left for the fields and Edith prepared to go to the clutch of dwellings on the beach to check on the parents and deliver a pie or pasty made up of left-uvvers or whatever was to hand, once Annie had skipped off to the schoolroom. The old folks had moved to live in the Fishermen's Alms-houses on the beach after Edith's father was incapacitated by an accident at sea. The hook attached to the arm that held the net on the sailing trawler had swung uncontrollably in high winds during a storm and hit him in the back. The injury had left him paralysed and bed-ridden and he had given up all hope of ever getting out of it again. Being an active man this situation frustrated him. Having been skipper of his own fishing vessel he was accustomed to giving orders. So, now his wife and daughter took the place of his crew, and he expected them to be at his beck and call, to do everything for him. Her mother at times was driven to distraction by his constant demands. The house move meant his bed was now positioned on the ground floor which saved her mother the constant task of traipsing up and down stairs to deal with his needs. Edith did what she could to ease her mother's burden and called in most days when she had finished her own home chores.

Having completed her washday routine, served and cleared the breakfast things, Edith slipped out of her working apron, hung it on the hook George had placed for that purpose alongside the mantle by the hearth and grabbed her bonnet and shawl from the peg on the back of the door. She popped a pie into her basket as well as a loaf of bread she had baked the previous day and nestled a couple of freshly laid eggs by the side of it which she knew her mother would enjoy. Her father would turn up his nose and complain that runny egg slops were not man food.

School was out so today Annie was accompanying Edith and danced around excitedly while she waited for her mother to be ready.

"Put on yow'n bonnet, Annie," Edith instructed, "then we'll be orf."

As she opened the heavy door angry, argumentative voices could be heard at the far end of the stables. The sound spiralled up the stone steps. Annie cringed, clapped her hands over her ears dropping her bonnet to the floor. Edith felt faint and sick to the pit of her stomach. She did not like confrontation. The ferocity of the language gripped her with apprehension.

"Pick up yow'n bonnet and put it on," she admonished her daughter more sharply than she intended.

Warily they negotiated the stone staircase. At the bottom step Edith looked cautiously around to see where the loud shouts were actually coming from. Annie nervously hung behind her mother. To the left of them an enraged cultured voice overrode frenzied ranting of the stable lads. Edith quickly decided to circumnavigate the commotion. She grabbed Annie by the hand. "C'mon, m'gal, we'll goo this way."

"But what about Pa?" Annie looked anxiously back over her shoulder.

"Doan't yew worrit. Pa be up in the fields by now, not involved in that frackhus."

CHAPTER EIGHT

"Up..."

As mother and daughter tentatively began to cross the cobbled stable yard they spied Lady Marion de Vessey strolling down the path from the Manor House.

"Good morning, Edith," her ladyship greeted warmly as she drew level with them. Edith dipped her head while Annie picked up her skirt, crossed her legs and bounced into a curtsey.

"Can you wait a moment, Edith, I would like to speak with you but first I need to ask the lads to prepare a carriage for this afternoon to allow me to pay a visit in Newton Lokesby." She walked graciously towards a stable lad not involved in the fracas further down the yard. Fred was busily engaged in mucking out a horse's quarters but stopped and looked up as Lady Marion approached to make her request. When her ladyship retraced her steps she drew alongside Annie to make comment on her pretty dress then turned to Edith to pass the time of day enquiring first about her father and mother.

"They be doin' noicely, m'lady. Mother be a'copin' an' oi try to goo uvver most days to lend a hand."

"Knowing how busy you are I hesitate to make further pulls on your time, but I would be pleased if you could make more baby gowns for this little one. Your work is so fine." Blushing prettily her ladyship's hand gently patted her slightly swollen abdomen.

Before Edith could open her mouth to reply Master Quentin strode up the cobbled road and rudely interrupted their conversation. He demanded a horse immediately of Fred, the stable hand whom he had seen speaking with his sister-in-law.

"What are you doing here, Marion? I should have thought this smelly place was out of your comfort zone," he spat out caustically.

"I came to ask for a carriage for a visit I am making after lunch."

“What! Why didn't you send a servant? That's what we pay them for," he commented critically. A slight sigh escaped Lady Marion's lips.

"I needed a walk and wanted to speak with Mrs Kemp," she replied patiently.

"You shouldn't fraternise with the peasants, Marion," he admonished loudly and unkindly. Marion felt uncomfortable and shook her head at her brother-in-law's demeaning manner towards Edith and Annie.

"Where is George?" he demanded.

"Up in Five Acre field," volunteered Fred diffidently.

"He should be here when I need him," Master Quentin roared brusquely.

"He’ll be back at dinner time," the lad spoke uncertainly. Quentin struck his thigh with his riding gloves. "That will be too late. I need him now." Impatiently he looked around the yard. "Those layabouts say they can't deal with the horses."

"They be field workers not hossmen."

"Where is everyone else?"

"Busy, sir, it bein' halfway through the mornin'." Fred knew that the stable hands not already out in the fields leading the horses, having completed their early morning chores, were catching up on sleep in one of the empty stables, following a late night down at the Fisherman's Arms.

"Ring the bell and summon them, now," Quentin commanded.

"Thass not ma job, sir."

"Do it, boy," he roared, impatiently.

"Yus, sir, oi'll g...git th...them," Fred stammered and stumbled towards a bell attached to the outer wall of a stable and pulled hard on the rope till the instrument rang out loudly.

Lady Marion winced at the loud clanking.

Annie cried out and quickly clapped her hands over her ears.

Master Quentin yelled.

Edith spoke sharply, "Not quite soo loud, Fred."

The frantic clanging brought a swift response from Jethro, Wilf and Sid who came running with jackets flapping and hats askew, while elderly Bert Bracewell, accompanied by Stan, followed unhurriedly his creaking knees slowing his gait. The farm labourers at the end of the block simply stood and stared.

When the stable lads stumbled into Quentin's view he pompously bellowed at them for their laziness. Spitefully he raised his whip to them when they appeared, slovenly and so very obviously bleary eyed.

Fred stood solemnly by and grimaced as his friends received the verbal and physical onslaught.

Quentin continued to rail at them about George's

absence.

Unfazed, Fred stood his ground. "But, sir, he be a' workin' in the fields along wi' the hosses."

"He should be here when I need him," Quentin spluttered with a daunting mixture of fury and ferocity.

"Don't be so unreasonable, Quentin, he is only doing his job," Lady Marion spoke softly.

"His job is to be here to get me a horse ready when I need one. He should have better control of his lads," Quentin snorted. He eyed the stable hands disdainfully.

"Look at this motley crowd. You are a disgrace."

"Ma would'n let us be wearin' ow'n bestest clothes fer work. They be at the pawn shop till Sa'urday," Fred offered.

"What is your name, boy?"

"Fred, sir."

"Right, Fred, can you get Champion ready for me?"

"Yus sir, but oi kin't git the saddle orf the hook nor git it on his back 'cos oi be too short. An' his head be too high fer me to fix his bridle."

Quentin stamped his foot impatiently. "So, what are you doing working in the stables if you cannot reach up?"

"Oi'm a'larnin', sir, an' oi be good at muckin' out, an' fillin' feeds, an' talkin' to hosses."

"That is glib talk but at least you seem honest."

"Yus, sir, Ma teached us to tell the truth."

"How old are you, Fred?"

"Twelve an' a bit, sir."

"Not a man yet, then?"

"Noo, sir."

"What's your pay?"

"Ha'penny a day, sir."

"Well, if you can get the horse ready for me you shall

have a rise. What do you say to sixpence a week? Despite your height you are worth more than all these rascals put together. It will come out of George's wages as you are here, and he is not, when I need a horse."

"Thank 'ee, sir." Fred touched his cap as he had seen the other hands do when in the presence of Master Quentin or his lordship.

"Get to it, then," Quentin snapped.

"Yus, sir," gulped Fred and scurried away.

Edith gasped. Lady Marion stepped forward shocked by Quentin's thoughtless words and cavalier treatment of the hands. She touched his arm. "Quentin, I do believe it is not within your gift to change the present wage arrangements."

Quentin bristled and shook off her hand. He puffed out his chest and between gritted teeth hissed, "Don't you dare question my authority in front of servants, Marion. I have said it, and it shall be so. Anyway, a spunky lad like Fred deserves a step up."

Marion paled at his forthright rudeness, held her tongue, and stepped back to Edith's side.

Edith's face had lost all colour. The loss of income would be particularly hard. Marion faced her.

"My dear, do not worry. I shall make sure you do not lose out. I know how conscientiously both you and your husband work for our family even if Quentin refuses to acknowledge it."

Edith's woe-begotten face dropped as she dipped in a curtesy. "Thank yew, m'lady."

Fred sweet-talked Stan to give him a hand with Master Quentin's horse. Annie slipped passed Edith and Lady Marion to skip alongside Fred and Stan as they made their way towards Champion's stable chatting amiably about one another's plans for the day.

"What is that child doing here?" Quentin barked.

"Annie lives here, Quentin."

"What do you mean?"

"She lives above the stables."

"What nonsense! She should not be here. This is no place for a child. Horses are sensitive creatures. Her carelessness could cause an accident. Champion's too valuable to risk that."

Edith could not remain silent.

"Annie hev bin wi' hosses since the day she wuz born..."

"Hold your tongue, woman!" Quentin cracked his whip angrily.

"...an' she probably handles them better'n yew, sir."

"How dare you!" Quentin raised his hand, his face screwed up in rage, unused to what he referred to as the lower classes expressing an opinion, especially one that reflected him in a bad light.

Edith stepped back, fearing he was going to strike her.

"Get rid of her. She is expendable, my horse is not," he ordered.

"Do not speak to my friend in that tone, Quentin."

"Friend!" he spat out. "I wonder what your husband will have to say about you taking the side of a peasant against his brother!"

"He, too, would regard Mrs Kemp as my friend, and Annie as a sensible person to have around horses," Lady Marion returned in a soft voice. "Quentin, why don't you go and see how Stan and Fred are getting on with Champion."

Quentin turned on his heel and stormed angrily towards his horse's stall, but Bert forestalled him by stepping into his path.

"Yew a'seein' them rail men agin, sir?"

"That is none of your business, Bracewell."

"Pshaw! It will be if they put them rails through ma cottage."

"It is my land and my cottage, not yours. So, I will do what I think best," Quentin bellowed pompously.

"Best fer who?" spluttered Bert angrily.

"The railway development will be for the good of all," Quentin declared emphatically.

Bewildered, Bert said, "But where will oi live?"

"That is your concern, not mine," Quentin snapped as he strode towards his horse.

"It wouldn't hev happened in yow'n father's day," Bert yelled after him. Then, he remembered Lady Marion was still standing close by. "Oi beg yow'n pard'n, m'lady." He touched his cap as he inclined his head towards her.

"That's alright Mr Bracewell. You are not to worry. My husband will make sure you are not put out of your home."

"He'll hev to curb that brother of his, then."

"Ralph is all for progress but not at the expense of foul play."

"His lordship be a gent, m'lady, but Master high-an'-mighty rides rough shod over anyone who gits in his way," the old man nodded sorrowfully towards Quentin's receding back.

Thankfully all the stable lads rallied round so that by the time Quentin reached Champion's stall the horse was ready to receive him. He swiftly mounted up on to the horse without so much as a thank you. With a flick of his whip he galloped out of the stable yard leaving behind a somewhat subdued little group.

Edith turned and watched absently as Master Quentin

cantered briskly across the parkland. A frown furrowed her brow. The events that had just taken place were not at all what she had expected when she rose early this morning. An extra 3d would certainly benefit Fred's family, as long as Hester didn't get hold of it, but would leave a big hole in George's pocket. *Oh, George, how are we to manage?*

Marion was first to break the silence. "Where are you off to this morning, Edith?"

"Annie an' oi be taakin' victuals up to Ma an' Pa."

"I do hope you find them as well as can be expected."

"Thank yew, m'lady." Edith inclined her head. "Oi'll do ma best to fulfil yow'n request fer more gowns."

Edith picked up her basket and called to Annie, "C'mon m'gal let's goo see Gramps an' Nans." Together they began to make their way to the Fishermen's Alms-houses on the beach.

CHAPTER NINE

"...early morning..."

As they departed Lady Marion stepped gingerly across the pebbled yard. Perturbed by the altercation with Quentin she thoughtfully followed the path to the Manor House knowing she had the unpleasant task of relaying her brother-in-law's obnoxious behaviour to her husband. As she approached her home the oak front door opened before her.

"Hanson, how kind," she greeted the butler. "Is my husband at home?"

"I believe he is in the study, my lady."

"Has coffee been served?"

"Peters is in the process of preparing it. Shall I bring another cup?"

"That would be good, thank you, Hanson."

The butler held out an arm to receive her ladyship's outer garment then walked ahead of Marion across the hallway. He tapped on the study door, turned the brass knob and announced, "Lady Marion, my lord."

Hearing the voice of his butler, Lord Ralph glanced up from the paperwork strewn on his desk. The sight of his wife caused his face to crease in pleasure. Smiling he rose and came forward with hands outstretched to greet her.

"My dear, is all well?"

Their union was a love match not a marriage of convenience nor arranged so that the estate might benefit from a substantial dowry. However, Lord Ralph knew Marion well enough to know that she would not normally interrupt the hour at his desk unless it were absolutely necessary. His eyes took in her countenance and although a smile graced her attractive features he sensed her blue grey eyes were dulled by an unknown anxiety.

"I am well..."

"But?"

A tap at the opening door indicated the arrival of Peters with the promised coffee.

"Come, sit down, my dear, and tell me what is concerning you." He led her to the settle. "Please pour, Peters."

"Yes, sir."

As his lordship seated his wife by the fireside, unobtrusively the maid served the coffee, placed the cups on the table near to them, then quietly withdrew.

Ralph sat beside his wife, turned towards her and tenderly touched her cheek. He smiled. "Now if your condition is not a concern what is causing this anxious frown?" His fingers moved gently up her face and affectionately traversed the contours of her forehead.

Lady Marion released a sigh she hadn't realised she was holding. Ralph's touch was soothing.

"Quentin!"

Since the death of their father Lord Ralph bore the responsibility of running the de Vessey estate but his headstrong younger brother was for ever meddling and causing upset to some of the staff particularly their parent's old retainers. This created tension needlessly.

Ralph stiffened. "What has he been up to now?"

"He has reduced George Kemp's wages by 3d a week in order to give young Fred Bemment a pay increase."

"What!" Ralph jumped to his feet knocking his coffee cup flying. Peters, who must have been hovering nearby, rushed in.

"Is... oh dear, my lady...umm... shall..."

"Yes, please, Peters." Ralph gestured with a hand the mess his actions had created which Peters' practised eye had already seen and her hands were promptly attending to.

"And that is not all. In my hearing he told Mr Bracewell that with the coming of the railway his cottage would have to be dismantled."

"Why?"

"Because it will be in the path of some rail track that is to be laid, and he will have to find somewhere else to live."

"He cannot do that! Father allowed Bracewell to stay on in that cottage when he retired. By then he had worked for many years passed his 65th birthday. I believe he is a sitting tenant for life." Lord Ralph began to pace the floor. He struggled to rein in his anger.

"That was also my understanding of the situation. I assured Mr Bracewell his home was safe."

“You did right, my dear." Ralph placed his hand on her shoulder reassuringly.

"I will need to check the contractual papers Father drew up with Marcus Capps, senior, but as far as I am aware Bracewell is a lifetime retainer, so the cottage remains his home for the rest of his days. I would like to know what Quentin is playing at. I have not given consent for the railway to go across our land. In fact, I have not been approached nor been party to any discussions regarding the railway. I am aware that Morton Peto and his cohorts are anxious to develop a harbour at Lowestoft and establish rail links to London and the mid-land counties in order to get newly landed fish transported more quickly to their lucrative markets. But I am unaware of any intent to expand in our direction."

Marion laid a restraining hand on Ralph's arm.

"Listening to him talk I fear some underhand scheming is going on. Quentin was very adamant about the track being laid and quite specific about the route it would take."

Ralph paced the room thoughtfully. "I cannot think what benefit a route in this direction would be. In contrast to the large quantities of fish the Yarmouth and Lowestoft boats land our fishermen bring in very small catches."

"Yes, sufficient for local needs."

"I'll broach these issues with Quentin and question him about the incidents you have mentioned. Meanwhile," he flashed Marion a smile as he sat back at his desk, "do not worry your head about it. I will also speak with Mr Jenner to find out what he may have heard on the village grapevine. I will instruct him to convey assurances to Bracewell and others that their homes and livelihoods are secure."

"As your brother is so anxious to increase Fred's wages perhaps it could come out of his allowance."

Ralph chuckled. "Can you picture Quentin's face when I tell him that?"

***

George brought in the horses from fieldwork at noon. He tethered Clover then unhitched Bessie from the shafts of the wagon in the stable yard. He took off his cap and wiped an arm across his forehead. Fred came running.

"Good bor, rub her down when her tackle be orf but doan't let her drink till she be cooled down."

"Yus, Mister George."

"Then, put her in the far meadow. Jethro or Stan can tend to Clover. Oi'll taak out Blossom this afternoon. Hev yow'n dinner afore gitting her riddy. Then juss maak sure all be spick an' span juss as it should be so his lordship will hev no call fer complaint when he comes to the stables."

"Yus, Mister George. Thank yew, Mister George. Lady Marion be wantin' a carriage this afternoon."

George nodded.

"Yew be doin' roite well, m'bor." He inclined his head towards the end stall. "Oi see Champion be out."

"Yus, Master Quentin rode out this mornin'. He increased ma wages."

"Is that roite!"

"Yus," Fred gulped, remembering that his increase was at George's expense. "Sorry, Mister George," he muttered and quickly took Bessie's bridle and led her across the cobbled yard to her stall calling out to Stan as he went by that Clover was waiting attention.

George pondered Fred's words as he walked passed the stalls. Voices of lads working in the stables carried through the open doorways. Bert sounded angry. Tittle-tattle between the hands was not unusual but what George was overhearing seemed incredibly outlandish - Bert threatened with eviction? Fred's pay rise coming out of his wages? The new railway cutting up the fields?

He called out. Jethro's head appeared round the stable door. "Aah! Could ye ready the small coach wi' the roans fer Lady Marion arter yow'n lunch?"

"Yus, Mister George."

George scrubbed up at the pump and dried himself on the scrap of towel Edith left out for the purpose. Then he plodded towards the steps leading up to his home perplexed beyond measure at what he had overheard. Automatically he pushed open the unlocked door.

"Oi be hum," he called out.

When there was no response and no evidence of Edith or Annie or of dinner his puzzlement increased. He ran back down the steps, tore round the corner of the building onto the vegetable patch.

"Edith! Annie!" He opened the privy door. Shook his head. He ran to the hen run, then passed the wood store into the orchard. "Edith!" He rushed back along the cobbles. "Fred! Bert! Jethro!" He yelled. "Ye seen Edith an' Annie?"

"Noo, not since early mornin'," they each affirmed.

George wrung his hands and shook his head in bewilderment. Then cautiously broached the topic he had overheard the stable hands discussing earlier thinking that might have some bearing on his family's absence. They acquainted him with their version of the confrontation that had taken place with Master Quentin.

Thoughtfully, George processed his next course of action. It was so unlike Edith not to be home when he was due in from the fields and even less likely that she would not have a meal prepared for him when she was expecting him. And she never let the fire die down. *Wherever can she be? Surely nothing hev happened to ma treasures.* His heart beat rapidly at the thought of anything untoward happening to Edith or Annie. Should he return to work or go up to the Manor? Mr Jenner was a stickler for punctuality. "It makes for the smooth running of the estate," was his mantra. George came to a decision. He gave precise instructions to the stable lads for their afternoon tasks and left messages for those yet to come in from the fields. He ran back up the steps to his home, grabbed the loaf from the bread crock, sliced off a chunk, spread it with dripping and cut an onion in half. He munched on his makeshift dinner as he hurriedly made his way up to the Manor House. With cap in hand he uncharacteristically approached the front door and pulled at the bell.

"Mr Hanson, could oi see the Squire? Matter of urgency." To his credit Hanson did not batter an eyelid or challenge George's audacity at using the front door, but graciously invited him to step inside. George nervously smoothed his hair with his free hand as Henson tapped on Lord Ralph's study door.

"Mr Kemp to see you, Sir."

Elias Jenner straightened from the books he had been pouring over on his lordship's desk and stood to one side. Lord Ralph looked up, raised an eyebrow, then gave a nod.

"What can I do for you, George?" He asked as his drayman cum stableman stepped uncertainly through the doorway.

"We...ll... hmm...." George looked down at his feet. *Now oi'm here where doo oi begin?*

"Spit it out, George," Elias Jenner spoke impatiently.

Lord Ralph looked at his estate manager and lightly shook his head. He sensed, by his behaviour, that George was seriously troubled about something.

"Edith an' Annie be a'missin'," George blurted out. "An' the fire be out. There be no dinner on, Bert be losin' his hum, an' Hundred Acre, Top an' Lower Fields are to be cut in half by the rail tracks an' Fred's wages be a..."

"Stop, stop, stop, my dear man," Ralph raised his hand to curtail George's outburst.

"Hanson," his lordship called, "another pot of coffee, please. And would you ask Lady Marion to spare us a moment."

Lord Ralph turned back to George. "Now, my man, you seem to have a bundle of concerns. Let us deal with them one by one. First of all, Mr Jenner is just leaving to assure Bracewell the tenancy of his cottage is secure." His lordship rose, turned round and made his way towards the door and gestured for Mr Jenner to leave. "We'll continue our conversation later. Let it be known that no one is losing their home, and we must check the issue regarding the railway is being dealt with," he uttered quietly as he ushered out his surprised estate manager. Closing the door Lord Ralph picked up a chair and placed it by the side of his desk.

"Secondly, sit down, George." Bewildered George did as his lordship instructed. Lord Ralph returned to his desk chair and proceeded to explain the secure tenure of tenants living in tied properties on the estate, including his own. Neither Lady Marion nor Peters passed comment on the unusual tete a tete when they entered the room. Peters unobtrusively poured the coffee and left. Ralph rose, greeted his wife and invited her to join them. George clutched his cap and quickly got to his feet.

"My dear, George is concerned about the issues that took place in the incident you witnessed in the stable yard this morning. I hope between us we can lay his fears to rest."

Marion smiled. "Of course."

"His chief worry is the whereabouts of Edith and Annie."

"They were both well when we parted this morning. A little upset by the behaviour and language displayed by Que.."

"But m'lady...umm...what...umm..." George interrupted diffidently.

"George is unaware what occurred at the stables. Would you explain, my dear."

Gently Lady Marion recounted details of the early morning row she had unwittingly been drawn into.

When she finished Ralph sensitively asked, "Edith wouldn't stay away fearful of your response to my brother's unfounded reduction in your wages, would she?"

George shook his head in disbelief at such a notion. "We will manage. Edith be a good manager an' together we'll trust the Good Lord to see us through."

"You will not have to manage, my man. Your wages will not be reduced. By the way, how is young Fred doing?"

George brightened. "Well, very well. The bor be a nat'ral wi' hosses."

"Deserving of an increase?"

George nodded.

"I do not know if you heard my words as Mr Jenner was leaving but the matter of the railway is in..."

The study door burst open.

"Sir, I beg your pardon. A word, please. In the hall," Hanson urgently entreated. Ralph raised his eyebrows but recognized firmness in Hanson's voice so instinctively followed his butler.

Lord Ralph returned a short while later dressed in outdoor clothing. Hanson close behind him.

"Your coat, my lady."

"My dear, I have given instructions to delay luncheon

and postponed your afternoon visit because I believe your presence will be needed elsewhere. I have sent Williams to the stables with orders to bring the chaise up here, immediately."

Lord Ralph turned to George. "Come, my man, I believe we may have some answers to your queries. I understand there has been an incident at the Beach village. I will explain as we travel."

CHAPTER TEN

"...all in a hurry"

The pleasure and promise of the early morning had become somewhat spoiled for Edith by the happenings in the stable yard. The angry exchanges kept playing through her mind. Had she been wrong to answer back Master Quentin as she had done? His conduct towards Annie had riled her. Their daughter had lived and moved amongst horses since the day she was born. Like her father Annie displayed a natural empathy with them. On numerous occasions she and Fred worked together in the stalls, topping up mangers or brushing coats and combing manes. Mixing with the stable hands, moving in and out of the stables helping groom the horses was a normal activity for Annie. It had been hard to hold her tongue. But her forthrightness could have serious consequences. Master Quentin's actions were known to be unpredictable. *How am I going to tell George about the loss of his wages? He can't be in two places at once. That be unreasonable, an' the other stable hands be quoite capable o' saddlin' up a horse. Master Quentin's attitude to Annie be illogical. He be well aware that we live above the stables.*

Lost in her own thoughts Edith had momentarily forgotten her daughter. She frantically looked about her, but Annie, too, had been affected by the angry outbursts and instead of skipping ahead as was the norm, exploring the fascinating aspects of the country lane, she walked subdued just a few steps behind her mother. Edith shifted her basket and held out a hand to Annie with a smile.

"Well, m'gal, thass be a rum ole dew. Doan't know why men hev to shout so!"

"Pa will sort it out." Annie replied solemnly.

"Yew be roite. Mussn't let their crossness spoil this day the Good Lord hev blessed us wi'." Edith tossed her head towards the hedgerow bordering the lane. "Yew want to pick a posy fer Nans?"

Annie nodded reluctantly then dragged her feet towards a clump of primroses and bent to pick the sunny flowers, welcome harbingers of spring.

Within a short while Annie became enthralled in her task, but the burgeoning life all around them was lost on Edith. Her eyes missed the emerging green of leaves, and her ears failed to catch the warbling of the song thrush or the nest building activity in branches above her. Her mind continued to be tangled in the conversation of the morning. It was as well she had traversed this path so many times before that unbidden her feet knew which direction to tread. Annie recovered her spirits as she added to her posy and began to chatter in her usual manner unheeded by Edith who was still juggling the implications of the altercation with Master Quentin. *The gowns will bring in extra but woan't maak up for the regular loss of 3d a week.*

They had turned left out of the track leading from the stables. The hedgerow on either side of the lane erupted about them in all its green finery, a plethora of spring flowers springing up beneath its canopy occupied Annie's busy fingers as Edith mulled over the dilemma Master

Quentin had created.

"Look, Ma, it be as tall as me." Edith paused to smile at her daughter's delight, discovering clumps of ferns unfurling their coiled fronds above her head as she bent to add to her floral bounty.

"We best be quickenin' ow'n steps or Ma be a'thinkin' we not be a'comen' a'day."

Annie obeyed her mother's direction and, pressing her fist tightly round the bunch of flowers, darted onwards to the bend in the lane that led down to the mouth of the river.

Swooping gulls noisily followed an incoming fishing drifter. The boat hand called out and waved as the vessel sailed into its mooring in the harbour.

"Thass be Gramps ole mate. Hope he hev a foine catch," Edith commented as she lifted an arm to return the fisherman's greeting.

They passed the riverside hostelry and turned right just beyond the harbour lookout, each step drawing them closer to the dwellings on the beach. Across the way Norah Tuttle, shaking mats outside her doorway, raised a hand as Scruffy Leckie Rackham clopped by with Bluebell pulling his rickety cart laden with an assortment of wares. A bevy of children with runny noses were squabbling next door. Edith grabbed Annie's free hand and quickly crossed the lane. Turning the corner that faced the frontage of the Fishermen's Alms-houses she was alarmed to see smoke escaping from her parent's home. "Dear Lord, what be a'happenin'?" She dropped the basket, picked up her skirt and ran.

"Annie," she shouted over her shoulder. "Run back to the lookout. Hurry! Git Mr Willets, the harbour master, to raise the fire alarm. Can yew do that?"

Annie nodded and sped off. In her haste the posy of flowers intended for Nans fell from her hand and scattered on the ground. Before she had gone many yards she bumped into the bulky form of Scruffy Leckie who had stopped to shout his wares.

"Whoa! Wass the hurry gal?"

Annie blurted out her tale of woe.

Instantly, Leckie grabbed a pan lid from the back of his cart and proceeded to bash it with a hammer, shouting at the top of his raspy voice, "Fire! Fire! Fire!"

"Can yew do 'ee?"

Before Annie could reply he thrust the utensils into her hands, then leaped back on to the cart, whipped up a startled Bluebell to a pace to which she was quite unaccustomed.

"Oi'll goo fetch the harbour man wi' the water tank," Scruffy shouted over his shoulder.

Annie nodded, unable to speak for the fear that gripped her caused by Scruffy Leckie's fierce appearance and the picture of smoke and flames coming through the windows of her grandparent's home. Fired by urgency she ran along the lane shouting and banging the lid for all she was worth.

Doors opened and heads appeared through windows. Voices yelled.

"Wass the matter?"

"What ye maakin' that racket fer?"

"Where be the fire?"

"Nans and Gramps," Annie yelled back, sobs breaking in her voice.

"Oi'll goo git Doc Cooper. "

Within minutes neighbours' feet were scurrying to help. Scruffy Leckie, accompanied by Mr Willets, speedily clattered back to the scene of activity with the water tank attached to the rear of the cart. As the hose was unfurled, willing hands worked the pump on the tank. Water gushed in spurts through a smashed window of the cottage. Other hands manhandled the well in the backyard of the alms-houses to fill buckets and pans neighbours had taken from Leckie's cart. All in a hurry these were then passed along a line of bodies so the water could be thrown through the open door which Edith had pressed her way through. Frightened beyond measure she pulled her shawl across her mouth and nose. She could barely see. As smoke engulfed her she held up an arm to shield her eyes.

"Ma! Ma! Pa! Pa!" she cried urgently, peering through the curtain of smoke. Flames jumped up from a burning rug. She automatically stamped on them. Her foot caught on something more solid. She heard a groan beneath her. "Ma?" She bent down and reached out to touch the burning bundle but quickly drew back her hand from the heat.

"Quick! Quick!" she screamed. "Water! Water! Here, quickly here," she pointed frantically to the bundle at her feet. An arm brutally pushed her out of the way as water was sloshed onto the smouldering mound.

"Mrs Kemp, get out!" A voice ordered.

"But it be Ma," Edith's voice broke hoarsely. Another bucket of water was thrown. In the murky gloom someone grabbed her arms and thrust her aside.

"Get out, get out." Edith stumbled, her knees weakened, the sloshed water and soaked skirts clinging around her ankles hindering her balance. With practised hands her would be rescuer concentrated on the casualty.

"Doc, how be Ma?" she asked in a faltering whisper, of a voice she recognized, coughing between each gasping breath. The smoke masked the doctor's shaking head as he bent down to lift the soaking rug from off Ma's body.

"Help needed here!" he called urgently. A couple rushed forwards raising free arms to protect their eyes and noses from the smoke as they swung water from the pans they held.

Annie screamed. Someone with bucket free hands put their arms around her shoulders. "Shush."

"It be Nans." Annie shrugged off the kindly hands and darted for the open door. "Where be Ma?" She shouted frantically.

"Noo, Annie."

"Grab her afore she..."

"Come back, Annie."

"Ma! Ma!"

Edith was fumbling around the cottage through the dense fog following the sound of her father's raspy cough. She leant across his bed, pushed open the window and wafted the smoke out with her arms.

"Git me out, gal. Git me out," he gasped.

Edith put her hands under his armpits and heaved. But he didn't budge an inch. The smoke stung her eyes. She took a deep breath but choked on the acrid air that caught in the back of her throat. She coughed and spluttered. "Dear God, be ow'n help."

"Hurrit, gal," he barked impatiently.

"Pa...oi'm a'doin' ma best," she gasped as she tried again to move him. A pain shot through her belly. Strong arms rough handled her to one side.

"Mrs Kemp, oi'll do this. Goo yew outside to yow'n gal," Scruffy Leckie gruffly rasped.

By the time the contingent arrived from the Manor House flames had been quenched, smoke all but disseminated and helpers were dragging from the smouldering cottage what might be salvaged. Pa had been taken into next door and attended by Doctor Cooper. Lord Ralph strode up to the harbour master who seemed to be in control of operations to ascertain what had happened.

"Doan't roitely know, m'lord."

Lady Marion spoke soft words of comfort as she mingled with the weeping group of women who were shocked at the devastating event that had befallen their neighbours.

George found Edith awash on the floor kneeling beside the still, prone figure of her mother. He placed an arm around her shoulders. She turned, "Oh, George." He pulled her head onto his chest. She sniffed and sobbed, swallowing the moisture that was gathering in the back of her throat to prevent it cascading in a torrent. Through the lifting smoky fog his eye caught sight of Annie cowering in a corner of the room, shoulders shaking as sobs escaped her lips.

George gently raised Edith to her feet and beckoned Annie to join them. Like a mother hen he protectively shepherded his precious treasures into the daylight away from the devastating gloom.

Ma was laid to rest in St Andrews churchyard under the ministrations of Parson Wisbey who was chaplain to the Fishermen's Alms-houses. From Pa it had been learned that Ma had spent time cleaning the lamp that fateful morning, refilled it with oil, then bent down to stoke up the fire. At the inquest the coroner pronounced it to be accidental death. It was assumed that Ma spilled oil onto her clothing as she refilled the lamp and a spark from the fire jumped out as she bent to poke the coals that flared up so rapidly she had no opportunity to put it out.

Pa followed a month later, his weakened body succumbing to the smoke inhalation. Before his passing Edith had returned to the cottage. Frantically she had scrubbed and flung wide the scorched windows to eliminate the unpleasant smell. However, Edith's persistent cleaning to rid her parent's home of smoke residue to make it habitable for her father to return, and subsequent daily care of his needs to the end, took its toll. The baby within her quickened. She drew short, sharp breaths. Slowly she ceased her busyness and took measured steps along the path towards home, pausing at intervals as abdominal pain gripped her. Tears filled her eyes. Strangled sobs fell from her lips, "Too soon! Too soon!" The result was the premature birth of her little son. His fragile life held on for two days then he joined his grandparents to the grave.

The stable loft family clung to one another in their grief. As earth was thrown over the tiny box till the mound stood proud of the ground, George stood upright with cap in hand. "The Lord giveth and the Lord taketh away. Blessed be the name of the Lord." From that moment George engaged strictly in the normal round of chores drawing strength to go on from God.

Annie seemed to grow-up overnight. But Edith kept the sadness tucked away in her heart. It only surfaced when doubts about the goodness of God threatened to overwhelm her. *Noo good askin' why. Dear Lord, juss keep me a'goin'. Help me hold things together 'cos thass be what Yew allus do.*

For weeks to come Scruffy Leckie's tankard was seldom empty no matter which local hostelry he frequented and for some while custom for his wares increased. A communities' recognition of his heroic action on that distressing day. His quick actions had prevented the fire spreading into adjoining properties and causing further tragedy.

CHAPTER ELEVEN

"Bustling about..."

As the villagers bustled about with the customary humdrum pattern of life Edith slowly adapted to a new daily routine.

At the Big House a son and heir made his entrance into the world just as a radiant morning sun burst in rays across a calm, early summer sea. The commotion his arrival caused to a household that normally ran like clockwork took some adjustment. The lusty lungs of Edmund Ralph de Vessey resounded along the corridors of the Manor House incessantly.

"Can't you keep that brat quiet?" Master Quentin bellowed.

"Really Marion, you should have more control over the child," her mother-in-law admonished. "The constant noise he makes is unacceptable."

Lady Marion became fretful, the baby fractious and the Squire uncharacteristically snappy. Kitchen staff clattered pans more loudly than usual. Maids and footmen bustled about the house, conducting their tasks in a noisy fashion, rattling grates and coal skittles. Voices were raised, doors banged and footsteps less restrained in an attempt to drown the baby's distressing cries.

It was on a particularly chaotic morning that Edith called at the Big House with garments she had sewn for the new arrival. Hanson was reluctant to allow her an audience with her ladyship. "She's in great distress." The cacophony of exaggerated household noise rang out above Master Edmund's persistent cries from the distant nursery; so loudly Edith could hardly hear the butler's words. Puzzled by the unusual din Edith raised a hand to her ears.

"Wass be a'goin' on, Hanson? Can't yew put an end to this racket?"

"We are trying to drown Master Edmund's cries so that Master Quentin will quit yelling and Lady Araminta cease her persistent complaints, Mrs Kemp."

Edith shook her head in disbelief.

"Hanson, put yow'n foot down. Stop this noise. Tell Cook to maak some chamomile tea an' send it up to her ladyship's room along wi' some honey."

Although unused to receiving orders from a villager Hanson complied with Edith's suggestion knowing that her ladyship held this young woman in high esteem. He had witnessed before Edith Kemp's common sense in action. So, swiftly he sent the parlour maid with the message for Cook and issued instructions to a nearby footman to pass on the news to household staff to carry out duties in a normal calm manner.

As he turned to escort Edith up the stairs Hanson was amazed how quickly quietness pervaded the air in the Manor House. The renewed silence was only broken by a baby's cries.

A door opened into the hall. Lord Ralph stepped from

his study, looked about him, then called up to his butler, "Is all well, Hanson?"

"I believe it will be, my lord," he replied confidently.

***

Nursed by the warmth of midsummer sun Annie and Peggy danced midst the kaleidoscope of flowers which permeated the countryside. The hedgerows and wildflower meadows dripped with the sweet nectar of their blooms. Bees buzzed and took their fill of the plentifulness on offer. The two girls, delighted to be released for a time from the schoolroom and household chores, revelled in the freedom the morning promised. They stooped to pick stalks of oxeye daisies growing in profusion along the riverbank. Their nimble fingers busily wove them, in conjunction with blue corn flowers and red ragged robin, into jewelled coronets for their hair.

"Be careful o' the bees," Edith called to the girls as she and Hester picked elderflower heads from the abundance displayed along the edge of the lane bordering the fields. Hester had reluctantly agreed to accompany her friend, giving in to Edith's persistent cajoling and promise of help to make the delicious syrup for the drinks the children so enjoyed. Her natural ebullience had not returned but at least her dependency on liquor had been curbed. When landlord's tabs remained unpaid they refused her further credit and the threat of a bailiff's visit if she continued to run up debts frightened her and stalled her reliance on their services. Besides, with George and Edith continuing as custodians of her boys' wages that source of revenue dried up for her, too.

Moreover, with Peggy's assistance Hester gradually

picked up the reins of several chores about the house. However, under the Kemp's guidance, Stan assumed full responsibility for household finances to prevent temptation being in his mother's path again. At first Hester was annoyed but soon became resigned to the situation when she realised how much easier life was for her without the daily burden of juggling coppers to make ends meet. Stan ensured rent for the cottage was always paid on time and he became adept at eking out their meagre resources. Together the youngsters discovered how to be inventive with their thriftiness. With Edith's help Peggy learned to make meals that satisfied their hunger. Edith also gave her a couple of chicks and a laying pullet and under George's instruction the boys erected a hen house with an enclosed run. They also turned the remaining tangled garden into a productive space from which Peggy made tasty delights. She looked forward to the day when she could follow Edith's example and sell her produce in the market square. Despite her youth Peggy displayed a natural flare for cooking creative dishes which the boys enjoyed, quite in contrast to their mother's stodgy, mundane fare.

One evening after their day's work George quietly took Stan to one side then accompanied him to pay off his mother's debts at all the hostelries in the village. The young man received assurances from the landlords, grudgingly in some cases, that they would not allow Hester further credit. "Yew woan't be paid if yew do," he emphasised. Thankfully, Caleb picked up a couple of rabbits that week, but no one complained about the sameness of the meals set on the table each day. Honour had been served and Stan felt they could hold up their heads amongst their neighbours.

A few weeks later George again drew Stan aside and

after a quiet word they made their way to Home Farm where together they purchased the runt from a litter of pigs. When they arrived home with the squealing creature peeking from under George's arm the children's excitement knew no bounds.

"Hold yow'n noise," Hester admonished.

"But Ma, we soon be hevin' ow'n own meat, an' bacon, an' mekin' head cheese, an' brawn, an' drippin'."

"Pigs doan't maak best drippin'."

"But they do maak cracklin', an' scraps, an' sausages," Stan laughed.

"An' pork pies," Fred added.

"Peggs yew a'goin' to be soo busy," quipped Stan.

Peggy scowled. "When will oi hev toime to do all that!"

"Doan't yew worrit ma gal," George encouraged. "It be a joint effort, soo, we will work together. Come yew on, we muss find this little fellow a new hum. It will be some time afore he provides us wi' meat."

"Ee be pretty scrawny," Hester criticised.

"We will feed him to fatten him up," Stan replied confidently.

It had been decided to house the piglet in the wood store attached to the privy at the bottom of George's vegetable patch so, leaving Hester behind, they all trooped up the lane to help adapt the space to the creature's requirements. Clumps of mint grew prolifically around the wall of the new pigsty. It was hoped that its crushed leaves, emitting a pleasant aroma, would subsequently mask the distinctive smell created by its occupant. All scraps of food were saved from both households for his consumption, and they waited eagerly for him to fatten up, but Annie's soft heart couldn't bear the thought of him being butchered.

"We moite need to coddle him fer a bit," George whispered for Edith's ears alone. "Keep him close to the fire an' hand feed him." Edith raised her eyebrows at the thought of the creature being inside their home and started to protest but George raised his hand to stay her objections. "Juss till ee finds his feet. Can't disappoint the young uns." He inclined his head towards the children eagerly watching the piglet.

In the following days it was Edith, assisted by Annie, who nurtured the little creature by the hearth till he'd put on weight and was sufficiently established to fend for himself in his outside pen. He outgrew the small space so quickly that some weeks later George and Stan, with permission from the estate manager, built a pigsty adjacent to the privy wall jutting out into the de Vessey orchard. Fred and Caleb along with other boys from the village searched for stones and small rocks suitable for its construction. Annie looked through the window in her home overlooking the garden watching the boy's antics. She chuckled as Caleb and Bobby Castleton struggled with an extra-large boulder. Edith peered over her daughter's shoulder.

"Come yew on, we will taak some refreshment to those hard workers." She poured a little elderflower syrup into a jug and picked up a handful of biscuits newly out of the oven. "Grab a few cups, Annie. I'll top this up wi' water at the pump downstairs."

The wellbeing of the piglet became a village project. The children frequently came to clamber on the wall to feed him, tickle and play with him.

"What shall we call him?" Annie asked.

"Let's call him Spot cos he hev those spotty black marks on his back."

So few families could afford to keep a pig, but they were willing to contribute to the feeding of a neighbour's pig in the hope of being rewarded with a piece of meat at killing time. Being without a pig was often an indication of real poverty. Sharing one's bounty was a true sign of neighbourliness. Mothers saved household scraps for Spot, such as potato peelings, and children were sent to gather suitable food from the hedgerows. Spot's progress was watched with keen anticipation; the young uns amused by the cleverness of his antics such as the opening of his pen door latch with his snout, the old uns eagerly awaiting the day of his slaughter. Their hopes for an early taste of pork were dashed a few weeks later when the pig man from Home farm called by to see how the pig was faring. "Thass be a sow!"

George could not believe his good fortune. Sows could have two litters a year. A second pig could be kept for paying bills, the litters being sold for profit and the first be slaughtered to provide meat throughout the year.

"We be able to control our finances instead o' bein' controlled by economic circumstances," he explained to Edith cheerfully. He put an arm around her shoulders and hugged her affectionately. "No more scrimpin' fer yew, ma gal. The Good Lord hev graciously provided fer us."

Edith nodded, tears filling her eyes. "More than we could ever hev imagined."

The following morning Edith attempted to have a similar conversation with Hester but was met with abuttals.

"How can you be thankful an' continue to hev faith in a God who delivers such a blow to yow'n family? Brutal He be. Not one blow but three."

"The Good Book say He doan't promise an easy path, but

He do promise to be wi' us an' see us through ow'n difficulties. Oi taak comfort from that."

"Noo!" Hester shook her head vehemently. "Empty squit!"

"Yew may reject Him, Hester, but He will nivver ferget yew because He loves yew. The Good Book reveals His loving care fer yew."

"He ent very lovin' to taak away ma man."

"Would yew deny Jeremiah the presence of the Lord?"

"He didn't hev to taak him in such a way or soo young."

"Jeremiah knew the dangers of his occupation. He was also ready to goo whenever the Lord called him an' he knew where he be a'goin'. Where will yew be when it be yow'n time to goo, Hester, now that yew be hardened yow'n heart aginst the Good Lord an' thrust Him aside?"

"It really doan't matter. Oi be done wi' all thass squit."

"O'course it matters. The Christian life be a mixture of battle an' blessin'. We be foolish to despise His wisdom an' instruction."

"Yew be a preacher, now?" Hester threw at Edith sarcastically.

"Oh, Hester, ma friend, oi be juss a'tellin' what yew an' Jeremiah a'say t' George an' me about the love an' goodness o' God from the Good Book."

"Bah!" Hester's hand struck out dismissively.

"This life be preparation fer the life to come. Juss yew speak wi' the Reverend Coleman from the chapel. He'll explain far better than oi can."

"Oi tell yew, oi be done wi' all thass squit," Hester repeated bitterly. "Chapel not be fer the loikes o' me."

"My dear friend, at toimes loike these chapel be the best place to be."

CHAPTER TWELVE

"...all flustered..."

Nevertheless, Hester remained adamant and persistently refused to attend Chapel although Stan ensured he and his siblings were in their seats by 11o'clock each Sunday morning. He felt it incumbent upon him to continue his father's practice to attend the services and read verses of scripture at home after the evening meal, but his lack of literacy skills prohibited him assuming that responsibility, so he delegated it to Fred. "Despite all ow'n difficulties the Lord hev provided, an' seen us through the tough toimes, so we will give Him thanks fer all His goodness."

"Umph," muttered Hester.

"Ma, soon we will hev a regular supply of meat. Thass be suthen to be thankful fer. We hev good friends an' neighbours who be teachin' us t' manage ow'n resources. Oi be soo thankful fer them. We be larning t' work wi' nature to hev produce in the garden. God sends the seasons, the rain and the sun to ripen the harvest an' Peggy be a'provin' her skills at bakin' an' maakin' meals fer us all from what we be a'growin'. Fred an' oi hev jobs that pays wages to meet ow'n bills. We will larn to live an' behave from His Book."

"Thass yow'n father talkin'," Hester mumbled but did not curtail the nightly devotions.

"Be readin' the Good Book juss a ritual 'cos yow'n Pa did

it?" Edith asked Stan one day when he visited their loft home to hand over his wages for safe keeping.

"At fust oi thought it be a good habit to continue. Ma weren't too keen, but oi couldn't do it, soo oi asked Fred to do it. As I listened to Fred read oi realized the Good Lord be givin' us wise counsel fer livin' lives well. Miss Peskett still be a'comin' to teach Peggy an' Caleb, one day a week when school be finished fer the day, lessons they got behind in arter Pa died. One day Ma invited her to stay fer tea an' when Fred prepared to read from the Good Book she looked acrorst at me. Oi shook ma head. Now when she come she be a'helpin' me to larn ma letters as well as the young uns. Oi now be beginin' to read it fer m'self. One day it will be me readin' the Good Book arter supper." he said triumphantly. Edith smiled.

George clapped him on the shoulder encouragingly. "The Good Lord bless thee, ma bor."

"Oi'd rather be doin' that than whilin' away time down the Fisherman's Arms wi' the lads, an' wastin' ma hard earned wages."

"Spendin' time wi Miss Peskett or larning to read the Good Book."

Stan looked at George surprize in his eyes. "Both oi suppose." George's words lingered in his mind and gave him pause for thought.

***

Unlike Hester, who at times still dealt with her grief in introspection, withdrawal and inactivity, Edith bustled in constant activity. She thoroughly turned out their loft home, washing everything that could be washed or scrubbed. She used cooking and baking sessions with Annie and Peggy to make extra pasties and pies which she delivered to older residents in the village whom she knew rarely cooked for themselves. Chatting with those who lived alone in the village, like Bert Bracewell and Mrs Jenner, caused her to be grateful for the blessings that were still hers; a daughter and husband who loved her and an almighty Father who watched over them all. The girls loved these sessions and looked forward to helping Edith distribute the cooked goodies. The busyness obliterated the devastation that had been caused in her heart by the untimely death of her parents and loss of the little boy yet gave a sense of purpose to her day.

Her ladyship sent word more frequently for her to visit at the Manor House. Sewing was brought to her in the nursery or sometimes Lady Marion's drawing room for her nimble fingers to work as they engaged in conversation.

Master Edmund gradually settled after Edith's initial ministrations. Lady Marion had elected not to engage a wet nurse but feed the baby herself; a fretful experience for them both till Edith's persuasive patience taught her the art of suckling a newborn. Confidence in Edith's skill grew as her ladyship's baby responded contentedly. Less flustered Marion lovingly fondled his downy head as he snuggled in her arms guzzling noisily. Serenity embraced them as love cemented the bond of motherhood. The Squire strode about the estate, a smile creasing his face and a spring in his step, as tranquillity settled on his home giving his brother less cause to yell and upset the household and his mother no reason to grumble.

Forays into the countryside and woodland to forage were a necessity but also a blessing. Edith revelled in the beauty and bounty at her fingertips. "The Good Lord hev blessed us wi' such abundance. All we need to do is gather it an' use it wisely," she instructed Annie alongside Peggy. The hedges bordering the fields had grown high enough to tangle with the trees' lower branches and nettles nestled in among the scrambling brambles, their serrated leaves creased and erect, a dark and dusky green, hiding the burgeoning fruit. Edith was keen to point out to the girls the harvest yet to come from what was growing all around them but also what could be made from the munificence available now. She demonstrated how to pick nettles for soup without getting stung, then pointed out the dock leaves that would ease a sting if they brushed against exposed skin.

"Not everything that grows be good to eat."

"How will we know?"

"Be best to ask afore usin' suthen fer cookin'."

Swaying red-leaved grasses bowed with seeds, clover resplendent with flower heads and mallow competed for attention, displaying varying shades of purple everywhere. Not to be overlooked digitalis spears were beginning to push upwards laden with colourful cups vying for recognition.

"Doan't pick ’ee," said Edith forcefully, pointing to the majestic spires. "They be poisonous. An' hemlock, an' monkshood."

"Some leaves be good for medicinals others will maak yew sick."

The girls pulled faces. "We'll nivver larn."

"O'course yew will. Yew be allus in the woods an' fields. Larn a new one each time ye goo out. What hev yew larnt a'day?"

Peggy looked flustered but Annie replied confidently,

"Not to gather that pointed plant."

Edith nodded. "Mmm! Digitalis! What hev we picked yew can eat?"

Annie looked at Peggy and giggled. "Elderflower," they burst out together.

"When yew know what each plant is used fer yew'll remember."

The girls looked at her disbelievingly. "Ma, we'll nivver remember."

Edith smiled. "Yew will. Allus using the abundance that be there will bring to remembrance its usefulness."

She turned her head towards the foot of the hedgerow. "What do yew see there?"

"Cowslips," they chorused together.

"Cowslip tea be a delicacy. Goo an' pick a handful of the golden pips an' oi'll shew yew how to maak some on ow'n return hum."

Along the riverbank curtains of willow plunged towards the water, their numerous wands bowing down into the flowing river. They spied Slip Cook busily cutting upright rods from the base of the trees, binding them into manageable bundles.

"What be Slip a'goin' a'doo wi' the willow?"

"Weave baskets," the girls cried out as one.

Edith nodded. "Another useful plant."

Thistles that had gone to seed fascinated the pair. Their downy heads were as soft as fur. The girls plucked at the fuzzy tufts, threw them into the air and laughed as they tried to catch the tiny quills before they parachuted to the ground.

Edith was pleased to see the two interacting with pleasure the activity of nature surrounding them. Sadness had more than tinged their young lives. Being plunged into grief by unexpected and horrendous tragedy was hard for adults to cope with let alone little people. Frowns of sorrow had for too many months marred their childish faces and touched all aspects of their lives. To see them laughing and having fun brought joy to her heart and a welcome lift to her spirits.

Responsibility settled on Peggy's young shoulders like a comfortable mantle. She had adapted to the needs of her family remarkably quickly. Without any qualms she learned how to pluck and gut chickens, as well as skin and quarter the rabbits her brothers brought home from the woods; woods that quickly greened providing much bounty beneath its canopy. Edith was confident that in no time at all both Annie and Peggy would grasp the value of the natural provision God bestowed on them. Gradually she was teaching the girls to fashion the plentiful rabbit skins into useful garments ready for the chill of winter, Annie's nimble fingers more adept with a needle than Peggy's.

"'Waste not, want not," my grandmother used to say," Edith repeated to them time and time again. They hurried home with their collection and patiently Edith showed the girls how to steep some of the leaves overnight for tea and soup and demonstrated stringing herbs to dry for use in the future.

"Put the cowslip pips into this jug an' we'll pour over some boiling water an' leave them to steep while we git on wi' other tasks. When they hev infused we'll add some sugar an yew can sample what we hev made. The honey be all a'gone till Mr Rodney Brooks, the wheelwright, hev some more fer sale, or we could hev stirred a spoonful o' that in." She proceeded to portion the bread dough she had left to rise earlier in the morning. "Here yew are. Knead it as I shewed yew afore."

"Moine be a'stickin'," complained Annie.

"Sprinkle it wi' a little flour."

Peggy released a handful over the doughy mess in such a rush it burst in a fountain up into Annie's face and down her apron. The girls' burst into spluttered giggles. Edith's face creased in smiles at their antics as her skilled hands rapidly turned and pummelled air into her portion.

"Put yow'n loaves on this tray an' we'll leave them to prove while we goo to pick some beans an' bury ow'n hands in the soil to find taters fer dinner."

Hollyhocks stood sentinel to the back of the border in the vegetable patch below their loft home. The saucer-shaped blooms abuzz with plump fuzzy haired bumble bees seeking out pollen and nectar in the warmth of the late August sunshine.

"These be working hard to produce the honey that Mr Brooks will collect from the hives at the bottom of his garden."

How good it was to reflect that each season brought its own bounty that working with the elements and trusting in God's faithfulness provided so they had sufficient for their needs and oftentimes enough to share with others.

CHAPTER THIRTEEN

"..and flurry..."

Edith took Annie and Peggy foraging again a few days later. With baskets over their arms she advised them what to look for and warned them what to avoid. The girls ran ahead eager to search for the items Ma had suggested. But across the lane they spotted Fred working alongside ole Alf.

"What be yew a'doin', Fred?" Annie inquired as she dashed towards them.

"Hedge layering," he replied without looking up.

"What fer?"

"Strengthen the hedge."

Inquisitively the girls drew closer.

"How?"

"By splicin' these tall branches o' blackthorn an' hawthorn, then bending them over to weave along the top."

"Yew won't destroy the bird's nest, will yew?"

"The birds hev fledged an' flown long before now. Doin' this will thicken the hedge for next year so that there be more cover fer nest buildin," ole Alf explained gruffly, his eyes never leaving the job in hand.

"A thickened hedge provides homes fer lots o' mammals, an' food fer insects as well as berries fer birds an' it also keeps the cows an' hosses safely in the field," explained

Fred sagely.

"Muss git on," urged ole Alf, fingers skilfully intertwining the branches.

"We be foragin'."

"What fer?"

"Stop yer mardlin', bor," the older man reprimanded.

"Yus, Alf."

"Bye," the girls, sensing a dismissal, skipped off towards the woods on the other side of the lane. They could hear voices and sounds of axes chopping against wood. Curiosity drew them into the bracken beneath the canopy of spreading branches of majestic oaks, ash, sycamore, chestnut and hazel. Shafts of light filtered through the continuous foliage covering, shining like spotlights across the woodland floor.

They caught sight of Mr Jenner, his jacket off and sleeves rolled up, supervising, as well as pitching in with the management of that area of the wood.

Annie boldly stepped forward. "What be yew a'doin'?" she asked as she approached the group of men.

"Get back, girl," Mr Jenner shouted as a long pole-like trunk crashed to the ground near to them. Peggy flinched.

"Move those girls away!" He spoke sharply. Jem Capps, hatchet in one hand, swiftly stepped out and stretched his left arm protectively in front of the girls.

"Yew mussn't come closer. It be dangerous."

"Why be yew a'cuttin' down the trees?"

"To encourage new growth."

"What yew a'goin' to do wi' the branches?"

"The wood be used fer maakin' things loike fencing, an' gearts an..."

"Git back, Annie," called a familiar voice, firmly.

"Pa! Pa!" She started to run towards him.

"Annie, stay there!" George shouted sternly. "Where be Ma?"

"In the lane."

"Goo back an' stay wi' Ma," he ordered sharply as he held on to the horse's bridle as the harness was being attached to the fallen tree trunk.

"Yus, Pa," she hung her head disconsolately.

"Ask Ma abaht coppicin'," he called after her slumped retreating figure.

After the girls had explained their unfortunate exploits in the woods Edith admonished them for interrupting the men's work.

"Because o' the cold winter, an' late spring they be tryin' to catch up now that field work be complete. We mussn't hinder their work. They be already far behind this year."

"But they shouldn't be a'cuttin' down the boo'iful trees," Annie persisted.

"What they be a'doin' generates new growth, an' provides wood fer many uses about the farm an' hum, as well as fuel fer fires. An' Scruffy Leckie's brother, Jimmy, who lives the far side o' the wood creates charcoal out o' the seasoned oak an' maple."

"Oh!"

"We can't do wi'out coppiced wood. Most furniture be made from wood. Pa used it to refashion the spindles on ow'n chairs. An' it be needful to maak the flail, mend wagon beds an' other equipment on the farm. Ash an' blackthorn have their uses too, an' o' course Slip Cook uses the willow wands fer weavin' all manner o' baskets, an' the loike. He also supplies Sonny Cooper wi' suitable willow to form into hoops that goo around the barrels he puts together to hold the herrin'."

She peered into the girl's empty basket. "Where be the things yew hev foraged?"

They hung their heads.

"Too busy minding other's business," Edith scolded. "Now yew goo do yow'n work an' leave the men to do their'n. In that way we shall all help to keep a roof uvver ow'n heads an' food in ow'n bellies."

***

"Beatrice, fetch onions from the cellar, then peel an' chop them fer steak pie. While down there check if the gard'ner's boy hev left fresh carrots. Be quick. Noo mardlin'," Cook directed. Beatie had proved a good little worker. Mrs Sands was gradually introducing her to kitchen maid duties. Her competency far exceeded that of the young girl who was currently occupying that position. When she discovered Beatrice had a natural flair for baking she was also keen to exploit those skills. Her pastry was as light as a feather and much appreciated above stairs. Cook could have taken the compliments for herself but chose to give credit where it was due and continued to encourage her young protégé.

"Oi would loike yew to maak the pie fer today's luncheon, Beatrice. Maggie will prepare the vegetables."

"Yus, Cook."

Maggie glared crossly at Beatrice and sulkily retreated to the scullery. Beatie picked up a candle and placed it into the candle holder and moved quickly along the back corridor guarding the flame from the draught with her free hand. When she reached the cellar steps she held it aloft to light her way down. She had only gone down three steps when movement below alerted her to the presence of someone rushing upwards towards her. As a figure pushed passed her all in a flurry, the flickering light caught the startled face of the between-maid.

"Taak care if yew goo down there," she hissed.

"Oh, oi be watchin' ma step," Beatie assured her.

"Yew need to," Lily scoffed, as in a hurry she rushed up the remaining steps.

Puzzled by the warning, Beatie descended into the darkness ruminating as to why the between-maid would be in the cellar. As she reached level ground rustling alerted her to another presence in the dank space.

"Oh noo, not varmints!" She carefully moved the candlestick to locate the onions. The flame lit up male footwear.

"Are you calling me a varmint?"

Beatie jumped. A firm hand reached out to steady her arm.

"Don't drop the candle. I want to see who would refer to me in such derogatory terms."

"Oh, please 'scuse me, Master Quentin, sir, oi didn't know yew were a'down here." The brief dip in the flame told him that even in the dark this young woman had curtsied. "Oi be collectin' onions an' feared rats be rummagin' around the vegetables."

"You have the upper hand on me. You know my name, but I don't know who you are."

"Oi be the scullery maid." Beatie shifted the flame to find the onions.

"Does the scullery maid have a name?"

"Beatrice." She placed the candleholder onto a ledge and proceeded to corner the edges of her apron, lift the fold to her waist and fill the temporary pouch with onions, then cast her eyes across the shelves for the carrots.

Quentin was intrigued that this peasant girl appeared totally unfazed by his presence. The flickering light picked out the focussed expression on her face as she concentrated on the task in hand. She wasn't attempting to catch his eye with her pretty countenance as the previous chit had been trying to do.

"How long have you worked here?"

"Over a year, sir," Beatie replied without pausing in her task. That information surprized him. Why had he never come across this appealing girl before?

"Do you like the work?" He persisted, wanting to keep company with her a little longer so sought to engage her in further conversation.

"Oi be still a'larnin', sir, but it be in'erestin'." With one hand she scooped her loaded apron and with the other she picked up the candlestick and turned to ascend the stone steps.

"'Scuse me, sir," she bobbed again.

This encounter was passing too quickly for Quentin's liking. He stood to block her exit.

"What's the hurry?"

"There be lunch to prepare. Oi can't be a'mardlin'." She pushed passed him. What audacity! Yet her innocent naivety excited him; her unsophisticated simplicity such a contrast to the artificial finesse and flirtatious nature of most females of his acquaintance. Apparently she was here to stay, so for the moment he was content to leave the pursuit of this particular quarry till another day. With a satisfied smirk he leisurely ascended the steps in her wake and made his way to the stables.

"He ent grumbled," commented one of the stable hands.

"Yet!" retorted another sarcastically.

"Oi be a'waitin' fer him to bellow."

"Perhaps his luck hev changed at the tables," suggested Wilf. The stable lads were well acquainted with Master Quentin's propensity to frequent the gaming tables and the equal frequency with which he lost. Losses which were mounting up at an alarming rate. Losses which were resulting in swathes of the Newton Westerby Manor estate passing into the hands of strangers. Losses which were becoming increasingly difficult to keep from his brother.

CHAPTER FOURTEEN

"But soon..."

Unaware that his gambling exploits were the subject of common gossip Master Quentin mounted Champion. As he cantered across the fields a satisfied smile creased his face. The picture of the scullery maid's innocence filled him with anticipation. He sensed this conquest might well be a challenge, but the pursuit would be worth the trophy. Maybe meeting her would prove a good omen. Today his luck would change. His spirits soared. He urged Champion to a gallop anxious to reach the Crown Hotel in Newton Lokesby to seal the deal with the rail bosses from London based for the present in Lowestoft.

On reaching the Inn he dismounted, handed the reins to a stable lad. "Rub him down well," he ordered.

"Yus, sir."

"Don't let him drink too much all at once. Make sure the hay you give him is fresh and dry," Quentin instructed brusquely as he strode in confident arrogance towards the hotel entrance.

"Yus, sir," the lad nodded, undeterred by Quentin's belligerence. Used to Master Quentin's rudeness from frequent visits in the past he led the handsome horse into the stable talking softly to him.

Some hours later the heavy clink of gold coins in his

pouch enhanced Quentin's belief that the blue-eyed chit from the cellar was the inspiration for his portentous good fortune. He allowed that chance encounter with Beatrice to colour his thinking and actions throughout the day. The lucrative deal struck with Betts, Morton Peto's partner, and the Lucas brothers ensured he could satisfy some creditors and still have sufficient for future forays at the tables. What cared he for grazing and arable land or cottager's homes. This was progress. Soon there would be a station at Newton Lokesby. Hustle and bustle. Rail tracks right down to Newton Westerby harbour linking their sleepy village to enticing faraway places. That thought excited him. He strutted to the hotel's dining room with an arrogant gait unconcerned that his actions were a betrayal of family loyalty. Self-satisfaction emanated from him.

A further winning streak later that night raised not a few eyebrows and heightened disbelief amongst his fellow players at the card tables. Undeterred by the derision of his companions at this uncommon turn of events in his fortunes Quentin departed the Crown Hotel in a flurry of excitement. He rode carelessly and carefree towards home elated by his success. He must see her again. He spurred Champion to race faster across the fields; acres of land that unbeknownst to his brother no longer belonged to the de Vessey estate. Before the night was through he would search her out determined to reward her with his gracious attention and gratify the passion of his loins.

His achievements that day were worthy of celebration. There was no one more deserving of his favour than that bewitching child who had contributed to this fortuitous change in fortune.

***

Summer was mellowing, beginning its slow, almost imperceptible meander into autumn. As the early morning light cast its golden net across the land the rich colours of late summer flowers glowed like precious gems. Purples, pinks and yellows swayed in swathes vying for dominance. "Look at me, don't pass me by," their upturned heads seemed to plead as cottagers gathered garden produce, digging up late potatoes, cutting early cabbage leaves and picking the last of the peas and beans.

Harvested fields were ploughed and spread with muck from the midden and stables. Doors and windows were kept tightly fastened to keep out the stench. The surrounding hedgerows, tangled with brambles laden with blackberries whose red and black fruits, glistened with dew in the morning sunlight beckoning as tasty morsels. Harvest thanksgivings in chapel and church gratefully acknowledged the bountiful provision of the Lord Almighty. Tangs of autumn rose from homes around the village, tantalising taste buds with fruity puddings, meat and vegetable pies and stews, as householders made the most of nature's generosity. At the Big House surplus produce from the kitchen garden that could not be stored in the cellar, or salted or bottled, was being turned into chutneys, relishes and preserves and placed on the pantry shelves. Nothing was allowed to go to waste.

Beatie refrained from mentioning the nauseous feelings she experienced each morning. At times some of the kitchen aromas churned her stomach so badly it was hard to keep her suspicions hidden. In those moments her face reflected the same dull, stunned horror of disbelief that was displayed in her mother's countenance following the news of the untimely death of their father. Breathing deeply and chewing slowly on a dry crust she refused to succumb to self-pity. Giving in was not her way of dealing with difficult situations.

Since the night an unwelcome nocturnal visitor had tricked her from her bed in the servants quarters, with notions that something was wrong at home, she had adroitly avoided her persistent pursuer. Never descending to the cellar alone or walking the Manor corridors unaccompanied. Making certain, as far as she could, that she was always in company with one of the other maids. Till one day as she walked through the kitchen garden on her afternoon out he accosted her. He blocked her path and would not let her pass. He took hold of her arm. She shook him off.

"How dare yew, sir!" She spat out angrily. She looked him full in the face her blue eyes blazing fiercely as she addressed him in measured tones.

"Yew hev dishonoured me, sir. Brought disgrace on ma family an' when yow'n family learn of my condition they will throw me out. Oi, an' our child, will be outcasts for the rest of ow'n lives because of yow'n selfish actions. May God hev mercy on yow'n soul."

The contemptible blackguard chortled. "Oh, I do love it when you are fired up, Beatrice."

Beatie stamped her foot. "Don't yew dare maak fun o' me, sir!" The colour rose in her cheeks.

Her accoster dared to put out a finger to touch the flaming skin, but she quickly stepped back out of his reach.

"You are wonderful when roused!" He declared raucously.

"Be yew a'goin' to acknowledge this child?"

His countenance changed. "You can't prove it is mine. If you say a word you'll be laughed at for your audacity."

"Sir, everyone knows oi not be a'walkin' out wi' a young man. Thass be a condition when oi be taaken on as scullery maid, an' oi keep ma word. Yew, sir, yew only, be the one who hev deflowered me an' put my life to shame. Now, let me pass."

With a queenly deportment not dissimilar to that of Lady Marion de Vessey she walked past him. He watched in admiration tinged with regret. What a woman! What a pity she is only a scullery maid!

***

"Oh, you foolish young man! What have you done? What tangled web of deceit and dishonour are you weaving?"

Beyond the clipped hedge, unseen, the conversation between the despicable blackguard and the Manor's scullery maid had been overheard. Dismay and trepidation filled the heart of the unwitting listener. "But soon there will be such repercussions! Dear Lord have mercy!"

***

Now that she was no longer welcome at home on her afternoons out Beatrice decided to call in on her Grandpa Bemment more frequently. Cook had allowed her to take a portion of meat pie left over from lunch to warm up for his supper which she knew he would savour. Grandpa always warmly welcomed visits with his eldest granddaughter. She never messed with his tools or fiddled and left things in disarray as the other children did. He sensed Beatie had a genuine regard for what he was trying to achieve with the materials and tools in his hands. She watched carefully and listened intently.

She found the workshop an interesting place to visit because her grandfather's work intrigued Beatie. Jonas had held a soft spot for his eldest granddaughter ever since she was a small child probably because her comely appearance reminded him of his beloved Sally. Since she was a little girl Beatie had liked the smell of leather and was fascinated as she watched Jonas shape flat pieces of hide into shoes, boots, belts, bags and saddles.

"Yew'll not larn by gawpin' m'gal. Yew pick up that tool an' copy me." By capturing her interest and getting her involved in the process when she was young and eager he taught her to repair all manner of articles, hammer nails and segs into soles and heels, stitch threads to hold them together and prolong their life. Occasionally Jonas was required to repair horse saddles, bridles, reins or anything else anyone cared to bring to his workshop and Beatrice absorbed all that her grandfather was performing at his bench.

Some considered Jonas Bemment mean and miserly, but Lousia Kemp who 'did' for him once a week remarked, "He be of a kindly nature, gruff an' at toimes obstinate, but allus good hearted."

Grandpa always welcomed Beatie no matter how busy he was. He worked. She watched. Occasionally they spoke. Sometimes he involved her in the task he was engaged in. But one afternoon when she rapped on the stable door he glanced up from his workbench and was startled. He knew at once from her countenance and the looseness of her garments that all was not well with her. At once he laid down his hammer.

"How noice to see yew m'gal. Oi be parched. Will yew put on the kettle whilst oi finish orf here? Oi be roite riddy fer a break an' will enjoy a mardle wi' yew."

Beatrice, who knew her way around Grandpa's scullery, promptly picked up the kettle, filled it with water and placed it on the stove. The back wall of the scullery was hung with bunches of mint and sage, thyme and lavender. A rope of plump onions was strung from a nail to the left of the chimney breast which Beatie avoided bumping her head upon as her busy hands made the tea whilst Jonas completed his task and washed his hands under the pump in the yard. He wandered through the open back door wiping his hands vigorously on towelling, his look shrewd and penetrating as the tea was being poured.

"Now, ma gal sit yew down here fer a mardle." He indicated the one chair by the side of the stove to Beatie and pulled out a stool from under the table for himself and sat down.

"Now, yew be a'tellin' me what be ailin' yew." He picked up the earthenware pot in both hands Beatie placed before him and sipped the scalding liquid while waiting for her to reply.

"Oi be juss foine, Gramps."

"Best be honest, ma gal. The pinched look on yer face ent juss from the nip outside."

Tears spilled down Beatrice's face. Gradually Jonas wheedled sufficient from her to acquaint him with her condition, but she adamantly refused to reveal any details.

When Stan arrived to escort his sister through the dark lane back to the Manor House Jonas drew him aside to his workshop while Beatie washed up the supper pots on the pretext of showing him something out there.

"Keep a watch on her, m'bor. She be wrongly used?"

Stan nodded regretfully.

"The gal needs her Ma," Jonas remarked with a tinge of sadness.

Stan shook his head.

CHAPTER FIFTEEN

"... they are ready..."

Some months later Annie walked along the path across the Common towards the broadleaved woodland. It was a straight, single track and provided plenty of opportunity to appreciate the melodic murmur of the breeze, the scent of emergent foliage mingling with the faintest taste of the sea and movement of nature as it reawakened with the gentle promise of spring.

A succession of warm dry days exuded the kind of warmth that sinks through the skin and into the bones, so very welcome after the harshness of winter. With the arrival of spring and the lengthening days the hens had returned to laying eggs. Edith had entrusted Annie with the responsibility of setting up their pitch at the weekly market. The sun brought everyone and everything into the outdoors. As Annie stepped down the burgeoning lane, carrying the basket with her precious wares carefully across her arm, a thrush sang in the low branches of a sycamore; the sycamore's red-tinged buds yielding to the emerging leaf. Not to be outdone in melodic song a robin competed higher up in an ash tree. To her left she heard the humming of a bee. "It be all a'happenin', they be ready for the changin' seasons," she thought, a gentle smile creasing her rosy cheeks, but in youthful innocence she was totally unprepared for the forthcoming changes in the lives of her friend's family.

She started to skip, then was mindful of her fragile load so walked at a more sedate pace scanning for Peggy whom she had agreed to meet where the footpaths crossed. Peggy had perfected her pastie making and now sold them at the village market where they were quickly snapped up by those who lacked baking skills or were too lazy to be bothered knowing their menfolk appreciated Peggy's tasty morsels at their dinner break in the fields. Both Bemment girls were blessed with the lightest touch when it came to pastry making. "Thass juss boo'iful. It melts in ma mouth," were frequent comments from the villagers who enjoyed Peggy's baking. Whilst up at the Big House "delicious" was the more restrained compliment of Beatrice's offerings.

Around Annie the elder and hawthorn sported full leaf, but the oak was only just getting started. Low down on some trees scaly, brown buds were still tightly closed whilst on others whippy branches reaching to sunnier skies were beginning to open into feathery fronds with fresh, vivid colour that only a young spring leaf displays.

Some meadow plants were high enough to reach her knees. Annie trailed her free hand through them, plucked a stalk of sweet vernal grass and shredded it absentmindedly as she walked, scattering a trail of seeds and releasing a sweet warm fragrance. Bursts of daffodils and primroses jostled at the foot of the trees and beyond open fields beckoned. Through a gap in the hedge she could see in the distance some of the farm hands busy with field tasks; some tilling, others sowing, and a plough pulled by a team of horses probably with Fred at the head and Seth behind the shafts. Up and down they would go ploughing the furrows in straight lines until the whole field was turned. Birds followed or flitted in and out from the hedgerows grabbing whatever morsel was unearthed and available. A smile curled across her mouth as she thought of Fred preparing the horses for their day's work. Growing up so close to the farm she was fully aware of the succession of seasonal activity; the repeated process with the harrow to get rid of clods and weeds. Then the working of the earth to a fine tilth for seed sowing followed by hoeing, manure spreading and ditch clearing. She quickened her steps eager to see if it was Fred till she remembered her mother's earlier admonition about not keeping the men from their work.

"Oi'd best be lookin' out fer Peggy. Oi'll see Fred later." A warm contentment settled around her heart knowing Fred would be in the stables when she returned home later in the day. She looked forward to spending time together and chatting while doing the end of day chores with the horses.

Peggy had never returned to school full time but continued to participate in the running of the Bemment household. She relished the time spent with Edith and Annie developing her cooking skills and was delighted that others too appreciated her accomplishment and were willing to pay for her produce. This income enabled her to ensure she always had food on the table for her mother and brothers.

After chapel service on Sunday morning Edith drew Peggy to one side. "T'morrow oi'll ask if Butcher Cooper hev a bone marrow. Yew git a bakin' tin from hum an' call in to moine on Tuesday mornin' an' oi'll shew yew how to maak a washin' day cake."

Ahead of time Edith boiled up the marrow bone. "Ma hev it on the stove all yusterday." Edith raised her eyebrows. "We...ell, very near," amended Annie with a mischievous grin.

"We'll skim all the fat orf the top o' the bone marrow thass be in the pan an' put it in this bowl. Like this. What be left behind we'll turn into pea soup fer dinner wi' the bread oi hev a'bakin' in the oven." The girls watched Edith's actions carefully then set about their task to separate the solidified fat from the liquid.

"Now git some o' this flour an' a little sugar an' some water. Throw in a few currants. Mix it all up together loike this into a cake batter." Midst a few mishaps Annie and Peggy followed Edith's instructions then poured the mixture into two tins.

"Cover the tins wi' a tea cloth. Now taak them up to the baker's shop. Oi ha'ent room in ma oven. Here be a farthin'. They'll charge this to cook it. Later yew can goo an' collect them when they be riddy." With a smiling face and a corner of her apron Edith leant forward and wiped floury streaks from both girl's cheeks. "Come yew straight back an' we'll maak the pea soup."

Annie and Peggy left on their errand carefully carrying the precious sweetmeat they had created eager to reach the bakers. The sooner their cakes were cooked the sooner they would be able to taste what they had made. This particular catering practice was a time honoured one that the baker adhered to for people who didn't have an oven in their homes. Dickie Brooks, the baker, was well aware that many of the beach cottages were without this piece of equipment so for a small sum, while his ovens were still hot but not in use for the bakery, he would cook dinners for people or bake the occasional cake. There was nothing scrawny in his looks or his manner; a fine testament to the labours of a man who enjoyed his work.

"When it be baked an' cooled oi'll cut the cake up fer yew an' put it on a dish," he beamed at the girls.

At the appointed time Annie and Peggy returned excitedly to the bakery to pick up the results of their handiwork. Pleased with her efforts Peggy took the cake home to share with her family. However, her mother screwed up her face in disapproval when there didn't appear to be many currants in it.

"Oi reckon yew stood on top of St Andrew's church to throw them in, an' missed by a mile," Hester commented disparagingly. Stan saw Peggy's glum expression. "Thass be roite good," he complimented.

"Oi loike it, Peggs," said Fred.

"Me too," Caleb mumbled as he stuffed in the last mouthful. "When yew maaken' it agin?" They all burst into laughter, restoring Peggy's spirits.

"Another item to sell at market?" asked Stan.

"Oi'll see."

When Annie also left school her parents were reluctant to allow her to go into service. She continued to acquire some home-making skills with Peggy under Edith's guidance but particularly looked forward to the weekly gatherings at the market in the heart of the village below the church. She missed the interaction with her school fellows so enjoyed the market's bustle and busyness. Chatting with stall holders and customers and meeting up with Peggy brought a broad smile to her lips. Listening to the old folk of the village talking about bygone times and reminiscing about old customs and traditions, songs and ways of doing things intrigued Annie. Nothing went unnoticed by Annie. She locked away words and actions in her memory; small things and occurrences delighted her and gave such pleasure.

Edith began to go more frequently up to the Manor House assuming many of her former responsibilities as ladies maid. Annie often accompanied her, learning sewing skills till she was sufficiently proficient to be entrusted with mending Master Edmund's clothing. Annie enjoyed the time spent in the nursery with the growing baby. She made up stories and games to amuse Edmund about what she had seen on her walks along the country lanes and by the seashore. Lady Marion seeing the attachment that was developing between her son and her friend's daughter suggested Annie become a nursery maid.

"You must agree, Edith, that Master Edmund is such a spirited little fellow that he does wear out his things amazingly fast now that he is on the move. Between you, and Nannie, Annie will learn to cater to all his needs." Edith discussed the possibility of such engagement with George and Annie's eyes lit up when he agreed. "But she muss come hum to sleep, fer now."

Lady Marion was ready for further changes to take place in the nursery arrangements before long. Increased early morning visits to the closet confirmed her suspicions that in a few months' time Nannie's duties would be doubled. Nannie Biddle had held sway in the de Vessey nursery since Lord Ralph and Master Quentin were born and whilst her affection and loyalty could not be faulted her agility was diminishing somewhat. Lively youngsters had the ability to dictate nursery rule and Lord Ralph, and his wife were anxious that their children learned discipline and respect in a loving environment. Much thought was given concerning whom they wanted to engage to be involved in their offspring's upbringing.

"It's important to have someone who will guide and influence our children in the values that we hold dear."

***

Against convention Lady Marion had refused to dismiss Beatrice. Following the conversation she had overheard in the garden between the deplorable young man and the scullery maid Marion sent for Beatrice. It was a particularly difficult day for Beatie and her pasty, peaked face reflected the sickliness she was experiencing. When she saw the young woman as she stood outside the door of her sitting room Marion was shocked at the change in Beatie's normally comely appearance.

"Do come in and sit down, Beatrice," she invited kindly. Beatie's stoicism almost gave way at Lady Marion's benevolence towards her.

"Thank yew, m'lady," she stammered as she gratefully took the proffered seat. Marion sat down opposite the frightened maid, smoothed down the skirt of her gown and wondered who was the most apprehensive at this unprecedented meeting.

She smiled directly at Beatie hoping to put her at ease.

"Beatrice, I won't prevaricate, for I am sure you know why I have asked to see you."

Beatie gulped. Tears flooded her eyes. Her shoulders slumped dejectedly. *How hev m'lady found out about ma predicament?* Her sickliness had caused her to lose weight, so she managed to conceal her expanding waistline under her apron.

"Please, ma'am, do not dismiss me," she pleaded. "Oi

hev nowhere else to goo," she mumbled. In the silence of the sitting room Marion only just picked up the barely inaudible voice.

"Please explain, Beatrice."

Beatie raised her eyes. She saw compassion, not censure, in the face of her employer. "Ma won't hev me in the hus. She say oi be brought disgrace on the family." Her head hung down and her hands fiddled nervously with a fold in her apron.

"Do you have feelings for the father?"

Beatie's head jerked up angrily, her eyes blazing indignantly.

"Noo!" she adamantly blurted out.

Marion pressed gently, "Were you compromised?"

Tears splodged on to Beatie's snowy white apron as slowly she nodded her head.

Seconds ticked away.

"Here, wipe your eyes and blow your nose." Marion passed the scullery maid her lace-bound handkerchief, clasped her hands decidedly in her lap and declared, "We will move you into the Nursery wing. In due time we'll work out your duties. Nannie will soon need an extra pair of hands." Her hand fluttered over her slightly swollen abdomen. "Initially, you can prepare Master Edmund's meals. Would you like that?"

"Yes, ma'am, but Cook woan't."

"Leave Cook to me."

"Thank yew, m'lady."

When the interview ended Beatie walked thoughtfully to her room in the attic. In a daze she gathered her things together in readiness for the move, scarcely believing what had just taken place. In the meanwhile, Lady Marion sent for Mrs Sands. Quietly but firmly she explained the changes that would be taking place in the household.

Mrs Sands tutted, pursed her lips and shook her head. Lady Marion looked her directly in the eye. "I shall rely on your discretion to curb any unwarranted gossip, Cook."

Before the sun set Beatie's few possessions were moved and she was settled in the nursery maid's small room close to Master Edmund's nursery, a provisional list of duties to hand and arrangements made for a change of uniform. A sigh escaped her lips unbidden as she laid her head on the pillow in her new quarters. In amazement the day's events tossed about in her thoughts. *A day that started out quoite rough hev ended soo unexpectedly.* Her troubles were not over but for the moment her body and mind were more at ease.

***

Early the next morning there was a knock on the kitchen door of the Manor house. "Answer that," Mrs Sands called out to Maggie as she beat eggs for breakfast 'upstairs'.

On the step stood Colin Jenner nervously passing his cap from one hand to the other. "Oi'd loike to speak wi' Cook."

"Step inside then," instructed Maggie her face lit with curiosity which Cook immediately knocked on the head.

"Fetch up carrots and potatoes from the cellar store, Maggie, and start preparing them for lunch," she ordered.

"Yus, Cook," the kitchen maid replied sullenly, miffed that she was being sent away.

"Well, m'bor, what do yew want?"

Colin cringed at Mrs Sands' forthright tone.

Falteringly he answered, "Permission to walk out wi'

Beatrice."

Momentarily Cook ceased her beating and raised her eyes to her unexpected visitor. Her brief perusal confirmed he was in earnest. “I’ll pass on yow’n request to her ladyship,” she clipped.

“Thank you, Mrs Sands.” Colin inclined his head and quietly exited the Manor kitchen.

Thass a pretty kettle o' fish! Cook vigorously continued beating the eggs, but her thoughts raced decidedly ahead. *An answer to that young lady's predicament, fer sure!*

CHAPTER SIXTEEN

"..and off they go."

Beatrice settled into her new role as quickly as possible. A small stove and preparation area were set up in a corner of the day nursery and in consultation with Nannie Biddle she planned young Edmund's meals. It was quite a learning curve for her as she adapted from cooking skills needed for family meals to the requirements of one small child.

"Nothing rich, and nothing too heavy."

"Yus, Nannie."

The menu was sent down to the kitchen weekly and the necessary food delivered to the nursery each morning.

When Beatie's sickliness was long passed she began to bloom. Lady Marion advised a daily walk would be beneficial, so the Squire's family garden was made available to her, much to Lady Araminta's displeasure.

"What are you thinking of, Marion, to allow servants to walk in our private gardens?" She complained at dinner.

"Oh, Marion, thinks nothing of fraternizing with the peasants, Mater. Calls them her friends," Quentin scoffed with disdain.

"Quentin!" Lord Ralph admonished his brother on his wife's behalf, but Marion gently shook her head.

"Why don't you take Edmund for a walk in the garden

after lunch before his afternoon nap. Make the most of this fine weather. The fresh air will be good for you both," Marion suggested to Beatrice the following morning in an attempt to make the situation more acceptable to her mother-in-law. She was aware this advice would also help protect Beatrice from prying eyes and unwarranted gossip about her condition as her girth increased and hopefully appease Lady Araminta.

On her afternoon out, with her ladyship's permission, Beatie met Colin outside the far kitchen garden gate. Quietly and without fuss they conducted their courtship unseen as they walked along the back lane, shielded by hedgerows, towards the bottom end of Grandpa Jonas's back garden. Beatrice was astounded that this gentle, quiet man should care so much for her that he was willing to accept another man's child as his own to protect her from further disgrace. His gracious kindliness touched her heart. As they visited in his home Jonas witnessed the genuine affection that developed between them as they got to know one another and welcomed the way his grandaughter blossomed in Colin's company. Such a contrast to a few months earlier.

However, in other areas within the community things were not looking so good.

In the estate manager's office the continuing fine, drought-like weather was causing grave concern. Farmers, gardeners and villagers waited patiently for rain. It had been hot and dry for weeks. Everything was crying out for water. Whilst the diminished river still flowed out to the sea many of its tributaries and freshwater ditches only had trickles of water in them or were entirely silted up. The situation became desperate when a well in the hamlet of Newton Common dried up completely and the children from the families were sent to the beach village with pots and jugs to beg for water. The ground was so parched, crops were wilting, garden vegetables struggling or dying almost before they put their heads above ground, animal troughs constantly had to be topped up, but there was expectancy in the air.

"Nivver knowed it be like this a'fore," grumbled Norah Tuttle to her neighbour.

"Not enough t' drink let aloan t' wash pots an' clothes," came the reply from Gertie.

"Not much change there then, be there," muttered Norah under her breath. Norah struggled with housekeeping and household chores with her brood of children and a husband who was constantly out of the home working at sea on boats but her slatternly neighbour Gertie Saunders, slovenly in dress and manner, never made the effort and was always on the cadge.

"Mark ma words thass a'gooin' t' pour," commented Bert Bracewell to Annie and Peggy as they passed him in the lane. The girls giggled and shook their heads at his words. They were on their way to give peelings and foodstuff to the pigs.

"Suthen moite haapen quoite soon," he nodded sagely and pointed towards the sky.

"Is that roite," Annie replied.

"Ye best be quick to be hum an' dry a'fore tea-toime."

"Yus, Mister Bracewell."

"Now, orf yew goo."

In no time at all, as if to give credence to Bert's words, distant flashes in the darkening sky and the odd rumble of thunder became evident as storms worked their way across the sea and hurried their young feet towards the gate which led into the orchard. A rush of air surged across the veggie patch as the first splodgy drops of rain fell releasing earthy scents from the dusty ground. The girls swiftly deposited the repast they carried for Spot and her piglets. She had proved to be a good mother and had managed to nurture all eleven of her first litter. Even the runt had survived being carefully reared by Peggy and Caleb; Hester being assigned to keep a close eye on it and feed it when they were elsewhere. A task she assumed reluctantly, at first, but when she saw the piglet thrive under her care she began to relish feeding him. Stan was delighted his mother was once again taking an interest in something.

Soon it would be time for the piglets to be taken to market, much to Annie's dismay. They were almost ready. George had always warned her not to get too attached because that was their destiny. "When it be their toime then orf they goo."

The rain became heavier. Annie lifted her face to the sky and raised her arms, spreading wide her hands, relishing the welcome bathing. Peggy joined her and soon they were laughing, singing and dancing together.

"Peggy why doan't Beatie come hum, now?" Annie asked tentatively as the girls stopped to enjoy their unexpected bathe. "Oi miss her."

"Ma hev forbidden her."

"Why?"

"She say 'cos she be wi' child out o' wedlock an' brought disgrace on ow'n family name."

"An' who be the Pa?"

"Beatie clamped up an' woan't say."

"Be she a'walkin' out wi' anyone?"

"Noo," Peggy promptly replied, unaware of the close

friendship quietly developing between Beatrice and Colin Jenner.

"The Queen's new baby be called Beatrice."

"She do hev lots o' babies, doan't she."

"Oi moite want lots o' babies, too, but oi shall wait till yow'n Fred an' oi be wed."

"Come yew on thass not fer a long toime. Let's goo get some soap an' wash ow'n hair." They ran home gleefully.

At first the welcome downpour brought cool relief for farmers and animals, fields and garden patches as well as the two young girls. But the deluge didn't abate. It continued for the next three days. And the north-easterly wind that accompanied it was relentless. It whipped up everything in its path including the sea which, with the evening high tide, surged with unstoppable vengeance towards the beach village.

The morning it ceased Lord Ralph walked with a worried Mr Jenner to survey some of the storm damage in the kitchen garden and the pastureland closest to the Manor House. The animals seemed to have fared well, but great swathes of the meadows were still under water, the heavy rain having been unable to penetrate the parched land.

"So far I have only given the premises a cursory glance, sir, but there is no evidence of serious damage or harm to the main house. However, I did notice broken tiles in the courtyard which I believe are from the large storehouse and there appears to be an abundance of debris on the front lawn."

"Thoroughly check all the outhouses and the stable block, Jenner. Then have the lads examine the fencing and the trees for breaks in boundaries. Take Seth with you and draw up a work schedule. Get Donald to cast an eye over the flock if he hasn't already done so. Other land work will be impossible till the water level subsides."

"Would you mind if I took young Fred Bemment along, sir?"

"Oh?" Lord Ralph raised his eyebrows.

"He's a bright lad and although his heart is with the horses I feel it wouldn't hurt for him learn more about the running of the estate."

"You think he has potential?"

"It may come to nothing, but I think there's more to that boy than mucking out stables."

"I trust your judgement, Jenner. He appears to be a bright lad. Let me know how he fares. I'm sorry to leave this situation for you to deal with. My brother is never around when there are matters to be addressed."

Concern at the devastation surrounding their home emphasized his exasperation at his brother's non-appearance when so much needed attention.

Mr Jenner sensed the Squire's frustration but wisely held his tongue. In his mind Master Quentin's blustering presence would be more of a hindrance than a help.

"I'll pick up a horse and ride over to Home Farm to see what the state of affairs is there while you attend to matters here. I'll meet you in the estate office after lunch to evaluate the situation."

"Yes, my lord."

They discussed further remedial plans as they walked towards the stable block, then as his lordship made his way to Prince's stable Mr Jenner sought out the gardeners and stable hands and issued instructions to carry out essential repairs.

Lord Ralph elected to ride along the main thoroughfare

between the Manor House and Home Farm rather than across the countryside byways believing it would provide more secure footing for his mount. His heart sank when he saw swathes of early cereal fields flattened by the torrential rain. Not only would that affect income for the estate but also the staple diet of his workers. The paddock by the dairy was a quagmire and he could imagine the state of the cows as they were herded in for milking.

As he dismounted by the side of the hay barn dogs began barking. A young lad came running out of the farmhouse.

"Hullo, Johnny, is your Pa about?"

"Mister Squire sir, he be in the milkin' hus wi' Ma an' the girls."

"Thank you Johnny. Could you tether Prince for me?"

"Yus, sir," the boy rushed forward eager to take hold of the reins.

The earthy odour of beasts, mud and freshly pulled milk filled Lord Ralph's nostrils as he entered the milking parlour.

"Good morning, Baldry," Lord Ralph greeted his farm manager then nodded towards the ladies busy on the milking stools. "Mrs Baldry, Violet, Blanche."

"Mornin' Squire," they chorused, the motion of their hands not ceasing as the warm milky liquid pinged continuously into the pails.

"We...ell, thass a foine ole doo, Squire." Farmer Baldry continued executing his pitchfork action as he tossed hay into feeding troughs.

"I agree, Mr Baldry. I have called to see how you are faring and check on conditions here."

"We be late startin' this mornin', sir, as we had to clear the muck an' mess round the farmhus a'fore we could git out o' the door agin an' acrorst the yard, but as soon as possible oi sent Tom an' Billy to assess the damage in the meadows."

"Is there any adverse battering to the house?"

"Noo, as far as oi can see there be juss a smashed window in the scullery, some slates orf the cowhus, a panel loose an' a door orf it's hinges at the big barn. Thass wind be moitey powerful. It mostly be the rubbish thass causin' problems; tools an' farm tackle blown into the wrong place an' branches an' the loike left behind in the storm's wake."

"Mmm. Send word when the boys get back with the assistance you need to set things right. Mr Jenner will send up the necessary help."

"Yus, sir."

"Is the well affected?"

"Noo, we managed to anchor the lid afore the storm got fierce."

"Good thinking. If the boundary fences or hedges are breached don't put the cattle in those fields. Fixing them will take priority."

"The meadow nearest the hus on the far side appears intact an' has the least amount o' laying water soo oi plan to put the cows in there."

"I'm afraid a number of the early wheat fields have not fared so well." Ralph proceeded to acquaint Baldry with what he had observed on his ride over to the farm.

"Thass bad, sir. Growing corn thass be snaffled by wind an' storm be bad news, sir. It may pick up in coming weeks but grain thass remains unharvested in wet weather can start to sprout and be loikely to develop mould an', as yew know, sir, will be rejected as useless an' we'll git a lower price fer it."

"Let's pray for a drying windy spell and then review our

options."

"Roite, sir. Oi hear some hev had it rough down on the beach."

"Oh?"

"Zeb returned from early deliveries wi' the news. The storm surge hev flooded the end cottages; the Bemment's, Elsie an' Jem's, an' some of the others."

"Stan and Fred's," mused his lordship thoughtfully.

"Yus, he spoke wi' Stan as they were sweepin' the water from the cottage an' takin' the furniture out to dry out."

"It seems we shall all need a helping hand."

"Indeed we will," Baldry agreed as he continued to fork hay into feeding troughs as Lord Ralph turned to bid farewell to Mrs Baldry and the girls.

"Will ye be a'tellin' the railway men abaht Low Meadow bein' prone to floodin', sir?"

Lord Ralph turned abruptly, puzzlement creasing his brow.

"Why do they need to know that?" he queried Baldry.

"In case they need to make adjustments afore they place the tracks."

"I'll look into the matter," Ralph replied sharply, striding briskly out of the milking shed to his horse. He was seething. *Something is going on of which my workers are apparently conversant, and I am totally ignorant.* Uncharacteristically, the squire rode Prince hard back to the Manor House recalling the conversation with George Kemp earlier which he had neglected to follow through because tragic events had intervened. His annoyance increased his determination to get to the bottom of the matter.

CHAPTER SEVENTEEN

"Leaving the women..."

Fortunately over the next few days the sun shone, and a drying breeze rustled gently through the fields. It tossed mats and curtains hung on lines to dry and blew around drenched furniture that had been dragged from the flooded beach cottages.

Neighbours pulled together to help one another. Edith baked extra pies and made stew with whatever she had to hand and, with Annie's help, carried it along to share with the cottagers who were endeavouring to cope with the disaster to their homes as best as they could.

After work George and some of the stable lads took a wagon to the beach hamlet laden with straw. "We'll strew it acrorst the floor o' the cottages to soak up excess water that can't be swept out. Then it can goo on the midden heap."

"We'll leave the women to lend a hand as home an' work duties allow." So their wives and sweethearts came when they could to help wipe down walls and wring out sodden linen. "Be best if we rewashed these clothes an' linen to get rid o' the awful smell."

When her chair had been carried outside Hester sat down on it looking sorry for herself till Edith came along with food. She unceremoniously yanked Hester up.

"Come yew on, ma friend, there be work to be done. See,

Peggy an' Caleb hev done a foine job draggin' things out an' Stan hev swept away the water from the floor. Now yew need to wash out yow'n kitchen cabinet drawers an' stand them on end soo they can dry in the sun. Oi'll leave yew some pie an' stew."

As soon as his mother and siblings were organized Stan smiled his thanks at Edith and walked over to assist their neighbours.

"Here, Jem, oi'll gi' yew a hand." Together the men humped a dresser from the kitchen, dripping water all over the place as they processed out of the house. When they set it down in the front garden Elsie opened the cupboard doors. Her shoulders shook as she sobbed.

"What a waste! What a waste!," she cried when she pulled her hand out from the flour bin. From her fingers hung a glutinous glob. "We hev noo food." Their meagre supply of dried goods was completely saturated and unusable.

"Nivver yew mind, ma gal, we'll manage. Juss thank the Good Lord there be none o' us harmed," said Jem as he paused with the load he was carrying out of the cottage. "We be a deal sight better orf than those miners caught in thass explosion in the north." Elsie's tears would not be stopped as she gaped at the waterlogged devastation.

"Ev'rywhere an' ev'rythen be emersed in a muddy liquid concoction. All be wasted an' spoiled," she sobbed. The loss of life 189 families were suffering in Wombwell didn't, at this moment in time, penetrate her thinking. The loss at hand appeared more overwhelming.

But Edith understood and her kind heart missed a beat when she saw the distressing destruction and her neighbour's despair. Life was hard enough without this additional difficulty. *Dear Lord give us strength.* Carefully she placed her pan of stew onto the table the men carried outside. She fixed a smile on her face and reached out to place a hand on Elsie's shoulder. "Elsie, dear, doo yew hev clean bowls fer some stew?" Despite her smile Edith's voice faltered. Bewildered, Elsie shook her head.

"Oi can't foind any."

"Let's look together." Edith rummaged through a pile of kitchen things that had been quickly dumped on the table.

"Ethel," she called to Elsie's daughter, when she located some bowls and spoons. "Will yew rinse these under clean water from the stand pump?" Edith drew a tea-towel from the waistband of her pinafore. "Yow'n Ma will dry them then yew can hev stew an' fresh bread fer supper." Ethel did as she was asked and passed the bowls to Elsie who, almost in a dream, dried them.

"Where be Benny, Ethel?"

"Wi' Fred, they be helpin' the men throw straw on the floors o' the swept-out cottages."

"Goo call him fer supper, good gal."

Once she had served Elsie's family Edith moved next door. The disgusting odour emanating from the open door hit her as she walked through the broken gateway and stepped cautiously up the flooded path. She swallowed and took a deep breath. From the front door she could hear voices in the distance so tentatively called out, "Norah, it be Edith. Oi hev brought yew some supper."

At the sound of her voice Polly, Prue and Patsy sloshed through the water that swirled around the living room floor shouting as they splashed one another eager to grab food to satisfy their hungry bellies. Edith cringed at the sight of their pinched faces streaked with grime.

"Where be yow'n Ma?" Edith asked as she fought to keep her balance in the quagmire as the children pushed and shoved to be first to snatch pies from the basket Annie was carrying.

Silent Pete held back.

"Stop!" Edith raised her voice to stay the grubby hands knocking the pasties into the water. "If yew doan't stop yow'n clamourin' noo one will git anythen 'cos they be all plunged into the mud." Patsy began to scream. Prue started to shout. Edith repeated her question, "Where be yow'n Ma?" Silent Pete pointed back through the open back door to the back yard.

"Prue, hold yow'n noise. Goo fetch yow'n Ma," Edith ordered. Sulkily Prue stomped off creating waves that thoroughly wet Edith's feet and clung to the bottom of her skirt and apron.

"Polly, oi said wait." Edith tapped Polly's hand away from the basket of pasties. Polly yelled. She squeezed the pie she had grabbed. The contents oozed out and she flung the remainder into the water. "Thass a wicked waste, Polly Tuttle," said Edith sharply. "We all be hungry, an' the food is to be shared wi' ev'ryone who lives in the row o' cottages." Polly stuck out her tongue and stamped her feet in temper saturating Edith even more, then balled her fists to hit the basket. Annie instinctively stepped back to protect the precious food, missed her footing and started to fall.

"Whoa!" Hands reached over the broken fence, caught her under the arms and saved her fall. "Thass be a close call, Annie."

"Thanks, Aunt Louisa," Annie responded as she regained her balance.

"Anything I can do to help?" Louisa called out over the

cacophony of sound as Edith continued chastising the unruly children. The pitch of the howling increased. Only Pete remained silent, but tears streamed down his dirty, snot-plastered face.

"Oh, Louisa, oi be roite glad to see yew. An extra pair o' hands will be soo helpful." Edith greeted her sister-in-law who lived in the cottage at the far end of the row.

"Would yew hold Annie's basket of food? Annie run back an' tell Pa o' the need at this end o' the row." The basket exchange was quickly made with no more mishaps and Annie ran to fetch help.

"Where be Hezekiah?"

"Out fishin'."

"Aren't yew flooded?"

"The sea didn't breach the wall soo badly at ow'n end of the row. Hezzie put the storm barrier acrorst the door entry when the storm were a'brewin' an' as soon as it abated he went out in the boat wi' Charlie Huggins an' Sol Cooper."

"Be Mr an' Mrs Armes alroite?"

"Water in the yard, like ow'n, an' some in the scullery, but Hezzie swept it back afore leaving. They be too afeard to goo out."

"When Annie gits back goo fetch some bowls an' taak them some stew an' pasties."

"Yew be soo good, Edith."

"Noo, juss sharin' what the Good Lord hev blessed us with. How be Maud?"

"She say they be juss foine. That husband o' hers be a lazy good fer nuthen' an' wuz not around so Hezekiah helped the eldest bor clear the yard. Maud peered through a chink in the door to say the huss be foine but she wouldn't come out. I think she hev bruising on her face."

"Oh dear! That poor soul! What a lot she hev to put up with."

"She won't say anythin' against him but when Bert be in his cups we can hear him a'yellin' an' carryin' on at her an' throwin' things abaht. When I called this mornin' she be holdin' a cryin' Aggie an' pacifyin' the young uns. For all her timid ways she loves her children. I could see the pinched faces o' Dennis an' Minnie peerin' through the gap."

The clattering splodge of horses hooves coupled with the creak of turning cartwheels and jingling harnesses as well as the chatter of numerous voices drowned further conversation between the women as Annie returned accompanied by the men. When Annie resumed her role as basket carrier Louisa called into her elderly neighbours with a couple of pasties and picked up bowls to hold stew for their supper. At the same time Norah waddled through the watery mess in her home shouting and cuffing her children. "Hold yow'n noise," she screeched. Above it all a raucous voice yelled from the next-door upstairs window, "Why ent yew bin to moine? We be hungry too. Ent we good enough fer yew?"

Irritation crackled up Edith's spine. *Oi'd loike to give that woman a piece o' ma mind.* Possible confrontation with an unreasonable, demanding Gertie Saunders brought out the worst in her. *Lord, keep uncharitable thoughts at bay. That woman hev cadgin' an' grudgin' behaviour down to a foine art.*

“We be gradually movin' along the row, Mrs Saunders," George called up to the disgruntled neighbour. "We'll sort out Mrs Tuttle then yew be next."

"Oi be roite pleased to see yew, George," Edith whispered in his ear as he walked by her. Relief flooded her whole being at the sight of her husband. He would help deal with the truculent Gertie.

"It ent roite," Gertie continued to complain. "Why do we always hev to be last?" She was determined to get her point across with the sharp end of her tongue.

"Come yew downstairs an' shew us what needs a'doin'," said George calmly.

"But there be water everywhere," she moaned.

"Hold yow'n noise Gertie Saunders," shouted Norah up to her. "We all be as drowned as rats soo quit yow'n squit an' move yer backside down here."

"Bring the children out onto the lane an' hev a bite to eat." While George continued to coax Gertie, Annie handed pasties to Norah to apportion to her children. Edith ladled stew into bowls Lousia held out for Mr and Mrs Armes and filled a large basin for the Tuttle family to share.

Curdling screams that accompanied the Saunder's exit from their flooded home could be heard across the village.

"What be all that racket fer?"

George sent Stan to assist them. Once the family were safely out onto the muddy lane gesticulations and whispered conversation between Stan and George resulted in Fred being despatched post haste for the rat catcher.

Gertie Saunders stood defiantly with wet feet and ankles, legs ajar and her arms folded across her ample bosom. "We ent hevin' dregs an' left-uvvers."

Edith's hackles began to rise. George saw her pursed lips and shook his head. "Everythin' be freshly baked today, Mrs Saunders. Where be Harry?"

"Down the Fisherman's wi' Arnie."

"Might hev known," muttered Norah, "skivin' as usual when there be work to do."

"He be delicate, as yew well know, an' juss needed fortifyin' afore he started a'clearin' the water," Gertie retorted haughtily. "Anyway, where be yow'n Bill? Doan't see him about," she added in a nasty tone.

"Fishin'."

"A loikely tale."

In a flash the cumbersome Mrs Saunders leaped towards her aggravating neighbour to defend her husband's honour.

"At least he works to supports his family!"

Stan stepped between the women before they tore each other's eyes out.

"Mrs Tuttle, oi think yow'n children be ready fer stew." Gently he steered Norah back to where her youngsters stood around the table in the front of their own cottage.

Meanwhile Edith served up stew into dishes Seth brought from the Saunder's scullery that Lousia had washed and placed on the rickety table George and Jem carried outside. As soon as the bedraggled children had scoffed the stew they snatched at the pies Annie and Louisa offered to them.

"Louisa there be a pie fer yew an' some fer Maudie's family an' a little stew fer you both."

Wearily Edith glanced around for Annie. "We'll maak ow'n way hum," she called to George. Dusk was falling and it had been a tiring day.

"It won't be long afore we be finished. We hev strawed Norah's an' now Sid has collected the vermin it woan't taak long to sweep out the water an' lay straw at Gertie's. O'ill be along a'hum shortly," George assured his wife.

Edith shivered. The sight of Sid's pole with the creatures strung across it turned her stomach. The children gleefully counted thirteen as he walked passed them. She had closed her eyes until she was certain he was out of view. Purposefully she and Annie walked home, along the lane and up the score. *Lord, thank Yew for strength to help ow'n neighbours today an' oi pray Yow'n comfort for those families who be sufferin' worse than we be, today.*

The steps up to their front door seemed a long haul but never had they been more welcome. When she reached the top she could not believe her eyes. Leaning against the foot of the door stood a sack of flour, a basin of dripping, a basket of vegetables along with a lump of meat and a dead fowl waiting to be plucked.

CHAPTER EIGHTEEN

"...to knead the dough."

Clearing up operations occupied everyone's thoughts and energy for some while in the village as well as on the de Vessey Estate. Trees that had blown down in the storm were sawn to make them safe and the timber cut into usable sizes by the estate carpenters. George harnessed others to Ditton to convey them to the side of the big barn to season. Slates were replaced and fences mended. Hedgerows that divided fields, battered down by the gale-force winds, were re-layered carefully to ensure nesting birds were not disturbed. Minor repairs were necessary to numerous properties throughout the neighbourhood. Joiners and builders were kept busy. The row of cottages on the beach that belonged to the Estate were inspected by Elias Jenner, once the straw had been removed, to establish they were thoroughly dry and fit for habitation. The wall at the bottom of the back yards facing the sea, that had been breached, was quickly rebuilt and the privies adjacent to the wall given the necessary attention.

Unfortunately, the three cottages in the middle of the row were the property of different landlords. Maud and Bert Maddox's cottage belongs to Mrs Hardiman while Mr Bilton owns the Saunders and Tuttle cottages. Their reluctance to spend more than is necessary on their upkeep is the cause of much displeasure to Gertie, Norah and Albert. The whole village frequently has to give ear to their perennial complaints.

"They be quoite content the men o' the village sorted out the mess caused by the floodin' wi'out any input from them."

"See how we be ridden wi' vermin but they woan't do nuthen abaht it."

"Nivver come near the place to see if it still be a'standin' or if we be alroite."

"They won't fix the slates on ow'n ruf. Water pours through the bedroom ceilin' when it rains an' we hev to put buckets under to catch it."

"A gale hev bin a'blowin' through that gapin' hole in the window frame fer a year or more but the more oi mention it the more they ignore it."

"Nor will they hev the smokin' chimney swept but they soon be at the door if the rent int paid on the dot."

"The privy door be hangin' orf but they doan't want to know."

Edith shut her ears to their continual grumbling thinking that some of the repairs could be tackled by their menfolk if they spent less time whiling away the hours in the Fisherman's Arms or The Rising Sun. Painting a derogatory picture of landlords when the tenants were unwilling to help themselves was not conducive to good relations. She recalled the original state of their loft home when it was first offered to them. A shiver ran down her spine at the thought of its former four-legged furry occupants. *How hard we worked to maak it possible to live here with help from ow'n friends an' the generosity of the Squire.*

She never did find out who had left such bounty on their

doorstep that day of the flood clearing. However, the generous kindness enabled her to continue baking daily, and sharing the largesse with her neighbours, until such time as their homes thoroughly dried out and they were in a position to make their own meals. Annie helped to knead the dough for loaves of bread and cut out the pastry to make individual pies and pasties then accompany her mother to deliver them.

Annie also looked forward to the days when they visited the less active senior citizens in the village whose minds remained more agile than their bodies. Chatting and listening to the older folk in their community as they spoke about bygone times enabled her to learn about different ways of doing things as they remembered old customs and traditions that had long died out. Their memories of youthful days were vividly recalled and fascinated her. Then, as mother and daughter walked home Annie would question Edith about what she had heard but some of the tales that had been related were out of her mother’s experience. "That be a'fore ma toime, m’gal." Edith replied on more than one occasion.

"For once oi be thankful for these steps. Oi be so glad that own hum be situated above the ravages o' the sea," Edith exclaimed at the end of another busy and tiring day.

"Flood water be unloikely to reach this far inland," George reassured her. "We be too high up."

"Such a blessin'."

George turned to his daughter. "A'morrow, Annie, oi want yew to feed the pigs afore dayloite. The aftermath of the storm hev put us behind in some of ow'n tasks. We muss catch up. Oi’ll apportion fieldwork to Wilf and ole Alf and entrust the welfare o' the hosses to Stan. Seth an' young

Fred be a'comin' along wi' me to taak the pigs to market in Newton Lokesby. Stan has chosen to keep the runt to fatten up as it be a'doin' soo foine."

"Yus, Pa," Annie teared up.

"Yew knew they would hev to goo, m'gal." He patted her on the shoulder.

"Yus, Pa," she nodded reluctantly.

"We'll keep Twospot to fatten up fer meat, an' retain the female fer breedin' wi' the boor at Manor Farm."

"But Ma..."

"Yow'n heart be too sarft, Annie, m'gal."

"The cycle of life on a farm be care an' provision. Yew know that, Annie."

"Yus, Pa, but..."

"The Good Lord provides for ow'n needs. Ow'n part be to tend an' nurture what be entrusted to ow'n care, whether it be grain, garden produce or livestock."

"Yow'n Pa an' oi knows what it be loike to be wi'out. Remember the struggles Peggy's family had not soo long back?" Annie nodded.

"We be blessed wi' a good Ma who manages ow'n affairs juss foine an' works hard in the hum an' the garden. An' yew be a'larnin' foine to follow in her footsteps." Annie nodded. From an early age she had absorbed all she saw and heard; tasks and sights, sounds and scents of all the seasons.

"When do yew expect Twospot to be riddy for slaughter?" Edith asked.

"Chopper Cooper, the butcher, suggested we hev the killing in the first cold snap, possibly middle of November. That will help wi' chillin' the carcass an' supply ow'n needs till next Spring. Maak sure yew hev sufficient salt in hand."

"Soo much busyness to look forward to."

"Spot will soon be riddy to drop her next litter."

"An' soo the cycle repeats itself."

The following morning before dawn had pushed back the night-time sky Anne tripped down the stone steps leading from her home to the cobbles of the stable yard. She turned at the corner of the building and made her way to the pannage where the pigs were kept. Across one arm she carried the bucket of pig swill. With her free hand she picked sow thistle and dandelion leaves from under the hedgerow that bordered the vegetable patch, dewdrops glistening as the morning light began to dispel the darkness. Some dark clouds lingered but were unable to overcome the emerging light of a new day.

Annie heard the twittering of the birds, but before she reached the pigs the cockerel outdid them all with his early morning call. She petted Spot and spoke in soft tones to the younger pigs as they snuffled and grunted their way through the fresh leaves and pig mash Annie set out for them that Edith had boiled up the previous evening in the vegetable water from their own meal.

"Waste not, want not, as my grandmother used to say," quoted Edith.

"Do that include pigs?"

Edith laughed. "Certainly. Yew will see come November. Every part of the pig will be used except fer his squeal. Nuthen will be wasted."

Annie completed her task then walked towards home, listening to the hidden creatures rustling the undergrowth as they foraged for food as she passed. *Pa be tendin' the hosses for the day an' Ma hev left gruel on the back o the stove. Oi best be quick.* Before she left home Pa explained that plans had changed for the day because Edith had been sent for in the early hours of the morning to go up to the Manor. “Yew an’ Ma will not be attendin’ the village market t’day but yew doo be required fer duty in the Manor Nursery.” George had refrained from telling his daughter that Beatrice had gone into labour.

Annie served breakfast for her father and herself. After clearing away she walked up to the Big House to fulfil her duties as nursery maid to Master Edmund.

As Annie departed from her home Fred and Seth finished their chores at the stables and met up with George who stood waiting in the orchard by the pigsty.

"If we doan't git a'goen we woan't be a'comen back," he chivvied the lads.

Carrying the necessary staves they guided the young pigs across the fields to the livestock market in the much bigger village of Newton Lokesby hopeful of buyers eager to fatten them up. The anticipated return would help to replenish depleted provisions and see them through come winter months.

CHAPTER NINETEEN

"One works the hosses..."

"Marion, for goodness sake go and keep that baby boy of yours quiet," Quentin ordered with his mouth full, gesticulating towards the dining room door with his cutlery filled hands.

Marion smiled sweetly at her brother-in-law. "Our boy is no longer a baby, Quentin. If you were observant you would have noticed he is quite a grown little boy."

"Really? Then what creature is making that wretched noise?" he demanded irritably. Uncharacteristically, Master Quentin had joined his brother and his wife for luncheon but had spent the majority of the meal complaining about the crying of a baby.

"It is a newly born baby girl named Rebekah," Marion explained.

"Well, what is it doing here?"

"She was born here in the early hours of this morning."

"Why?"

"Her mother had nowhere else to go."

"Why come here?"

"Beatrice has been living and working here for quite some time. First as a scullery maid, then as a pastry cook and latterly she has been engaged to prepare Edmund's meals and care for his needs."

"Why have the monster here?"

"She is not a monster but a beautiful baby girl. Her mother was turned out of home by her mother as soon as it was known Beatrice was in the family way."

"What about the father?" asked Ralph.

"It seems the father has distanced himself from all responsibility leaving Beatrice to bear the brunt of disgrace and rejection alone," Marion quietly explained.

Ralph's brow furrowed. "Surely he should be made to acknowledge his actions and make provision for Beatrice and his child."

Marion's head shook sadly from side to side.

"Beatrice resolutely refuses to cite the father and one can hardly compel her to name him."

"Very noble of her," Quenton muttered.

"In contrast to the unspeakable cad who has left her in this predicament," Ralph emphatically expressed.

Quentin audibly gulped at his brother's remark.

Marion looked up from her plate and noticed the tips of Quentin's ears had turned scarlet. He took no further part in the conversation but put his head down and finished the food on his plate as rapidly as possible. Still chewing a mouthful of food he flung down his knife and fork, scraped back his chair, rose abruptly and excused himself before the next course was served.

"My brother's manners get more and more coarse and unacceptable," Ralph declared as Quentin made his hasty exit.

Marion slowly placed down her cutlery upon her plate and turned to face her husband. Quietly she said, "Your words touched on a raw nerve."

"My words?" Ralph raised his eyebrows questioningly.

"Quentin is the cad to whom you referred who has landed Beatrice in this position." Marion proceeded to share the conversation she had unwittingly overheard in the garden so many months previously.

Ralph thumped the table angrily. "Why didn't you tell me?"

"I thought at the time it was wisest to remain silent, for Beatrice's sake."

His lordship made to rise but Marion gently pulled on his sleeve. "The damage is done, Ralph. Let's see if your words have influenced his conscience. In the meantime we'll continue to support Beatrice in the nursery wing."

"Not a good example to our children nor a reflection of the values we uphold."

"Currently Edmund is too young to understand all the implications. The situation may have changed before this little one puts in an appearance." She placed a hand tenderly on her growing abdomen. "At present Beatrice has a job, one she fulfils exceptionally well, and a roof over her head and here she is shielded from the unpleasantness of village gossip."

"You know best, my dear," Ralph concurred with resignation. Marion refrained from enlightening him about possible changes in Beatrice's circumstances now that her child was born.

***

Later that day Lord Ralph was riding out with Mr Jenner inspecting repairs to the outlying boundaries of the estate. In the distance figures could be seen engaged in some sort of construction work.

"Whoa!" His lordship reined in Prince.

"Have we men working in this area today, Jenner?"

Elias Jenner pulled up his mount alongside his lordship.

"No, my lord."

"Then we had better check what is going on."

They cantered towards the workers.

"Excuse me, my man, can you tell me what is going on here?"

"Can't stop to talk I'd lose a day's pay."

"Direct me to the foreman."

"The one in the top-hat."

"His name?"

"Betts."

"Thank you."

The brief encounter elicited no information whatsoever. Men continued to dig, shovel cinders and move wooden beams or lever metal rails from wagons as though the men on horseback were not present. Their attitude made Ralph feel as though he were invisible.

Explosives could be heard going off not too far distant. The horses whinnied. Prince agitatedly pawed the ground with a hoof. Mr Jenner's mount bucked almost unseating him. Talking calmly to the horses they steadied them. When they were settled Lord Ralph and Mr Jenner rode towards the top-hatted man who had been indicated.

"There is something extra-ordinary going on here, Jenner. I am beginning to suspect unprecedented wheeling and dealing. I intend to get to the bottom of it. Do you know anything about it?"

"No more than you, sir." Elias Jenner refrained from mentioning unproven gossip that had recently reached his ears.

"Snippets I gleaned from my conversations with Kemp and Baldry, some while ago gave me pause to think something could be amiss, but I have been unable to get enlightenment upon the matter as each time I have recalled it some occurrence has arisen that required more direct attention which consequently put the issue out of mind. I never did get that needful conversation with my brother."

“Yes, sir, many unprecedented incidents do seem to have occupied our attention of late.”

As they approached the top-hatted gentleman they could see he was in earnest conversation with a couple of other men. They reined in their horses before dismounting. Leading the horses, as there was nowhere to tether them, they walked up to the group having decided as they rode across that Mr Jenner would initiate the discussion.

"Good day to you, sir," Elias spoke directly to Mr Betts. "As steward of this estate may I ask what you and your men are engaged in here?"

"Why, sir, can you not see? We are constructing a railroad that will link this area to the great metropolis and the rest of this country that will bring work and prosperity to the people living here," Betts explained congenially.

"That sounds very fine, but I would like to point out, sir, the Squire has not given permission for such construction. This is private land. You are trespassing."

Betts waved an arm dismissively. "No, no, no, sir, you are in error. This land has been purchased legally for this development. The documentation, signed, sealed and settled, is lodged in our Lowestoft office."

Lord Ralph stepped forward. "Mr Betts, the documentation you may hold is counterfeit. Whatever transaction has transpired between you and another party is illegal and fraudulent."

"You are wrong, sir. We had lawyers from London draw it up and it was thoroughly checked."

"No, sir, you are the one who is wrong. This land is entailed and can neither be bought nor sold."

Betts looked aghast.

"And who are you, sir, to so pompously issue such a statement and question our right to be engaged in this development?"

"I am Lord Ralph de Vessey. I hold this land in trust for future generations. I have not been approached by anyone nor consulted at any time about this venture you are engaged in, if I had been, you and your associates would have known the legal situation from the beginning. I therefore insist that you get your men to desist from their labours and remove this material and themselves from my land."

"We have paid good money for this land. I dispute your argument, sir. It is ours to do as we please."

"No, sir, you have been duped. This land cannot be sold, built upon, developed or used, for any reason other than as farmland and parkland pertaining to the de Vessey estate, as it is guarded by entail."

"Master Quentin took the money and signed the papers. It is legally ours," Mr Betts persisted.

Elias Jenner's eyebrows twitched. Lord Ralph did not so much as flinch.

"No, sir. Master Quentin has no authority to make decisions regarding the disposition of the estate. Marcus Reydon Capps, my lawyer in Norwich, will deal directly with your lawyers and sort out this mess if you will be so good as to give their name and address to Mr Jenner. In the meantime I ask you to leave the de Vessey estate."

"But... you can't order us off, sir. We paid for it and acquired it honestly."

"Sir, the transaction was fraudulent. Had your lawyer done his homework he would have learned the land could not be sold because it is entailed in perpetuity. However, I acknowledge you have been reprehensibly misled. My lawyer will ensure you are adequately recompensed. Good day to you, sir."

Lord Ralph and Mr Jenner mounted their steads and rode off at pace. Elias had never seen Lord Ralph display such anger. He was the calmest man he knew, never raised his voice or lost his temper. His lordship recognized there were two ways of looking at things and was always willing to consider the other man's point of view. This behaviour seemed totally out of character for the Squire.

At that moment Lord Ralph blessed the prudence of his forbears in the instance of the entail. Whilst some would consider the entail an encumbrance Ralph was grateful the legal requirement, in accordance with the peculiarities of the de Vessy mind, tied his hands. Entail may at times have been like a millstone around a former squire's neck but currently Ralph saw it as a safety net and a way out of the tricky situation his brother had landed him in.

"On return to the Manor locate Quentin immediately, Jenner, and direct him to my study," he instructed curtly.

"Yes, my lord."

"Also send word to Marcus Reydon Capps and ask him to attend at the Manor, urgently."

"Yes, sir."

The men dismounted at the stables knowing one of the lads would work the horses. They went their separate ways,

Mr Jenner to find Quentin and Lord Ralph to prepare for a difficult conversation with his younger brother.

The stable lads took care of the horses. Fred was on hand and took Prince's reins and led him to his stall talking calmly in his ear before commencing the normal routine following a canter across the parkland. Stan handled Mr Jenner's mount.

That evening the walls of the Manor vibrated for more than an hour to the raised voices that emanated from the Squire's study, an unprecedented occurrence.

Master Quentin eventually stormed out of the study, his face as black as thunder, slamming the door with such force a number of servants came rushing to see what might be wrong. He rudely pushed them aside and proceeded to stomp up the main staircase towards his mother's wing.

CHAPTER TWENTY

"..and one tills the soil."

In no time at all Lady Araminta came flouncing down the stairs in her arrogant, aristocratic manner. Alternately she shouted irritably for her eldest son, "Ralph, Ralph, where are you?" then muttered murderous threats against him as she descended each step.

Hearing the commotion Ralph stepped out of his study and greeted his mother pleasantly.

"Why Mater you look charming. Are you joining us for dinner this evening?"

"I most certainly am not," Lady Araminta shouted haughtily. "What horrid things you have been saying to my poor, dear boy!"

Ralph took his mother gently by the arm and led her towards the sitting room where their conversation would be less public. Huffily she allowed him to guide her. He knew it was going to be a difficult conversation because he had said some very straight things to his recalcitrant brother which had probably been embellished by the time they reached their mother's ears. Words Quentin did not want to hear, nor address, and as a consequence his mother would take exception to.

As Ralph seated his mother in a chair by the fireside she continued to rant and rave at him. Unperturbed he strolled with his arms behind his back to the full-length window overlooking the formal garden. He took moments to gaze at the tranquil scene it presented with its symmetry in form and colour before turning to face the torrent of abuse that was being hurled at him, longing for similar calm and order within his home. His mother's tirade continued almost unabated for a further ten minutes.

"Well, what have you to say for yourself, you cruel boy?" She finally threw at him angrily.

Ralph moved slowly towards Lady Araminta before speaking into the pause that she permitted.

"Mater, may I give you the facts. You may not find them at all palatab..."

"What do you mean fac..."

"Mater, you asked me a question, may I answer you?"

"Well, get on with it," she said crossly and shrugged her shoulders. "You are just like your father; so precise with details."

"Your youngest son has fraudulently purloined vast areas of the estate for his own gain, then frittered it away gambling. His debts are so vast he has crippled the estate beyond belief."

"Oh, the poor, dear boy. If only you had given him a larger allowance," she whined pathetically.

"What! And have him squander even more. No, Mater, it is time he grew up and learned to act responsibly. Quentin has stated quite categorically that he doesn't want to work for the estate, so I am giving him the opportunity to oversee Father's plantation and holdings in the West Indies. Not only will it put him beyond the arms of the law it will also be a formidable yet challenging adventure for him."

"What do you mean by saying 'putting him beyond the

arms of the law?'" she demanded angrily.

"Quentin's actions warrant criminal charges."

"No! Impossible! You are banishing him!" Lady Araminta snapped.

"No, Mater, seeking to instil in him a sense of responsibility and the opportunity of learning the value of knuckling down and getting something worthwhile accomplished."

"No, you are sending him away from me," she screeched.

"Not at all, Mater, seeking to keep him out of jail and giving him chance to grow up and show his true mettle. Whenever he got into scrapes as a boy he would inevitably come running to you and you pretended it, whatever it was, had not happened and it did not matter. When Papa said no, you consistently contradicted him on every occasion, so that Quentin always knew he could get his own way with you. It has made him weak. He needs a project to get his teeth into, prove he is capable of achieving something. He has to make this work because he has colossal debts that have to be repaid."

"You are cruel!"

"No, Mater, you are the one who has been cruel by refusing to administer discipline. By unfailingly giving in to him and letting him have his own way, teaching him to be underhanded instead of open, honest and forthright, you have failed him."

"How dare you!"

"I dare, Mater, because it is the truth and if you would only be honest with yourself you would recognize it is so. Quentin is going to have to work hard to make the plantation pay in order to live. It will be far from easy necessitating hard graft and toil. He may literally have to till the soil, which I understand is quite different to what we have here, in order to produce a marketable crop."

"But what about his allowance?" she wailed.

"There is no allowance. His deliberate foolhardiness has bankrupted the estate."

"Then I shall help out my poor boy from my allowance."

"Mother, don't you understand? There will be no allowance from the estate for you."

Araminta's voice faltered, "What do you mean no allowance?"

"Just that."

"But I cannot live on nothing!" She whined snappishly.

"You have the fortune Father left you."

Araminta turned her head hastily and would not hold his gaze.

Ralph balked at her crest fallen face. "Don't you?"

Araminta looked down at the fingers twiddling agitatedly in her lap.

"Have you given Quentin your money to fritter away?"

His mother refused to answer. She also refused to look him in the eye. Instead she rose abruptly to her feet and with back erect and head held high walked towards the door. She turned the doorknob and forcefully opened the door.

"If you banish your brother you also banish your mother," she brusquely spat out at him as she made her way across the hallway and up the staircase, chin erect, nose pointing arrogantly upwards in disdain, skirts swishing behind her.

"That is your choice, Mater." Ralph spoke softly as he stood in the doorway of his study watching her retreating figure with sadness in his heart.

Hanson was hovering nearby. Ralph turned to him.

"Hanson, please serve dinner. There will only be two."

"Yes, your lordship."

The butler laid the place settings himself and thoughtfully set them out close together so that Lord Ralph sat at the head of the table and Lady Marion to his immediate left. As usual when they dined alone the couple shared the day's happenings with one another.

Ralph reiterated his conversations with his brother and Lady Araminta.

"I fear I may have spoken rather harshly to both Mother and Quentin."

"Maybe they needed to hear those words."

Ralph shook his head. "Neither seem to recognize the severity of Quentin's actions. Mother brushed them aside as of no consequence, as is her usual reaction to what she terms his misdemeanours."

"How frustrating for you."

"After she had exited the study to storm upstairs in a huff she even hurried back a few moments later to remonstrate with me. "So, you choose to believe the words of a hussy in preference to the truth spoken by your own brother," she threw at me."

"Oh dear!"

"I never mentioned Beatrice or the fatherhood of her child so Quentin must have brought up the matter with Mother. My response was simply to remind her of Nannie's words to us when we were children, "Think the truth and you will find it will help you speak it too." I concluded with, "Mother, remind Quentin of those words"."

"What was her reaction to that?"

"Silence and the cold shoulder. I quietly quoted the next

two lines about that affecting our actions, but she turned her back on me, stormed out of the study again and marched angrily up the stairs. So I called after her, "The only other alternative to prison would be for Quentin to go to India and quell the mutiny." For which I received another icy stare."

Marion reached out and laid her hand on his arm. "I'm so sorry, my dear, that you have to bear the burden of your brother's wrongdoing. Would he have the backbone to cope with the life of a soldier?"

"Probably not."

"I hear Joe Jenner and Farmer Baldry's eldest boy, Tom, have joined up to fight."

"A means of getting away from jobs they detest and parental control, I suspect."

"I feel for their mothers."

"The newspapers report that the mutiny started because new cartridges for new rifles were greased with animal fat."

"Really?"

"Apparently it is against their religious beliefs to partake of such a substance. I understand they put the cartridges into their mouths to pull them apart. Pig and cow fat is offensive to both Hindus and Muslims. Mangal Pandey, a sepoy in the 34th Bengal Native Infantry, is credited with starting the mutiny because he shot British officers who were sent to arrest him for being one among many to raise objections to the new cartridges and rebel."

"It sounds like a lack of understanding of native cultural practices and beliefs."

"It reads more like the imposition of western values coupled with discrimination, exploitation and interference in religious affairs indigenous to the Indian people."

"A lack of respect for their traditional way of life?"

"It would seem so. I have always tried to look at all situations impartially and listen to the other person's point of view even if it differs from mine. However, with my brother I fail to understand his actions. His behaviour is reprehensible and beyond my comprehension. I fear I have not reined in Quentin as successfully as my father did and he has taken advantage of that. Mother was constantly far too lenient with him, never acknowledging the wrongness of his attitude or behaviour and certainly never administering punishment or correction. I guess as the eldest I underwent a far more disciplined routine, but looking back, I am grateful for the boundaries my father, in particular, set for me. I learned from an early age what was, and what was not, acceptable behaviour.

"Papa instilled in my tutors that the schoolroom was to be ruled with a rod of iron. For some reason that regime never pertained to Quentin, much to his detriment, I fear. We are now living with the consequences of that lack of restraint. Moral lassitude and a complete disregard for Scriptural truths cannot be concealed or covered up. They are clearly revealed by actions and words. One must eventually face up to the consequences of choices that have been made."

The following day Marcus Reydon Capps arrived posthaste. He was ensconced in Lord Ralph's study for quite a while as they thrashed through the implications of Quentin's criminal activities.

Troubled beyond measure Ralph listened as the lawyer itemised the legal ramifications of his brother's behaviour. He shook his head in disbelief and rubbed a hand across his brow.

"As Quentin has agreed to go to the West Indies rather

than face court proceedings I will cover the fraudulent debt he has incurred."

The lawyer tutted and shook his head. "The only way you can achieve that, my lord, is by taking out a bank loan."

"Despite what he has done to cripple the estate I will do whatever is required to prevent my brother going to prison."

Marcus Reydon Capps nodded.

"I leave you to address repayment and compensation to the railway men through their lawyers. It will also be necessary to settle any outstanding gambling debts Quentin still has to prevent further charges being brought against him."

"Yes, my lord. It will take a day to sort out the paperwork."

"I will come into town the day following tomorrow and meet you at the bank to draw up the mandatory documentation for the loan and call into your offices to attend to the other business matters."

***

Before the month was out Lady Araminta and Master Quentin had packed their trunks and vacated the west wing in the Manor House. They travelled on the newly laid railway track from the newly built train station at Newton Lokesby constructed by the Lucas brothers supervised by Messrs Betts and Peto. Mother and son took berths on a ship sailing from Liverpool to the West Indies.

However, they were not allowed to leave Newton Westerby until Quentin had reluctantly signed papers under the watchful eye of Marcus Reydon Capps promising to repay monies he had squandered from the estate. He also penned his name to a document agreeing to support Beatrice's daughter till she reached the age of maturity or such time as she married if that occurred first.

After their departure Lord Ralph's anxiety drew him to the family chapel at the heart of Newton Westerby Manor House. His heart and mind were in a turmoil. He gave no thought to where he sat but allowed the calmness of the cool space to envelope him in an embrace of peace.

Involuntarily his hands picked up the book of Common Prayer from the ledge in front of him. Ralph was acutely aware of his responsibility towards the many people on the estate whose families, lives and livelihoods were woven into the fabric of the place. They were going to be affected by the decisions he made today following the disclosures of the disastrous actions of Quentin. He could not risk the security and well-being of his tenants and loyal, hardworking servants. Almost unbidden his eyes were drawn to look up at the stained-glass window above the altar, erected by one of the de Vessey forebears, depicting the resurrection morning. "Dear God, what am I going to do?" Randomly his fingers flicked through the pages of the prayer book. His eyes lighted on words from Proverbs chapter three; 'In all thy ways acknowledge Him, and He will direct thy paths.' A lump rose in his throat. "Sovereign God, You know our plight. You are in control. Lead us in Your paths of righteousness."

CHAPTER TWENTY-ONE

"And one mends the fences..."

Following Lord Ralph's meeting with the bank manager and estate lawyer his lordship asked to see the senior members of his household staff. Hanson, the butler, Mrs Sands, the cook, Mrs Bertha Hanson, the housekeeper, Alice Housego, the senior housemaid, as well as, Elias Jenner, the estate senior steward, gathered as requested in the master's study. Having heard the uncharacteristic, raised voices, door slamming and foot stomping on the previous two days the assembled group were apprehensive about what they might hear from the Squire. They stood in silence, each absorbed in private thoughts; individual breaths creating an unseen breeze of crosscurrents. The mantle clock relentlessly ticked away every second.

Eventually, the Squire looked up from the papers strewn across his desk that he was working on, his countenance grave, deep lines etched upon his brow.

"Thank you for coming this morning and giving me precious moments of your time." Slowly, Lord Ralph rose from the worn, round-backed leather chair that had been his father's to address the group who stood before him. Such loyal dependable people. He cast his eye upon each of them and smiled; that warm friendly smile they were used to, which today didn't quite reach his eyes as it usually did. *A troubled soul* thought Mrs Hanson.

"I feel it incumbent upon me to advise you of a very serious occurrence that threatens the survival of the estate and therefore your position here and that of those working under you."

Hanson and Elias Jenner stood erect. Mrs Sands nodded knowingly. Alice nervously twisted her hands. Only Bertha gasped.

"I want you to know the facts from me rather than learn from unproven gossip about a situation that has arisen." His lordship paused, visibly distraught, and took a deep breath before continuing.

"My brother, Quentin, has engaged in gambling exploits which have caused the estate to be plunged into a very grave financial position. All our livelihoods are under threat. Mine included. In consultation with the estate lawyer certain actions have already been put in place. I have had to take out a vast bank loan against the value of the estate in order to pay compensation to the rail track men and others to buy back land that should not have been sold or gambled away because it is entailed. Had such been possible I would have liked to have avoided these stringent measures, but we are all going to have to tighten our belts."

Again, Lord Ralph hesitated. A coal dislodged on the fire. A baby cried. Outside a horse whinnied. A bird flew too near to a window brushing the pane with the tip of its wing. In the distance men worked in the fields. Across the garden dappled light shone through the trees as the morning sun moved across the sky. Normal everyday activities.

In the master's study it felt anything but normal. Different thoughts spun through each of the minds of the faithful servants as they stood listening to their master's words. They were hard to take in.

"Sir," Hanson stood tall and at attention. "You have always treated us well, all your staff. We will stand by you. I am sure I speak for each one of us" He looked at the others and witnessed their nods of confirmation.

"I do not want to lose any staff, but it is going to require a concerted effort to get us through this difficult patch. Everyone will be required to pull their weight. We cannot carry any passengers. Those unwilling to fit in to this new regimen will be released, with suitable references."

"I understand, sir." Hanson acknowledged.

"Yew mean no wasters or wastage, sir," said Mrs Sands.

"Yes, Cook. In the kitchen only prepare for meals what is actually needed. Nothing extravagant, simple nourishing repast."

"Yes, sir."

"There will be no lavish dinner parties for some time, nor will my wife be hosting ladies' lunches or afternoon tea-parties for the foreseeable future."

Mrs Sands nodded sagely. "I understand, sir."

"We can perchance look at selling surplus from the kitchen garden at market, Jenner." Lord Ralph looked enquiringly at his right-hand man.

"It's certainly a possibility, sir."

"I leave you to work out details for each of your responsibilities and instruct those under you accordingly. If you feel it would help I will speak with the household staff collectively at 9o'clock tomorrow following morning prayers in the chapel. Mr Jenner and I will be meeting and speaking with garden, farm and stable hands later this morning."

"Thank you, sir," Hanson bowed his head in response. "I

will direct the staff in a way that is appropriate to the particular circumstances we now find ourselves in."

"Are yew asking for no fires except in rooms actually in use, that sort of thing?" asked Alice tentatively.

"That's right, Alice, and possibly curtains closed in unused rooms and furniture covered."

"Cutting back on new purchases?" inquired Bertha.

"Yes, Mrs Hanson, conserve where we can and repair rather than renew."

"I understand the need for everyone to work to earn their keep, but if stringent measures are going to be implemented some may then not have sufficient work to keep them in employment," commented Hanson.

"In that case we may have to deploy several members of staff into other areas."

"But that might usurp another person's occupation."

"I hope that will not be the case. I suggest as we give thought to this we may find we are creating new jobs which at present are not being utilized. For the estate to remain viable we are going to have to be inventive and creative. If you or your staff have any ideas please share them with Mr Jenner. It is early days for us all. Now I have kept you all long enough. Please give thought to what I have said, how roles may be changed and consider where we can successfully save. Thank you for your attention and faithfulness. By God's good grace we will come through this crisis."

Ralph moved thoughtfully towards his desk. He slowed his steps and turned. "I'll suggest to Parson Wisbey that we sing John Keble's hymn 'New every morning is the love' at morning prayers in chapel tomorrow. It will remind all of us that God will make provision."

***

Despite Lord Ralph's carefully worded explanation the following morning after prayers in the family chapel there were ripples of disquiet throughout the household, which spilled over into the village, because so many families were impacted by affairs at the Manor. Gossip was rife as tenants and workers aired their fears that jobs, businesses and homes could be affected.

"Thass a pretty kettle o' fish, them expectin' twice as much work fer less pay."

"Not roite! Losin' yer job 'cos they be lost their money."

"Serves them roite fer lordin' it uvver us all these years," were the less charitable comments in the cottages on the beach.

"Hold yow'n noise, Gertie Saunders, be glad yew be still got a ruf o'er yow'n heads an' Maggie an' Arnie, an' now Nellie, still hev a job at the big hus, though oi doubt Harry will keep his. He be too bone idle." Norah Tuttle remonstrated with her neighbour knowing that though their homes were owned by tight-fisted landlords they were not tied into the estate as were others in the row.

Stan Bemment had chatted over this very predicament with his neighbours, Jem Capps and Hezekiah Kemp, fearful that if he lost his job his family would be evicted from the tied cottage that was their home. He and Jem worked full time for the estate whereas Hezzie followed the herring around the coast and wasn't reliant upon the estate for income, but Mr and Mrs Armes were retired estate workers and believed they were secure tenants for life under the contract they held from the late squire.

"What a predicament to be in!"

"We all pay rent money owed to toime, an' tend the gardens..."

"Unloike ow'n neighbours in the middle o' the row," interspersed Jem with a nervous laugh.

"...soo oi'm sure we doan't give cause for losin' ow'n hums. Oi'll hev a word wi' Mr Kemp an' see what he say," Stan assured him.

In response to Stan's query George Kemp doubted whether Lord Ralph would dispose them as long as they paid their rent. "But oi'm not sure."

When this aspect of disquiet reached the ears of Elias Jenner he brought it to the attention of the Squire.

However, Lady Marion pre-empted this conversation over dinner following concerns Edith Kemp had shared with her the previous afternoon giving Lord Ralph opportunity to formulate a plan to allay the fears of his tenants and workers.

"Jenner, when the workers come to pick up their wages from the estate office on Friday I will be in attendance with you, and we will speak to them individually."

"But sir..." Mr Jenner started to ague.

"We have fences to mend," Lord Ralph stated emphatically.

"...that will be time consuming."

"Yes, but I think time well spent. We will learn a number of things from this exercise. Who is with us and who is not. We'll listen to their concerns and voice our reasons for acting as we are doing. Find out who is creative and has initiative and discover who is flexible or willing to try something new or different."

CHAPTER TWENTY-TWO

"...for his daily toil."

Summer moved seamlessly into autumn, September absorbing the challenges of the last few weeks as effortlessly as seasons acknowledge the changing hue of the landscape.

The myriad changes in the Manor House, at Home Farm and across the estate did not create the hiatus the Squire had envisaged. Following the initial shock of the severity of the inevitable austerity that Master Quentin's treachery had caused there was, at first, considerable grumbling and anxiety amongst certain members of staff and workers. But, with tact and tenacity Hanson and Mr Jenner coaxed those under their authority. They emphasized the necessity and wisdom of pulling together to get everyone through the challenging times that faced the estate. A quiet word here and there sparked unexpected creativity and innovation as each person was made to realize the importance their contribution was to the success of the mammoth undertaking before them.

Mr Jenner had cause on numerous occasions to acknowledge that the Squire's insistence on the personal approach on the first pay day following his original announcement proved to be pure genius in many respects. Those servants who persisted in still engaging in murmurings of discontent against the estate were given the option of leaving the Squire's employ. However, on the whole most remained, admitting that the Squire had been open and honest with them, and they wanted to respond in kind. He had explained clearly that no one would lose his home or job unless he chose to give it up. "Rent and wages will remain the same for the next year but dedicated hard work will be required by all to pull the estate through this crisis."

"Can't tell us fairer than that, can he?"

That pay day was to prove pivotal in the long-term recovery of the estate fortunes as well as establishing confidence and good worker and management relations. There was soon a hive of additional activity in workshops, kitchen, garden and fields as well as in the dairy at Home Farm.

Mr Jenner worked tirelessly, travelling in person to contact possible outlets in Lowestoft and Norwich and even further afield, to raise funds for the estate by selling surplus produce. The Squire's approach convinced him that face-to-face conversations achieved more positive results.

Carpenters constructed crates to transport fruit and vegetables to the Covent Garden Market. Seth was seconded to organize the conveyance of cattle and sheep to Smithfield's meat market in London. They utilized the newly established Newton Lokesby railway station with its rail link to the London markets.

"Sir, we may not desire rail tracks to be built across de Vessey land, but does not reason suggest that we use the facility already in place to our advantage?" Mr Jenner argued with the Squire, reminding him that his neighbour had freely given consent for a station and rail tracks to be built across his land. "Transporting livestock and edible goods will be quicker and less time consuming leaving our own men free to continue working on the estate."

"Excellent thinking, Jenner," commended Lord Ralph.

"Not entirely my own reasoning, sir. Seth pointed out the value of conveying the cattle and sheep in wagons rather than driving them such a distance along the lanes. They would lose less weight and arrive at market looking in prime condition. Also drovers would not be required. Prove more lucrative overall for the estate despite having to pay transport costs."

Lord Ralph nodded thoughtfully, unable for a moment to speak. The gracious respect his employees were showing to the family in this period of crisis was overwhelmingly humbling.

Mr Jenner continued, "Abel Catchpole suggested that with correct packaging and cartage fruit and vegetables could also reach their destination in a fresher state if carried by the railway, so I instructed Josh Piper and his boys to construct suitable crates for their transport."

Deeply moved Lord Ralph was barely able to speak.

"What an unbelievable inspiration the staff are proving to be, Mr Jenner," he whispered.

"Yes, sir, ideas and abilities are cropping up from the most unexpected quarters."

"Hidden skills being unearthed like buried treasure and the fact that they are willing to give them for the benefit of the estate humbles me beyond measure," Lord Ralph choked back the emotion in his voice. To enable his master to recover his poise Mr Jenner proceeded to enlarge upon other enterprising activity taking place.

"In the kitchen Mrs Sands is supervising her girls in the

production of preserves, relishes and chutneys. Cook is in her element; her inventiveness knows no bounds. The junior staff can hardly wait for tea-time to come round for then they get opportunity to sample and comment on new receipts made earlier in the day. The most popular are then put into production."

Ralph looked up and smiled. "Isn't the drawing room allowed to be part of this tasting experience?"

Mr Jenner spluttered, apologetically, "Oh, my lord, I'll get Hanson to attend to it."

"Give her ladyship opportunity to put her seal of approval on the enterprize."

Jenner recovered his composure, "Quite right, sir, if the goods are to bear the name and insignia of Newton Westerby Manor, the Squire and his lady ought to be aware of the quality of the products being sent out."

"Any more unusual ventures I should know about?"

"Abel has given Jimmy, the kitchen garden boy, the task of collecting fruit and vegetables not suitable for crating up to transport to market and depositing it in the scullery each morning. There is much washing, slicing and chopping till the scullery and kitchen maid's hands seem to be permanently stained with the juices of the abundant crop. You may have noticed the pungent aroma of spices and fruits filling the lower part of the house. Fruit tarts, pâtisserie items as well as conserves are the result.

"It has also been discovered the under footman has a penchant for drawing and painting. He has designed distinctive Newton Westerby Manor labels which the parlour maid cuts out and sticks on the varied jars of produce."

"I would really like to see what is being sold in my

name."

"I'll arrange for a selection to be sent up at tea-time today, sir."

Hedges beaded with shiny blackberries waited tantalisingly for eager hands to pluck before the birds claimed them for their repast. Edith persuaded Hester to accompany her and when Peggy and Annie could be spared they joined them, ink-stained fingers rapidly dripping with juice and tastebuds enjoying soft flesh bursts in a mouthful of dusky, fragrant sweetness. Soon baskets of the luscious fruits were delivered to the Manor kitchen to be turned into jams, jellies and pies.

Mrs Sands ruled an organized kitchen but the glut of produce that descended on her domain almost overwhelmed her. Anxious not to let the Squire down Cook sent for Beatrice to come into the kitchen one day. "Beatie, just look at this abundance. Please, would you create your delicious fruit and vegetable pies?" Although unsure that her pies were likely to be to the standard required for such a select market Beatie nevertheless spent each Monday baking items using whatever fruits or vegetables were to hand. They were then conveyed to prestigious establishments by rail on Tuesday to supply discerning households with delectable sweetmeats including the impressive properties on the newly built seafront at Lowestoft designed by Peto's architect Clemence. Beatie's confections and savouries proved more than acceptable.

Demand far exceeded production so that Peggy, whose lightness of hand was comparable to her sister's, was also asked to give a hand in the Manor kitchen.

Crab apples grew in abundance in the hedgerows so some of the village children were sent to gather them. Annie and Peggy knew where to find them so armed with baskets they led a merry band of chattering youngsters along the lane adjacent to the common to pick the fruits. Caleb and Bobby Castleton, egged on by Benny Capps and watched by Silent Pete, darted amongst their playfellows and mischievously began to pelt them with the small round fruit they gathered from the ground till Peggy admonished them for wasting the produce. Caleb pulled a face at his sister and muttered, "Bossy boots!"

"Doan't see why we hev to collect these fer the Big Hus," grumbled Prue Tuttle petulantly.

"'Cos it helps keep some o' ow'n parents in work an' rufs uvver ow'n heads," replied Annie sagely.

"Ha'ent they enough other things to eat, then?" Prue persisted sarcastically.

"The Big Hus woan't eat them, silly. When the baskets be full we be a'goin' to help Ma maak crab apple jelly to sell in the town shops to get money fer the estate," Annie explained.

"Why doan't they pick them, then?"

"'Cos they be doin' other things."

"Ma say it be all Master Quentin's fault, so he ought to be helpin', not us."

"He be a'gorn," commented Florrie Saunders knowingly.

"Yus, acrorst the sea to foreign parts," enlightened Tommy Maddox.

"Wow!" Such daring travel to unknown lands was beyond their comprehension and there followed an imaginative exchange of the bold adventures Master Quentin and Lady Araminta might be caught up in. The crab apples became gun shot or cannon balls as they landed haphazardly in the baskets.

"Come on yew fightin' men we need yow'n strength to help carry these full baskets up to Mrs Kemp's hus," coaxed Peggy.

Between them they carried the bounty up the stairs to where Edith was waiting to show them how to turn the hard little fruits into a delicious jelly. They didn't like the tedious washing, stewing, straining, measuring, boiling and clarifying that was required before the filling of the row of glass jars which sparkled against the whitewashed wall behind the shelf upon which Edith placed them. But how they enjoyed the taste of the jelly when plastered on freshly made bread that Edith sent each child home with!

"Mrs Kemp has initiated one of the under maids and the second footman in the art of setting up a stall at the village and Newton Lokesby markets," Mr Jenner continued. "They attend each week with a selection of the goods that are being produced. We do have options to hold stalls at the Ipswich and Norwich markets, but I'm not convinced sending someone with goods that far afield will be cost effective."

"I agree. Transporting to established businesses is proving lucrative at present. If we spread our net too widely we may reach a point where we have insufficient produce to satisfy the customers."

"My feelings entirely, sir."

"Can you enlighten me about what is going on at Home Farm?"

"Farmer Baldry's wife and daughters have developed a tasty cheese and creamy butter which has been snapped up for the provisions counter at the newly established departmental store in Knightsbridge, London."

"Really?"

"As a consequence of the success of this initiative the farm has been able to take on extra girls to learn the process as well as the skill of coating and packaging the end product with animal-fat-soaked muslin to preserve the cheeses for conveying to their destination. The Royal Hotel in Lowestoft also placed a regular order as has a long-established hotel in Norwich."

At tea-time that afternoon, having sampled some of the attractively presented produce Hanson instructed Peters to set before them, Lady Marion remarked to Lord Ralph, "What amazing people we have working for us. We are well blessed by the Good Lord, as Edith would say. These are excellent aren't they?" Marion indicated the preserve jars, cheese and butter set upon the table. "The labels are distinctive and eye-catching."

"Yes, latent skills have become apparent for which I am truly grateful, but we must not allow ourselves to be complacent."

"I understand from Mr Jenner that thanks to the rail network, producers like Newton Westerby Manor, are now supplying the town and city stores as well as markets with fresher and cheaper food than had previously been possible."

"That is true. Our venture seems to have boosted urban demand for fresh foodstuffs and pushed up agricultural output still further. Newton Manor may have been the forerunner of such enterprize, but other farmers have realized the potential and we are now in a competitive market. The poorer people living in cities like London now have access to quantities of affordable fruits and vegetables. Such commodities are no longer the prerogative of the wealthy. Through our own want we have been given the opportunity of serving the requirements of two vastly different sets of people. However, we cannot rest on our laurels. We have a long way to go before the estate is solvent and I do not want our people to burn themselves out."

"The daily toil of many has completely changed direction."

"And in some instances I think for the better."

Within a week of this conversation the cogs that seemed to be running so smoothly in the recovery of the estate were thrown into turmoil.

Amidst the additional busyness a plentiful harvest had been gathered in and thanksgiving celebrated in church and chapel, the Squire insisting that the usual harvest home take place in the big barn albeit it on a more moderate scale. The children who had been instrumental in so much of the gathering-in returned to school where an unexpected and unseen affliction lurked.

CHAPTER TWENTY-THREE

"The others..."

In the whirlwind of additional activity to save their jobs, homes and the estate, some of the villagers, as well as the staff at the Big Hus, between them did not neglect the hum drum occupation of their day to day lives, whilst others became attuned to new pulls on their time and abilities. The parlour maid continued to rise at 5.30am to light fires and draw curtains back in rooms that were still in use.

George Kemp, unceasingly, daily descended the steps from his home before daybreak to give attention to his beloved Suffolk Punches. As day began to dawn the stable hands and farm labourers continued to engage in the routine of estate life.

After consultation with the Squire, Mr Jenner offered Fred an apprenticeship. So commenced an unexpected period of adjustment and learning. Such a pull away from his beloved horses.

In response to correspondence from the estate office as well as the Squire's study there were infrequent missives from Lady Araminta and even less from Master Quentin bearing the Barbados postmark.

Beatie and her daughter moved out of the Manor House nursery wing. A notification had arrived for her from Marcus Reydon Capps stating that a cottage in the village was hers with a promissory note that a monthly allowance would be paid for the child. It was the cottage adjacent to Jonas Bemment's cobblers workshop; the one that had formerly been the farrier's home but left vacant when the smithy had relocated nearer to the stables. At first Beatrice was reluctant to accept it but Lady Marion eventually persuaded her to take it and make the cottage into a home for her daughter's sake. When she agreed Jonas generously offered his grandaughter items of furniture and linen hemmed by his beloved Sally that was superfluous to his needs. He was so pleased to have Beatrice close by.

After his day's work Stan came to help Colin move the bulky pieces between the two houses and place them where his sister, Beatie, directed. With meticulous care she cleaned every nook and cranny ready to receive what her grandfather had so generously given. She beamed at the men as the bare rooms took on a homely appearance.

"Oi can't believe this be ours," tears of joy streamed down her face.

"Juss thank the Good Lord fer all His goodness."

With Beatie's departure Annie moved into the nursery maid's room at the Newton Westerby Manor House, with George's reluctant consent, and with occasional help from Beatie gradually assumed full responsibility for Master Edmund's well-being.

Edith went more frequently to the Big House to assist Lady Marion in whatever capacity she could so was able to keep an eye on Annie. Amongst her many duties Edith was training Nellie Saunders in the mending of linen because the young girl had demonstrated an aptitude for stitching. "I think it will be worthwhile cultivating her skill especially as we are having to be as thrifty as possible," commented Lady

Marion.

The only occasion Edith was unavailable for service to the Squire's family was when she was called out to birthings. Louisa went into labour while Hezekiah was still at sea so Edith asked Beatrice to accompany her believing it would be good for her to gain further experience. Beatie took her baby back to the nursery at the Big House where Annie and Nannie Biddle looked after Rebekah with Edmund till baby George put in his appearance.

The washing line at the end cottage of the row of cottages on the beach continued to be first with clothes billowing on washday. When home from sea, Hezzie continued to rise at dawn determined to make the most of his time ashore so that as Louisa prepared their breakfast his adoring eyes flitted between her serene face and the cherubic slumber of baby George. The joy within their home shone as brightly as the rising sun outside.

Their elderly neighbours pottered contentedly in their home and garden delighting in the "li'tle bor" who gurgled in his perambulator the other side of the fence.

Next door Tommy Maddox snivelled over his oatmeal at the breakfast table. Albert impatiently cuffed him. "Eat yew up an' git orf t' school afore oi gi' yew another one," he yelled. Maud cried out for him to stop, then quietly coaxed Tommy to take a spoonful till Bert turned on her,

"Stop babyin' the bor," he snapped as he swung out a clenched fist and caught her on the side of her head.

"Ma, m' eyes hurt," complained Florrie at the Saunders household.

"Yew juss want to git out o' goin' t' school. Now, hurry yew up, m'gal, an' git yew orf," Gertie ordered.

No amount of coaxing by Norah Tuttle could persuade

Prue to get out of bed. The hand she placed on her daughter's forehead quickly drew back as it burned at her touch. "Noo school fer yew, a'day, m'gal."

In the school room Miss Peskett struggled to maintain the attention of the majority of her pupils who did attend. Some children exhibited listlessness, the others, though not unruly, were simply inattentive and lacked the ability to concentrate. Ethel Capps, Tommy Maddox and Caleb were slumped across their desks. Silent Pete and Bobby Castleton seemed to be the most alert. Concerned at this unprecedented behaviour Miss Peskett quickly scribbled a note and gave it into Bobby's hand.

"Will you run to Doctor Cooper's house? Give this to him. Go straight there and come directly back to school."

"Yus, Miss," Bobby affirmed.

"You go with him, Pete," Miss Peskett instructed. Silent Pete nodded vigorously and side by side the boys ran out of the door to accomplish their errand.

In the sewing room at the Manor House tears dropped unbidden onto the pillowcase Nellie Saunders was working on.

"Why, whatever be the matter, Nellie?" Edith enquired in a kindly tone.

"M' head hurts suthen awful, Mrs Kemp."

Edith scrutinized her young companion closely and concerned by the girl's flushed appearance reached out a hand to touch her brow.

"Oi think it be best if yew goo hum, Nellie."

"But Ma will be cross if oi doan't earn m' wages."

"Doan't yew worrit abaht that now. Yew put yow'n work down an' git yew on hum."

Nellie didn't make it home. Her legs crumpled beneath

her as she blindly stumbled passed the stables on her way to the row of cottages on the beach. Stan found her in a heap as he brought Bessie and the wagon back from deliveries to Newton Lokesby market.

Gently he picked up her unconscious form and laid her on the wagon bed and delivered the girl into her mother's arms. For once Gertie's motherly instincts over-road her frequent curmudgeonly attitude.

Up at the Manor House Master Edmund was vigorously airing his lungs. Lady Marion stepped into the nursery to investigate why her son was being so vocal.

"As it is such a lovely morning, Annie, take Master Edmund out for his walk now rather than after lunch. Maybe a change of scenery will occupy his attention."

“Yus, m'lady."

As she pushed Edmund in his pram around the formal gardens of the Manor House Annie bumped into Fred striding purposefully along the path. Her heart leapt at the sight of him and a smile creased her face.

"Hello Fred," she greeted cheerfully.

Fred paused and toffed his cap towards her. "Good morning, Miss Kemp."

"Fred, it be me, Annie." She reached out to tug at his coat sleeve.

"Oi know, but Mr Jenner hev instructed me to greet everyone on formal terms when we be engaged on ow’n official duties."

"Oh, oi see," stammered Annie not really understanding Fred's aloof manner at all. When he heard the break in her voice Fred regretted his officious attitude towards his friend. Annie's crest fallen face tugged at his heart.

"Oi'm not allowed to be over familiar wi’ people known

to me in case sometime in the future oi be called upon to discipline them."

"But Fred, oi hardly ever see you these days, what wi' yow'n new role and me larnin' ma new duti..." Edmund started to grizzle.

"Shhh...shh." Annie comforted as she gently rocked Edmund's perambulator. "...you'd nivver git chance to discipline me."

Fred grinned, then nodded towards the crying child. "The little chap do seem to be out of sorts."

"Yus, he be a li'tle finnicky an' not himself at all today," Annie explained as she continued to push the baby carriage back and forth, but nothing seemed to pacify Edmund.

"Oi need to taak him back to the hus." Annie turned around and started to walk away.

"Annie, when be yew orf?" Fred called out after her.

"I usually hev an hour when Master Edmund goes down fer his nap arter lunch." Annie called over her shoulder.

"Oi'll meet yew by the far geart in the kitchen garden at 2 o'clock this arternoon," he shouted after her retreating figure.

Annie smiled. "Thass be good. We can catch up on news." She rocked the baby carriage as she walked, but Edmund's cries would not cease.

"Oi muss get on. Oi'll see yew later, Annie."

Warmth spread across her middle and Annie smiled again. How quickly Fred had reverted to familiarity. Briskly she pushed the irritable little boy home.

Back in the nursery Edmund continued to grizzle. He refused the lunch Annie prepared, clamping his lips together, rubbing his eyes, then holding his ears as he cried. She sat him on her lap, rocking the toddler to and fro in her arms in an attempt to soothe him but nothing would pacify him. Annie started to become frantic when all she tried had no effect on easing the child's distress.

Drawn by the persistent cries Nannie and Lady Marion appeared by the nursery door at the same moment. Marion scooped up her son from Annie's arms. Nannie hovered, observing the flushed countenance of the little boy and the spot like markings appearing on his skin.

"Oi'm sorry m'lady, but...um...he woan't settle, an' woan't eat, an' oi doan't know what oi be doin' wrong." Annie spluttered out falteringly.

Despite her age and increasing frailty Nannie Biddle recognised the little boy was ailing and the inexperienced nursery maid had done nothing untoward.

"I believe we still have a baby bottle in the nursery kitchen, Annie. Would you make up a weak camomile tea mixture for this little chap. Put in some honey. Reverting to sucking from his baby bottle might bring him some comfort."

"Yus, Nannie." Annie went to do as she was bidden.

"M'lady, I think it would be wise to seek the counsel of Doctor Cooper," Nannie advised and even before receiving affirmation from her ladyship she pulled the bell.

Within moments the under-footman was at the nursery door.

"Send at once for the Doctor. Master Edmund is sick," Nannie ordered. A glance towards her ladyship confirmed the instruction, by the slight inclination of her head, and the young servant shot off at the double.

When Annie returned with the filled glass baby bottle Nannie was seated with Master Edmund on her lap. Still snuffly from all his crying he at first refused the warm liquid. Finally, with patience Nannie persuaded the little boy to suckle. Annie stood looking on agitatedly.

"You did everything right to comfort Edmund," Lady Marion assured her. "Had I realized he was sick I would not have sent you out. In the meantime I want you to take your afternoon off. Nannie Biddle will watch over Edmund, and I will be on hand to listen to what Doctor Cooper purposes for him."

Loathe to leave her charge Annie dragged her feet to the nursery maid's room and changed out of her uniform. It was a glum, tearful companion that met Fred at the kitchen garden gate.

"Whatever be wrong, Annie?"

"Master Edmund wasn't bein' crochety this mornin'. He be very sick an' the mistress an' Nannie be a'waitin' fer the verdict from Doctor Cooper."

"He be not the only one. The Doc hev sent for yow'n Ma to help Miss Peskett turn the schoolroom into a sick room because there be soo many children ill, includin' Caleb an'...."

"Oi'd better goo an' help." Annie started to scoot along the track.

"Noo!" Fred pulled on her arm to draw her back. "Yew muss stay at the Manor. Fer the toime bein'." Gently he reached up and wiped a solitary tear from her cheek with the tip of his forefinger. "We muss all stay away unless we suddenly feel unwell. Yow'n Ma hev things well organized."

"Who else be sick?"

"Florrie an' Dolly, Walter an' Rodney Saunders; Stan found Nellie collapsed on the cobbles by the stables. Some from the Common, Jack, Milly an' Winnie; Tommy

Maddox an' Richie Castleton; Prue an' Patsy Tuttle; Ethel Capps an' Peggy..."

"Oh not Peggy!" Annie gasped as the tears flowed afresh.

"I was a'goin' to walk yew to Beatie's to see her new hum but visitin' be no longer advised so let's goo down to the shore." Fred smiled at her and put out his arm towards her in a gentlemanly fashion. Through tear washed eyes Annie looked up into his kindly face. This was the friend she knew. She placed her hand in the crux of his elbow and walked alongside him, her throat clogged with emotion and her heart bouncing in an unusual fashion.

***

"Maggie, be those vegetables riddy? The water be nigh boiled dry," Cook called, irritated that her repeated requests had gone unanswered from the kitchen maid.

How she missed Beatie's work ethic in the kitchen. When, after a few more minutes, the kitchen maid had still not appeared, Mrs Sands crossly made her way to the scullery calling loudly, "Maggie, hurry yew on."

Astounded to view unprepared carrots and cabbage still on the draining board and so few potatoes peeled and Maggie slumped across the sink Mrs Sands shouted again. Maggie jumped involuntarily, then slithered to the floor in a dead faint.

Cook quickly checked the girl then lifted the door latch and quickly yanked open the outer scullery door. At the top of her voice she called for the gardener's boy. "Jimmy! Jimmy come yew here! Drop everythin'! Run yew on to Doctor Cooper's."

Jimmy stood and gawped at Mrs Sands. Behind her he saw the prostrate Maggie.

"Now, Jimmy! It be urgent!"

Scared at the sight of Maggie on the floor Jimmy turned and pelted as fast as he could.

He ran into Doctor Cooper as the doctor was alighting from his pony and trap on the Manor House front drive.

"Whoa, boy, where are you going to in such a hurry?"

"Fetch yew, sir," gasped Jimmy. "Cook say it be urgent."

"So I understand," remarked the doctor as he strode towards the front door.

Jimmy ran in front of him to block his path. "Noo, noo, in the scullery... I think she be dead."

***

"Measles!" was Doctor Cooper's diagnosis. "Keep the room darkened, sponge their bodies with tepid water to bring down the temperature and spoon liquids if they are unable to drink from cups," the doctor instructed those caring for the sick at the Manor as well as other children who had been taken poorly in the village.

Lady Marion, alongside Nannie Biddle and Annie, never left Edmund's side. Meals sent up from the kitchen for them were frequently left untouched until Doctor Cooper insisted the women needed to eat to keep up their strength. "You must drink too, and get some sleep, or you will succumb to illness as well."

Anxious for the health of his son and heir Lord Ralph frequented the nursery constantly. The burden of the estate diminished into the background as the pall of life and death hung over the little boy who was so precious to him.

Concern at the toll on his expectant wife also tugged at his heart when he viewed her careworn features, sunken, tired eyes, furrowed brow and weariness of limbs. Helplessness pressed upon him. This was a situation beyond his power to control or sort out. When she saw her husband's worried face peering round the nursery door Lady Marion crumpled. Lord Ralph rushed to catch her and held her sobbing form in his arms. "Ralph, it seems there is no hope. Our precious boy is fading fast."

CHAPTER TWENTY-FOUR

"...between them..."

Heartache relentlessly pierced the community, for disease is no respecter of persons. Almost all the homes situated on or around the beach village were in some measure affected by the epidemic. Anxiety gripped them. An unprecedented number of villagers attended the call to prayer Parson Wisbey issued for the Sunday morning service in St Andrew's church. Lord Ralph sat alone in the Squire's family pew, a forlorn figure with pale and drawn features. Master Edmund had given up the fight for life in the early hours of that morning.

During the following week sadness pervaded the Manor House. Instructions were issued in whispered tones and staff trod in deft quietness to fulfil their duties. Between them they kept everything running smoothly. Lord Ralph and Nannie became perturbed by the calmness and strength Lady Marion exhibited at the loss of Edmund and voiced their concerns to Doctor Cooper.

"Doctor, her attitude frightens me."

"She is purposefully busy from daylight to dusk cleaning in the nursery, sorting and packing away Edmund's clothes, almost obliterating his short life. She is intent on re-organizing household matters, the kitchen menu, staff routines, excessive cleaning of drapes, and furnishings including even the beating of carpets."

"It's almost as though my lady is seeking to remove all evidence of the infection by cleansing everything in the house. She is scarcely taking a moment to breathe!"

"Her control is unnatural."

"Yes, her behaviour is out of character and irrational. She is exhausted, still unable to sleep, yet is displaying incredible energy. No tears have fallen since that moment when it became obvious Master Edmund was not going to survive."

"My dear wife appears to be acting as though she is obligated to punish herself for what has happened to our son. I fear for the child she is carrying."

"Grief of the heart displays in different ways and given her ladyship's condition the nesting instinct could also be prevalent. I will leave this potion. Add it to my lady's bedtime drink. I will call in again, my lord."

Annie's tender heart was devastated by the loss of Edmund. Tears would not be stemmed as she repeatedly went over in her mind the routine of the last few days. *Was there anything I should hev done differently?* She did not return home but stayed on at the Manor. Unobtrusively she assisted her ladyship in her daily tasks, quietly suggesting Lady Marion sit down when presented with cups of camomile tea that Lizzie sent up from the kitchen; a panacea Edith promoted for so many ills. She insisted on having a large jug always prepared which stood ready on a shelf in the pantry cupboard ready for heating up. She knew Mrs Sands also followed suit.

Whenever she could gain Lady Marion's attention Annie pointed out autumn blooms visible through the drawing room window in an effort to distract her ladyship and encourage her to take a walk in the garden. To oblige Annie, Marion mechanically went through the motions of strolling around the flower beds she had been helping to redesign, but her heart was engaged elsewhere.

Lord Ralph, his own heart aching with grief, regarded his wife with earnest anxiety. At mealtimes barely a morsel was touched. In the evenings, when she was eventually persuaded to refrain from her futile busyness, Lady Marion sat by the fireside holding a book, but no words left a page to penetrate her mind. In those moments he perceived she struggled to keep back the tears. Never had he felt less useful.

"Other than instructions there is no conversation. She appears locked within herself," his lordship confided to Doctor Cooper.

"Give it time, my lord."

"I fear for the life within her. How I wish Edith Kemp were available. Her down to earth common sense has brought calm to many situations in our home in the past."

However, Edith's ministrations were still engaged elsewhere. So many children had succumbed to measles that Miss Peskett closed the school. To restrict further spread of the infection in the village all the sick children had been carefully carried to the school room and placed on pallets or mattresses that had been arranged on the floor, desks and chairs were pushed back and piled to one side. Edith and Amy Peskett lovingly administered care to each child with gentleness, sponging regularly to reduce temperatures and patiently spooning liquid into mouths that had great difficulty swallowing.

Prue Tuttle and Florrie Saunders along with Tommy Maddox and Fred's youngest brother, Caleb, were struggling to respond to the treatment causing Edith grave concern. Daily, Bobby Castleton knocked at the schoolroom door to see if there was anything required or messages to be delivered. "Please ask the doctor to call in, Bobby."

Anxious mothers rapped on the schoolroom window each morning to get an update on the welfare of their children. As most of the Saunders family had succumbed to the infection Gertie insisted on coming to the schoolroom every day to help look after them.

However, Edith would not have her in the sick room unless she thoroughly scrubbed in carbolic and changed her filthy lice infested attire. To show she was not discriminating against her slovenly neighbour she and Amy did the same. "To protect the children from further infection."

Since the government had passed the Public Health Act in 1848 Doctor Cooper had been appointed Medical Officer for the area. Having carefully perused the documents issued he became aware of concerns that the spread of infection was linked to the lack of cleanliness because of poor sanitation and contaminated water supplies. With an epidemic on his hands he was anxious to minimize its spread. He instructed Edith that water be boiled to sterilize it and regular hand washing with carbolic soap take place.

Elsie Capps also came in to relieve an exhausted Edith and Amy, her daughter Ethel seemed to have only a mild dose of measles, whereas Benny remained well so stayed to help Jem. Old Mrs Armes proved a treasure, patiently watching over and assisting the recovering children, telling stories of her life on the farm and crooning lullaby songs to assist them fall asleep as well as helping feed them with broth or stew that village mothers, Mrs Castleton in particular, delivered regularly to the sick room.

Joseph Castleton and Jem Capps between them manned the pump to ensure there was always fresh water available for the schoolroom as well as fuel for the stove. All of the Castleton children, apart from Richie, remained free of infection, so Dora kept them busy, collecting eggs and picking vegetables for broths to run up to the sick room with sustenance for those engaged in nursing duty as well as their patients. Harold had been taken on at Home Farm and under the auspices of Farmer Baldry was learning alongside the farmer's sons how to mind the farm. One evening he was sent home with a plucked chicken for the pot to be turned into nourishment for the sick. Millicent was working in the dairy, learning the skill of butter and cheese making as well as the intricacies of milking.

Susan Castleton assisted her mother in the preparation of vegetables and meat for the pot then stood on a stool in the forge kitchen to watch and stir the broth on the stove.

In between his errands for the schoolroom Bobby became Joseph's right-hand man in the forge. One village family's involvement in restoring the prosperity of the estate and giving a helping hand to neighbours' in need. Actions that were replicated in many other homes throughout the closeknit community.

When Caleb and Tommy appeared to be getting worse rather than better Edith sent messages to Hester and Maud to come and nurse their sons.

"Orf yew goo, Ma," Stan encouraged Hester. "Oi'll manage juss foine. Yow'n mind be more settled if yew see fer yow'n sel' how Peggy an' Caleb be a'doin'." The possibility of losing any of her children stirred Hester to action. The vitality that had been the essence of his mother's personality before their father's untimely death suddenly emerged from the bond of grief that had held her in its grip for so long. Peggy had been the mainstay of her mother during those early difficult weeks, but Caleb, despite his growth spurt, was still her baby. A weight lifted from Stan's heart as he watched Hester step out of the door with a definite intent.

Maud's reaction to the request was thwarted by Bert's aggressive selfishness. "An' who will cook ma dinner if yew goo a'skivin' orf?" He raised his arm to hit her to enforce his will. Minnie yelled. Bert turned his venom on her. "Hold yow'n noise," he shouted as he pushed the little girl violently to the ground. Maud bent to comfort her sobbing child and was rewarded with the force of Bert's boot. He yanked open the door. "Maak sure ma dinner be on the table when oi git hum," he ordered.

"How can oi when yew gi' me no money to buy victuals?" She timidly called after him from her position on the floor.

Coins chinked in his pocket. Angrily he threw two halfpennies at her and stomped out of the doorway without a further word.

There were not many who were wanting Albert Maddox to turn up at the estate office on pay day expecting receipt of a wage believing that he was bone idle and a tyrannical wastrel. He merely filled a space four or five hours a day slyly pretending to be working with an implement in his hand but was never seen to bend his back or hump his shoulders more than was necessary, sneaking off to The Rising Sun or Fisherman's Arms whenever opportunity presented itself. Such a practised idler was considered dishonest by his fellow labourers who felt it expedient to ignore him as they found it difficult to pass the time of day congenially with him. Albert, on the other hand, considered himself to be a deeply injured individual. He was of a suspicious nature, always acted in an uncivil manner towards everyone and was angered by their treatment of him demonstrating his aggression in physical violence, particularly when he had been imbibing at one of the village hostelries. But mostly Maud and the children were the victims of his brutal temper, unseen, behind closed doors. To Maud's distress Archie was beginning to copy his father's attitude and actions.

As soon as Albert's footsteps died down in the distance Maud attended to the breakfast pots and shooed her remaining children, who were free of the infection, into the backyard.

"Stay yew here till oi git back," she instructed as she bent to rub her hurting shin. Mr Armes was tending his vegetable plot.

"Oi'm a'goin' to the schoolroom," she called over the fence. "Will yew watch the children?" Mr Armes grunted an assent, as was his wont.

Burning up with fever Tommy was barely able to open his eyes at the sound of Maud's voice. Weakly he clutched her hand. "Ma," he hoarsely gasped as the last breath escaped his body. Maud's strangled sobs churned Edith's heart, and her tears mingled with those of the grieving mother.

"Oh, my dear Maud." Gently Edith laid a comforting hand across her back. Maud flinched. *Dear Lord, what be a'goin' on here.*

Later that same day Florrie Saunders's tenuous hold on life was relinquished as she lay in Gertie's arms. Gertie's uncontrollable howling reverberated off the schoolroom walls as she held Florrie to her bosom, the gentlest, quietest offspring of her brood. Edith placed an arm around Gertie's shoulders. The head of the distraught mother slumped onto Edith's shoulder. Edith swallowed the lump in her throat.

"The Lord be yow'n consolation, Gertie, dear." *Lord, this woman hev for so long been a thorn in ma side but roite now she needs compassion. Please taak away ma irritability an' animosity towards Gertie. Lord, she needs Yew, be her comfort.*

Edith could identify with Gertie's anguish; the rawness of loss overcame her as remembrance of her lost little boy surfaced afresh.

Caleb's life hung in the balance during the night-time hours. Anxiety enveloped Hester. "The darkest hour is just before the dawn." Words her beloved Jeremiah had so often quoted from the theologian Thomas Fuller whenever she showed concern about him being on the sea at night came unbidden to Hester's mind as she meticulously sponged her youngest son's fiery body.

Tears fell. Uncontrollable tears. “Forgive me Lord.” Years of anger and hurt were released. "Dear God spare this child." She held Caleb in her heart as the final evidence of the love she and Jeremiah had shared. "As Yew came to Yow'n disciples in the watches of the noite come now to m’bor."

As morning dawned and the darkness of night was pushed away by the emerging light of day Caleb's fever broke and healing sleep settled over his body. "The Lord be praised." Tears of joy mingled with those of sorrow in the schoolroom.

Meanwhile, at the Manor, Annie, along with other

members of the household staff, was woken up in the early hours as the sorrow of Edmund's passing and subsequent frenetic busyness caused Lady Marion to go into premature labour. Despite Edith being occupied in the schoolroom and unavailable for the birthing Annie remained calm. Nannie Biddle was appalled.

"An unmarried chit of a girl like you should not be in attendance at a confinement. It is unseemly."

"Needs must!" retorted Annie as she organised the household staff in necessary tasks, sending a footman to fetch Beatrice, then handing Rebekah into Nannie Biddle’s capable hands, arranging with Mrs Hanson for necessary linen to be brought to her ladyship's room, instructing the parlour maid to ensure hot water was available. However, the young women were reluctant, at first, to allow Doctor Cooper into her ladyship's bedchamber as he had so recently spent much time with the sick children in the schoolroom. So, instructions, along with warming pans and other needful implements, were passed carefully through the door.

A tiny baby girl was born, making her appearance into the world far too soon. The undersized scrap of life was not expected to survive.

"Leave her, Annie, she will not live," Doctor Cooper had advised but Annie was determined to fight for the life of this child, the first miracle of birth she had witnessed. Patiently and tenderly, she tended the baby's needs.

She was awestruck by this miniature person entrusted to her care. She fingered the child's perfectly formed feet and hands with wonder and gazed with fascination on her petite facial features. Lifting the warming pan from the crib and putting it to one side Annie tentatively cradled the undersized newborn in her hands. Wrapping the little girl tightly in a blanket to keep her warm Annie tenderly laid her in the heated hollow left in the crib. Constantly she checked the baby remained snugly tucked in and felt warm to the touch.

In the night-time silence, as some of the household slept, Annie's eyes remained glued to the child watching the imperceptible rise of the tiny chest as life-giving breath passed in and out of her minute lungs. At the slightest whimper Annie ensured her needs were met, the moon lighting the dark corners of the nursery enabling her to carry out each small task. As she watched and waited in the stillness tears stung her tired eyes as she recalled the little boy who had formerly occupied the nursery.

"Li'tle one yew muss live. Yow'n Ma needs yew t' fill her heart wi' joy."

The following day Louisa Kemp came in to assist wherever necessary. She handed George into the capable hands of the maid assigned to help Nannie Biddle and walked into the baby Nursery to relieve Annie.

Meanwhile, Beatie concentrated her efforts on the wellbeing of the mother who seemed to be sinking fast. Concerned for his wife Lord Ralph insisted the Doctor be allowed in to examine her. For some days her ladyship's life hung in the balance. Doctor Cooper remained in attendance instructing Beatie, until he was called back to the schoolroom, when the news concerning Tommy and Florrie reached him. Within that sickroom he drew Edith to one side.

"Despite the sadness here all seems to be under control, but I think your presence is more needful at the Manor at this time. If you're not too tired I'll take you up in the trap after first checking the other children here." Edith caught his eye and gave a knowing nod.

"Oi'll come. The mothers an' Miss Peskett can cope here now. I'll need a change of clothing and a carbolic scrub."

"Of, course," the Doctor sagely nodded.

***

Between feeding their own babies Beatrice and Lousia took it in turns to provide a little breast milk that Annie dribbled from a scrunched-up muslin rag into the tiny mouth that she coaxed to open by putting a finger gently under her chin. Drip, drip, drip. With each droplet that hit its target Annie prayed for the life in her hands just like she'd heard her parents pray so often at home.

"Dear Lord, help her breathe, may her limbs fill out an' grow strong just as baby George an' Rebekah be a'doin'." When she was able to suckle the mothers wet nurse the little girl named Rosamund by Parson Wisbey who had been called in to swiftly perform baptismal rites.

Day after day, night after night, Annie gave the baby relentless attention and was careful about every detail, till tiredness encroached. Louisa again came to relieve Annie, insisting she got some sleep. Reluctantly Annie made her way to the nursery maid's room. She kicked off her shoes, but sleep claimed her before she could undo even one button of her uniform.

***

Leaving the care of the recovering children in the capable hands of their mothers Edith, scrubbed and freshly attired, travelled with the doctor to the Manor House to take the place of Beatrice who was beside herself with weariness. Edith's practised eye took in the situation in the confinement room at once. She commended Beatie on her care of Lady Marion but was concerned by the young woman's bleary eyes that were underwritten with lines of anxiety. With experienced efficiency Edith immediately set to work.

"Now, let's get some sustenance into m'lady, then oi think it be high toime mother an' daughter be introduced to one another. Both need the nearness of the other. An' yew need some proper rest, m'gal." Edith crossed the room and pulled the bell.

"Will yew ask Cook to send up some broth fer Lady Marion an' camomile tea fer Beatrice," she instructed the footman. "Tea always helps." Beatie shook her head. As if copious cups of camomile would make her sleep deeply rather than toss and turn seeking to solve the problem of getting her ladyship to pull through and baby Rosamund to thrive.

Edith called Louisa from the Nursery and together they adjusted Marion's pillows and propped her into a sitting position. The baby was brought through and held close to her ladyship. The sound of the mewing-like whimper of her baby stirred Marion's breast. Unbidden, milk flowed. In her weakness she reached out a hand and lovingly caressed the downy head nestled against her. A faint smile kissed her lips. Gradually, with gentle words and careful movement, Edith coaxed Lady Marion to partake of the delicious broth Mrs Sands had sent up while Louisa cradled Rosamund.

Edith looked in on Beatie when she had settled her charges and was pleased to find the young woman sleeping. She moved on to the nursery maid's room and her heart eased when she saw Annie, too, enveloped in peaceful slumber.

CHAPTER TWENTY-FIVE

"...mind the farm..."

As winter edged closer the cycle of labour at Home Farm and in the Manor House and village kitchens intensified. Livestock not transported to the London market but retained for home use was ready for slaughter. This would supply households with enough supplies to get through the coming months.

The epidemic had taken its toll on many families, but they had pulled together and supported one another through the tough times. Miraculously, Lady Marion and her baby daughter had also survived, and both were doing well. "The Good Lord be praised," was on the lips of many at the Manor and in the surrounding community.

Ensuring there was provision for all in the coming lean days was another collective focus.

Measles had by-passed residents and workers at the Manor Home Farm so that dairy production continued unabated, providing valued income for the estate. Accommodation had also been made available in the attic rooms of the farmhouse for Harold and Millicent so that they were away from the epidemic and readily on hand for chores in the early hours. Whilst the women concentrate on butter and cheese production Farmer Baldry and Donald Ashby, the shepherd, mind the farm. Along with Seth they passed a keen eye on the stock before deciding which to sell and which animals to keep for home consumption and which to retain for building up the flock and increasing the herd of breeding cattle.

“Maakin’ the roite decisions now will ensure the continuity o’ the farm an’ aid the recovery o’ the estate,” Baldry explained to the men. Though Seth displayed a penchant for husbandry his involvement in the early days of the estate crisis revealed an instinct for working with the animals.

"Baldry, foster this natural ability Seth exhibits," Elias Jenner advised.

Whilst the men at Home Farm organized the slaughter of the animals at the slaughterhouse, the kitchen at the Manor House was thrown into a frenzy of activity in preparation for the reception of the carcasses. Beef was dealt with on one day, mutton and pork on separate occasions. Mrs Sands supervised an army of press-ganged workers to ensure the walk-in pantry and cellar were thoroughly cleaned and whitewashed. Shelves were mostly of thick slate or stone to keep supplies cool. A few were made of slatted wood to improve circulation, and the kitchen and scullery maids were commissioned to scrub them down thoroughly ready for use. Repairs were carried out where needful and ceiling hooks for holding sides of meat were checked for stability.

The war against vermin was arduous both in the cellar and pantry; rats and mice were a constant menace, but cockroaches, flies and beetles could be even worse. A window in the pantry covered with a fine mesh screen to allow for ventilation while keeping out flies was brushed and checked for holes. "Doan't snag yew're fingers on broken wire," warned Mrs Sands.

"They be a'comin'," Jimmy, who had been put on watchman duty, hollered through the open back door.

The wagon pulled up. Seth and butcher, Chopper Cooper, humped the carcasses across their shoulders into the Manor kitchen and laid them onto the prepared kitchen table. Following Mrs Sands instructions they portioned the meat into useable sized beef and mutton joints. Salting was one way to slow down deterioration and Cook quickly set Maggie and Cora to their task while she and Lizzie cut up the suet to render into lard. When it was ready they proceeded to coat or smother some of the meat with the lard then hung the larger joints from the ceiling hooks in the cellar. Other cuts were stored in casks of rendered fat mixed with herbs and flowers that had been dried to flavour the food.

In the village preparations were underway for the pig killing. Chopper Cooper had undertaken to carry out this process but not until his task at the Manor House was completed. Then he visited the very few pig owning cottagers in turn before returning to Home Farm piggery to attend to the Manor's pigs. Mrs Sands insisted on a gap between the different meat carcasses because pork had so many different components it took longer to prepare. Chopper was paid in kind, cuts and joints, which were then made ready for sale in his butcher's shop in the village.

There was great excitement when the turn of the Kemp's pig arrived, particularly amongst those who had contributed to his food supply throughout the year. Young and old waited with eager expectation. The children jiggled up and down by the side of the sty in the orchard till Chopper arrived to lead him to the empty stable that had been allotted as a preparation area and storage place as the Kemps didn't have an outhouse. Stan and George, with help from Jethro, had scrubbed and whitewashed the disused space to make it suitable for storing the meat.

Walking behind the animal with a stick lightly touching his back Chopper guided him out of the orchard and along the side of the loft house passed the vegetable patch to the cobbled yard leading to the stables. The youngsters trooped after him determined to miss nothing of the thrill of the occasion. The adults stood outside the stable ready for the action.

After the killing Chopper and George lifted the pig carcase on to the bench that George had built for the purpose, with a bucket strategically placed to collect the blood, then with sharpened knives they cut out the backbone or chine, as some called it.

"Yew want me to sever the head, Mrs Kemp?" Chopper enquired. Edith nodded. "Oi hev the pan ready on the stove upstairs to maak it into head cheese." Swiftly Chopper executed the necessary chop and handed the head to Edith.

"Roite, oi'll leave yew to it, George," and with a brief wave of his hand Chopper moved on to his next customer and George began to singe the body to rid it of as much hair as possible. Edith, having left the head cheese to simmer, descended from her kitchen and along with Peggy, Hester, Ethel and Louisa used pig scrapers to remove the rest.

"We'll save these long hairs fer Jonas," she said, "they may be useful fer sewing some o' his leather items."

Normally the whole carcase was hung from the roof until it was wanted for cutting up and kept open to the air by a pair of pig stretchers. However, with such an eager audience and tongues hanging out in anticipation, George commenced to portion the carcase into various cuts of pork, bacon, ham and the like.

"Come yew on, bor," he called to Stan. "Come an' larn where an' what to cut so yew'll know what to do when it be yow'n turn fer the killin'." The runt the Bemments had raised was due for slaughter the following week.

Painstakingly George portioned the cuts of meat. Scraps were placed in a pan to be eventually made into sausages; the skin of the intestines being put to one side to be washed and used for casings. He tossed the bladder to Bobby Castleton.

"Goo wash this out under the pump. Blow it up, tie a knot an' yew hev a ball. See what pleasure yew can hev wi' it." Eagerly the little boys followed Bobby to the pump keen to see what fun could be had with this unusual part of the pig. Other oddments went into the making of brawn and haslet, the saved blood formed the main ingredient of black pudding along with chunks of fat and pearl barley. Further internal parts would be slow cooked, when Edith had time, into tripe or chitterlings.

Nothing was wasted. George showed Stan how to cut out the heart, kidneys and liver, separate them from the suet, then sliced them up and along with a piece of bacon passed a parcel, "sufficient fer a fry-up" to the families who had helped feed the pig.

"Yew want a trotter, Elsie?" His offer was greeted with a grateful smile. Mixed with herbs the resulting jelly-like loaf would be a tasty morsel served with vegetables or sliced between slices of home-made bread.

"Norah?"

"Thanks, George."

"What abaht us?" shouted Gertie Saunders impatiently.

"Give me toime to chop them, Gertie. There be one fer yew an' another fer Maud."

"Where be Maud?"

They looked around. Heads shook. "Ha'ent seen her."

"Yew want to bring this acrorst to ow'n kitchen, Edith, to maak up the sausages?" Dora asked indicating the growing mound of meat pieces. "Save yew traipsing up an' down the steps." Edith nodded gratefully and helped gather up pots of meat scraps. Peggy picked up the natural skins that would provide the casings and they followed Dora along the cobbled lane to the forge at the end of the stable block.

"What a blessing yew are now soo close by," Edith commented as they ambled along the cobbles.

"At first oi missed living at the centre o'the village but it be easier fer Joseph to be situated here an' there' be soo much a'goin' on at the stables." Her nimble fingers quickly attached a mincer to the kitchen table. Peggy, aided by Susan who stood on a stool next to the table, fed the funnel with small pieces of meat as Dora turned the handle and Edith held the washed skin to receive and form into sausage shapes, amidst much laughter, as they learned to master the process.

"How oi miss Annie helpin' in the kitchen. She an' Peggy worked soo well together. She would hev loved this, but yew be doin' a foine job, Susan." However, in her heart she thought it best that Annie's tender heart had not witnessed the slaughter of the pig.

"How be things up at the Manor?"

"Annie be workin' flat out, determined to pull that li'tle life through. She say the babe be slowly fillin' out an' startin' to flourish. Beatie an' the Doc be nursin' m'lady through this ordeal. They do say she be a'gettin' stronger each day. Louisa be up at the Big Hus a'helpin' out while Hezekiah be at sea. Nannie Biddle hev her hands full wi' George an' Rebekah, but one o' the maids be assistin' wherever there be need. Since the estate crisis, staff doo seem to hev become adept at adjustin' to different work schedules."

Both in the Manor and cottage kitchens the curing of ham was an important part of the preserving process and to get it right was considered an art.

"It may be tedious but worth it in the end," Mrs Sands told the kitchen maids. "It be essential to hev a ham pot with deep upright sides, preferably one made of glazed earthenware. Yew'll find one at the back of the bottom shelf of the pan cupboard in the scullery, Maggie."

"Yus, Cook."

"Roite, Lizzie, oi want yew to mix some salt, salt-petre, sal-prunel, dark brown sugar an' treacle into the bowl Maggie brings back. Follow this receipt for the correct quantities."

"Yus, Mrs Sands," Lizzie reached out and took hold of the proffered page. Lizzie Capps, younger sister of Louisa Kemp and Jem Capps, had been taken on to replace Beatrice and to Mrs Sands satisfaction was proving to be quite an asset in the smooth running of the Manor kitchen. Lizzie didn't have Beatie's panache at pastry making but was quick to pick up and execute other useful skills and had such a pleasing personality. Her cheerful spirit brightened the darkest day and was a welcome contrast to Maggie's sullen attitude which remained unchanged despite her brush with measles. Cora Brooks, the baker's daughter, a quiet shy girl, blended well with the kitchen staff and was willing to tackle any task Cook asked of her.

Mrs Sands picked up the pot of common salt kept by the stove and placed it on the table next to the ham. Deftly she commenced to rub salt into the ham.

"Maggie, pass the ham pot to Lizzie, then come give me a hand."

They worked together for a few moments.

"When yew hev the mixture riddy Lizzie we'll put the ham into the pot. It must be turned daily, an' the mixture ladled over it. When it be thoroughly pickled we'll drain it an' bake it slowly in the oven to dry. Cora, oi'll shew yew how to sew it into muslin then we'll hang it on a ceilin' hook in the pantry till it be wanted fer the table upstairs."

"Yus, Cook."

When the day for the slaughter of the Bemment's runt arrived Peggy's heart was in her mouth in trepidation of the task before her. However, neighbours stepped up to give assistance. George took time to come down from the stables to guide Stan in the division of the various cuts of meat. Edith alongside Dora Castleton offered willing hands with the preserving of the joints and young Susan eagerly waited to join by turning the handle of the sausage machine as she called the mincer.

Caleb, fully recovered from the measles, ran errands and

joyfully caught the bladder Stan threw to him. Together with Benny Capps, Bobby and Silent Pete he rushed to rinse it with water. Dennis Maddox hung over the fence watching longingly.

"Come yew on an' play," Bobby called. Gleefully Dennis jumped the fence to join them. When the bladder was full of air Caleb tied a knot in the neck then with lots of noise they ran to play on the beach, the other side of the newly built wall at the bottom of the beach cottage gardens, while the women and girls worked over the stove in the kitchen, a rejuvenated Hester readily participating in proceedings, much to Edith's delight. *Thank Yew, dear Lord, fer answered prayer.*

CHAPTER TWENTY-SIX

"And see the animals come to no harm."

The concerted collective effort of so many ensured that at the Manor House and in most cottages in the village, pantries, store cupboards and cellars bulged with sufficient provisions to satisfy appetites throughout the winter months. Only those inclined to laziness or incapacitated by ill health or old age suffered the strictures of bare shelves, though the latter were frequently beneficiaries of the kindness of their neighbours.

Peggy's young heart, remembering those days of emptiness and hunger, swelled with thankfulness as she viewed the well-stocked outhouse and pantry that would provide for the needs of her family. She also gave thanks for the restoration of her mother's participation in family life. Each morning Hester now ensured the boys always went off to work with full bellies. After the evening meal at the end of the day, when he had read from the Good Book following Amy Peskett's tuition, Stan never ceased to give thanks to God for the blessings that were theirs. None of them could forget the struggling journey they had travelled along to bring them to this place of sufficiency and more. "The Good Lord hev kept His promise to supply all ow'n needs." When his eyes met those of his Ma and a smile accompanied a nod of her head his heart almost burst as it overflowed with joy.

"Yus, m'bor, we hev more than sufficient fer ow'n needs an' enough uvver to share thanks to yourn diligence and persistence."

***

A chill wind caught the naked branches of a cluster of hawthorn and sycamore trees as early morning frost glistened on roof tops and paths. Fred shivered and pulled his muffler tighter round his neck, thankful he had obeyed his mother's insistence that he put it on. The icy coating made the stile into the field slippery. He took it with ease then hopped down onto the frosty grass below that scrunched under his boots as he landed. His feet left dark footprints on the icy footpath as he walked down the lane towards the stables his boots crushing the delicate thin layer of crunchy frost to the earth beneath.

He passed the pond, its water greyish blue, smudged and glassy, like breath on a mirror. Thoughts pranced back and forth in his head as he mulled on Mr Jenner's conversation last evening.

"You work well with horses, Fred, but I believe you have the ability to do more. In the last year you have seen how they fit into the overall working of the estate. You give attention to detail and are willing to learn new things. You have also proved that you have an aptitude for assessing how all aspects of the estate and farm knit together and seeing that the animals come to no harm; checking boundaries of fields, hedges and fences, are as important as correct footcare, feed and adequate pasture. The Squire agrees that you have competently fulfilled all that was expected of an apprentice and on my recommendation would like you to become under steward for the estate."

Locked into his thoughts Fred momentarily took his eyes from the path and almost skid over. *Look where yew be a'goin', bor! What would Mr Jenner think o' yow'n lapse o' concentration,* he chided himself.

"Each day you have conscientiously watched, listened and participated in many tasks, grasping much about the running of the estate, but there is a great deal more to learn. However, with Mr Kemp's approval you may still work with the horses one day a week and also help train young Caleb to take your place, whilst continuing to add to your knowledge by performing other duties on the estate."

Fred's heart was overwhelmed by the trust that was being placed in him but also apprehensive at the expectation Mr Jenner had of his ability to fulfil the undertaking. He must be honest. He had enjoyed the challenge of the apprentice position but... How he would miss the horses! They had been his life for so long.

What would Annie have to say about his new situation? The pit of his heart felt heavy. He hardly saw her these days. They were both so busy, caught up with their daily responsibilities in different areas of the Newton Westerby Manor estate. Mr Jenner had intimated that a cottage would go with the new appointment. They could get married! Was she still of the same mind? *Oi must speak wi' her afore oi accept Mr Jenner's offer,* he resolved.

Mr Jenner had been pleasantly surprized at Fred's quickness with figures, his awareness of income and expenditure, which helped in his understanding of balancing the ledger books of the estate but delighted that his intuition of Fred's potential had been proved correct.

"He is quick to see ways of doing things more efficiently," he commented to the Squire. "I guess the times of economy during his upbringing, particularly the frugal months following his father's death, has enabled him to see where wastage can be avoided, and savings made."

"The lad certainly seems to have picked up the reins of management incredibly quickly."

"Yes, for one so young it is remarkable that already Fred has the workings of most aspects of the estate and farm at his fingertips and sees how each element dovetails together with the other components."

"It is more than pleasing to see how the young man has developed. A wise choice, Jenner."

"Yes, sir. Fred is also able to articulate what is required in such language that whomsoever he is speaking to understands what is needed to be achieved. Having been brought up in the village and worked alongside the lads he knows how they think and act and the best way to get them to tackle new things."

"There is no resentment amongst them?"

Mr Jenner shook his head. "Fred doesn't lord it over his old stable mates nor act superior to them. He has a knack of drawing alongside them and getting them to listen to him. I think it's because he also asks their opinion on different matters then listens to what they have to say that they respect him. They also see him implement some of their suggestions."

"An important factor when dealing with other people."

"Yes, sir, yet, when we have to deal with city men he instinctively knows the correct way to approach them with whatever issue is under discussion, but he won’t be drawn into any dishonest scheming."

"It is gratifying to know that the management of the estate is in good hands for the foreseeable future."

"I think, sir, we should also be looking at training up other younger people in management in different areas of the estate."

Lord Ralph raised his eyebrows as he looked directly at his estate manager. "You do?"

"Mmm," Elias Jenner articulated thoughtfully. "It would need to be done in such in a way that those who currently hold senior staff positions do not feel threatened but acknowledged as an important part of the teaching process. Suffolk men are so opposed to anything allied to change that it will take a month of Sundays to render their acquiescence in the way new things are executed."

"What do you have in mind?"

"Well, looking at who we have working in different sectors of the estate and consider who appears to have the potential, not only to take on more responsibility, but be willing and able to learn and put into operation new things. People who will be good at leading as well as delegating to others."

"Do you have men in mind?"

"I haven't thought this through in detail with regard to each sector, but watching Fred blossom beyond all expectation I felt it might be worthy of consideration for all other senior positions. None of us are getting younger!"

"Excellent idea, Jenner."

"Experience is a valuable commodity. You have those who have been in loyal service for an exceptionally long time, sir. Could they be persuaded to pass on their expertise to others? They know those working under them far more intimately than I so would know who the best candidates would be to consider for training up."

"It would require a careful and sensitive approach to get

them on board, otherwise mismanagement could ensue, and subsequent negligence of the livestock and property of the estate could result. We can't allow that, Jenner, especially when we consider how these faithful people have worked so hard to pull the estate back towards solvency. Permitting harm to come to any part of the estate that has been entrusted to my care is not on the agenda."

"Of course, sir. Progress must run alongside stability. I think George Kemp saw Fred as the one most suitable to eventually take over the running of the stables from him. We've snatched that possibility away."

"So, what alternatives come to mind?"

"Stan and Seth are both excellent horsemen."

"I would be inclined to consider Stanley's gifting to be more on the equine side of things. Like Fred he has an empathy with the horses and Seth's inclination is towards field and farmwork. He is in tune with the requirements of the seasons and can read the signs of wind and cloud."

"He surely has an instinct for what is required for crops to grow well but he also has an eye for the livestock as he proved when he organized the transportation of the cattle to market."

"Apportioning responsibility is not going to be an easy decision, is it? We also have to consider Baldry's boys. How are they shaping up at Home Farm? Is the eldest lad likely to remain in the army or expect a place back on the farm? I believe young Harold Castleton is also proving his worth."

"Mmm, I believe more so than at the forge. That sphere of work seems to be more in Bobby's line."

"Let's not be too hasty," Lord Ralph advised caution. "We'll keep an eye on the young men we've mentioned and see how they shape up in the coming months."

"Yes, sir. It might be advantageous to additionally watch the young women with regard to posts within the household. Whilst Beatrice is an excellent cook she has furthermore proved herself capable of many other responsibilities within our community so may not be available for our consideration, however, I am inclined to think that young Peggy has potential to one day fill Mrs Sand's shoes. Following her father's untimely death she assumed the running of the Bemment household. Even at a young age she exhibited remarkable capabilities."

"But mostly simple requirements for a village home, I would guess."

"I am sure Mrs Sands could train and initiate the young woman in the refinements suitable to the kitchen and table of the Squire."

"You think she would be teachable?"

"I believe Edith Kemp had considerable input to Peggy's early cooking and baking skills which led to her serving our community well with her pastie making. More recently she has been contributing the pâtisserie delicacies which have graced the drawing room tea-table and are in demand in local establishments. So I am convinced she would adap..."

A knock on the estate office door interrupted their deliberations and announced the breathless arrival of the senior footman.

"Sir, forgive me, but Constable Huggins has arrived at the Manor and is desirous of speaking with you, urgently."

"Thank you, Haggard, I will come at once." Lord Ralph at once scraped back his chair and stood up.

"We'll continue this conversation at a later date, Jenner." The Squire left the estate office and strode swiftly after the footman.

At the Manor House Hanson hovered in the hall. On arrival his lordship had ushered the constable into his study and shut the door. The butler remained available should he be required. Within minutes the study door reopened. The Master's face was very grave. "Hanson, arrange coffee for the constable and please order the chaise. Would you locate her ladyship. Is Edith Kemp in the house today?"

With his usual efficiency Hanson put all the wheels in motion. He ordered a footman to the stables, directed a maid to the kitchen, sent Alice Housego for her ladyship and enquired of Mrs Hanson if Edith was on the premises.

On learning that Edith was at home his lordship wrote her a note and a footman was sent posthaste to deliver it to the stable loft home. Her ladyship on descending from her drawing room was closeted with his lordship and the constable for a short while till the chaise was announced. Directly, Lord Ralph grabbed outer garments and with Constable Huggins walked out of the house and stepped up into the conveyance. Once he was seated his lordship took up the reins, the wheels crunching the layer of frost as the horse trotted cautiously along the drive towards the wrought iron gates. As soon as the gateman had opened them the chaise exited, turned right and proceeded with care down the slope in the direction of the village. As the chaise neared the market square the Squire spied Edith walking along the icy road.

"Whoa!" Lord Ralph pulled up alongside Edith.

"Good day, Mrs Kemp. I'm sorry to bring you out on such a cold day."

Edith acknowledged his lordship with an incline of her head.

"It be a situation that hev to be dealt wi' regardless o' the weather, m'lord."

"Yes, indeed. Hop in Mrs Kemp. It will be a tight squeeze but only for a short journey. Thank you for responding so promptly to my missive. Constable Huggins informs me that Sergeant Coleby and Doctor Cooper are already investigating at the rear of the Maddox cottage."

"It be a sad day, m'lord."

Silently, her companions nodded their agreement.

Meanwhile, back at the Manor her ladyship slowly climbed the staircase, clinging unsteadily to the banister, and returned to her drawing room, her countenance drawn and sombre. Moments later Peters knocked and opened the door having been quietly instructed by Hanson to bear to her ladyship a pot of camomile tea.

Lady Marion's heart was exceedingly heavy from the disclosure her husband had shared with her. Disturbing news that Constable Huggins had brought concerning the Maddox family.

CHAPTER TWENTY-SEVEN

"And when..."

A short while later the chaise pulled up in the lane adjacent to the row of cottages on the beach.

"The challenges of life seem insurmountable, at toimes, doan't they?" murmured Edith as Constable Huggins prised off the wooden batten that had been hammered across the front door to prevent it from opening.

As they entered the house the intruders gulped as the stench which pervaded the room reached their nostrils. Edith gathered her shawl to her nose. It was unbearable. In the centre of the littered space stood an overflowing chamber pot. Next to it was a saucepan with similar contents, and more spilling on to the floor.

Through the gloom they saw children huddled together in the only chair in the room. Lord Ralph stepped forward. Minnie, curled up on the floor, started to cry. "Where's your Ma?" he asked in a kindly tone.

Vacant eyes stared back at him, but no one made a response.

Constable Huggins pushed passed his lordship and demanded loudly above Minnie's increasing screams, "Where be your Pa?"

Dennis and Aggie cowered into the corner of the chair.

"When did you last see your Pa?" The constable sternly

persisted in increasing decibels.

The children retreated further into the chair, arms clinging around each other. The howling Minnie got up unsteadily but struggled to clamber up to join them.

A shivering Carrie unsteadily gave her weak, little sister a helping hand then attempted to stand her ground, facing the grown-ups who had broken off the wood Pa had hammered between the door and the jamb to prevent them from opening it and getting out.

"Answer me, now! When did yo..."

"Stop, stop, stop," Edith stalled the constable's harsh words and actions by rushing forwards and flinging her shawl around Carrie's quivering shoulders, drawing the girl into the warmth and comfort of her motherly arms.

"Can't yew see these children be afeard an' perishin' cold. It be freezin’ in here," she chided.

Ignoring Edith the constable took another step towards the children intent on his lawful mission.

"And when did yew last see your brother, Archie?" His aggressive approach caused the howling to intensify as Dennis and Aggie joined in Minnie's distressing wails.

"Shh...shh," Edith whispered soothingly, "all will be well." She turned to the men.

"Gentlemen, pass yow'n coats, please," Edith held out a hand expecting them both to comply with her request. Lord Ralph was so shocked at the conditions they had encountered he unquestioningly complied with her demand. Edith tucked the garment carefully around the children noting that not only were they shaking with cold, but their faces were pinched, hair matted, eyes sunken, lips cracked and dry. They appeared lethargic and incredibly undernourished.

Constable Huggins affronted that a villager should give orders to the Squire, and himself, stood his ground.

The Squire, however, having quickly assessed the situation was sensitive to the immediate needs of the children charged him, "Constable, fetch the blanket from the chaise, now." The constable mindful of his Sergeant's instruction stubbornly remained where he was. "But we must find out when they last saw their parents and brother, sir," he spluttered.

"All in good time, my man. Fetch the blanket and organize a carriage to come from the Manor stables. Now, constable," his lordship issued decisively when the policeman made no attempt to move. Sullenly Constable Huggins complied.

Edith endeavoured to calm the children, then spoke to the Squire, "Not only be these children cold, but they be also starvin', m'lord."

"What would you recommend, Mrs Kemp?"

"Why don't yew go wi' Constable Huggins out the back to speak with Sergeant Coleby and assess the situation there while Carrie an oi hev a li'tle chat. Then we need to get some victuals into them an' git them warmed up as soon as possible."

When the constable returned Edith grabbed the blanket, scooped up Minnie, sat down in the chair with Aggie and Dennis and wrapped the blanket round them all.

"Come Carrie, sit on m'lap an' tuck yow'n cold toes in the folds."

"Mrs Kemp hev yew some more o' thass stew?" Dennis lifted pleading eyes up to her.

"Yew hungry m'bor?" she asked sympathetically, knowing full well from their appearance the children had not eaten for some time.

"Yus."

"When did Ma last maak yew a meal, Carrie?"

"Can't 'member."

"Years ago," whispered Aggie tearfully.

"Oi'm soo thirsty," cried Minnie.

"Shh...soon we be a'goin' t' see what we can find fer yew t' eat an' drink."

While Edith settled the children as closely and comfortably as she could the men strode swiftly through the debris into the filthy kitchen. As the constable broke open the boarded up back door Lord Ralph glanced around the kitchen.

"Constable, why would a huge branch like that be in the kitchen?"

"I don't roitely know, sir."

"Suggestive, don't you think?"

"I'll mention it to the Sergeant," Constable Huggins called over his shoulder as they trod carefully into the yard following a trail of blood which led to where another constable stood by the outhouse door. Sergeant Coleby and Doctor Cooper stepped through the outhouse doorway and greeted them with a solemn nod.

"A bad business, sir."

"Life extinct. A very bad business," the doctor confirmed.

"Battered almost beyond recognition, sir," the Sergeant informed the Squire as his lordship peered round the outhouse door.

"Foul play implicated?"

"Cursory examination would suggest that the injuries are consistent with that view."

"Any sign of Mr Maddox or his son, Archie?"

"No, sir."

"I'll leave you to deal with the necessary details with regards to this situation, Sergeant."

"Yus, sir."

"Didn't the neighbours hear anything?"

"Albert's outbursts are such a frequent occurrence they paid no attention."

"Didn't they think it strange that Mrs Maddox nor the children were out and about?"

"They assumed the cold weather had kept them in the house. The schoolmarm called as the children had not been in school for quite some time and was concerned when there was no answer to her knock. She raised the alarm."

"It is essential that alerts are put in place at once to discover the whereabouts of Albert Maddox, in the meantime, the Union's Relieving Officer at the Blything House of Industry will need to be notified with regard to the welfare of the children. They have been sorely neglected and are in a deplorable condition. Doctor, you as medical officer to the institution will be required to examine the children, so in addition to you and myself we will need another two from the parish council to form a quorum who will agree to payment for them under Poor Law provision."

"I suggest Parson Wisbey and Reginald Capps, the parish clerk, my lord. If they are not available then Joseph Castleton, the blacksmith, or Dickie Brooks, the baker, could be approached."

"Excellent suggestion, Doctor."

"I'll go and cast a brief eye on the condition of the children before they are moved and carry out a full examination when they are admitted into the Workhouse."

The Squire nodded his assent.

"But sir, we must get information from those children about what happened here before they are removed from the scene," Constable Huggins indignantly persisted. "Surely they know the whereabouts of Albert and Archie. They must have seen something."

"Leave it with Mrs Kemp, constable," Lord Ralph stated firmly. "I am confident that before the day is through we shall have the information you require." The constable looked askance at the Squire disbelieving what he was being told.

"Sergeant Coleby, I leave you to carry out your duties here. Constable, I hear the approach of the carriage. Will you assist in carrying the children across after the doctor has looked at them," the Squire instructed.

Gingerly the men walked back through the cottage. Lord Ralph drew Edith to one side while the doctor and constable moved the children to the carriage.

"How long?" he quietly enquired.

"Possibly a couple of weeks. Maybe longer, judgin' by the amount of excrement an' the state o' the children. Oi've tried to piece together what happened from the disjointed things they hev said. It seems they devoured all the food they could find an' when it ran out, coupled wi' the lack of water to drink, they became disorientated an' lost count of days."

"Why?"

"Albert blamed Maud fer Tommy's death. The bor be getting' to an age fer bringin' in a wage. Bert was incredibly angry. Shouted at Maud an' hit her repeatedly with a branch he had broken from one o' the trees in the lane."

Lord Ralph nodded perceptively.

"Then in temper he threw a hot saucepan full o' stew from the stove at Maud. It caught her on the side o' her head. She fell. Bert kicked her to get up. When she didn't he yelled fer Archie to come in from the yard. Together they dragged her to the backhus. The children saw it all. Bert came back inside, went upstairs, an' □□ returned carryin' a bag. He told Carrie to watch the children an' wait inside. Bert went out o' the backdoor. Archie nivver came back indoors.

"The children heard hammerin' aginst the back door, then the front door. Carrie tried to pull at them, but they wouldn't open. She scraped from the floor what she could salvage o' the stew to feed them. When they couldn't go outside to use the privy she brought the chamber pot downstairs. They stayed huddled together in one room because they were cold. They ate all she could find till there be nuthen left. There be nuthen to drink as they couldn't get to the pump. She tried to open the windows, which had been nailed down a long time ago to keep out drafts, but only succeeded in maakin' her fingers bleed."

"Quite a sorry state of affairs."

"Yus, sir."

Lord Ralph felt a deep sense of responsibility, almost a feeling of guilt, that such violence could remain undetected in their village for so long.

"Where was the community spirit that is usually prevalent amongst the villagers?"

"The wintry weather will hev kept people indoors."

"You know the children will have to go to the Blything House of Industry?"

"But, sir, they be soo weak an' malnourished. They need nourishin' food an' lovin' care not the strict regime o' the

Workhus," Edith looked at him imploringly.

"They also need a roof over their heads. We have to be realistic, Mrs Kemp. Where else can they go?"

"Oh, sir, they be too young to be subjected to the strictures o' the Workhus. Such roughness be there."

"We have no other option than to entrust their welfare to the Board of Guardians at the Blything House of Industry until such time as their father can be located. They will have bed and food, school and ultimately work." Determined in his resolve the Squire stepped stridently through the doorway towards the carriage where the children waited, despair dogging his footsteps that the desperate circumstances dictated such drastic measures.

Edith shook her head sorrowfully as she followed him. If only...

As the horses pulled the carriage steadily through the village plodding cautiously on treacherous surfaces coated with snow and ice four pairs of frightened eyes fixed their gaze on her. Their plight churned within her heart. They had witnessed the brutal death of their mother at the hands of their father and suffered days of dreadful deprivation. She could give them warmth, bathe and feed them, but nowhere in the loft house was there space to bed them down. Could she...?

The horses lumbered meticulously up the hill. Not a word was spoken.

The carriage neared the lane just prior to the gates of Newton Manor.

Edith sat bolt upright. "M'lord, can we call at the forge?"

Without questioning her meaning the Squire tapped with his cane on the roof of the carriage. The small hatch slid open.

"Coachman, please stop at the forge."

When the carriage drew to a standstill Edith nimbly alighted and carefully picked her way to the door of the forge cottage. Before she had opportunity to knock the door drew back. Dora Castleton stood there expectantly.

"Why Edith whatever be wrong? I saw the coach pull up," she pulled her friend through the doorway out of the cold.

Briefly Edith conveyed the needs of the Maddox children. Very quickly the women devised a plan. Dora called Joseph from the forge.

"Joe, we need yow'n help."

Edith returned to the carriage and explained her plan of action to the Squire. The children were swiftly conveyed into the cottage.

"I will return in ninety minutes, Mrs Kemp. Ensure the children are ready. We must reach the Blything House of Industry and return before nightfall."

"Thank you, Sir."

***

Consternation at the troubles of the Maddox family was at the heart of many a conversation in village homes as well as the Manor House later that night. The violence that Albert had demonstrated towards his wife did not come as a surprize to most, but his cruel treatment of his children shocked them.

"Did he intend them to die as well?"

"Hev he no feelin' fer them?"

"Callous brute!"

"Heartless! Thass what he be."

The situation did not rest easy in Edith's heart. As she snuggled up to George in the warmth of their bed that night she prayed for a workable solution to the dilemma.

CHAPTER TWENTY-EIGHT

"...the night begins to fall"

But sleep did not come. The scenes from earlier in the day constantly played over and over again in her mind.

"Such evil!" Tears poured down Edith's cheeks as by candlelight she busily sorted through a drawer.

"Excess liquor causes a man to lose his good sense. It seems nothin' can restrain his anger an' actions when he be a'taken that way unless the Good Lord touch his heart."

"Knowin' that doan't help the children's plight roite now," Edith replied with a shake of the head as she continued her task.

"What be yew a'doin'?" George asked.

"Seein' if any o' these clothes that Annie's outgrown will fit Minnie or Aggie."

A smile touched George's lips. "An' what else be a'goin' on in that head o' yow'n?"

"Juss a' thinkin'..."

When she had finally reached home earlier that evening, having reluctantly left the dejected Maddox children at the Workhouse, with a heavy heart Edith recounted to George all the details of her day.

George simply listened, occasionally shaking his head, as Edith described the deplorable conditions they found at the Maddox cottage.

"The li'tle uns be doin' sadly. They be soo weak they could barely walk. At Dora's we gently bathed them by the hearth an' wrapped blankets around them, cuddlin' them on ow'n laps to give added warmth. Dora had chicken broth on the stove which we had to spoon feed into them because their mouths were so cracked an' sore, an' their arms lacked energy to lift a spoon."

"What be Albert a'thinkin' on to do such a frightful thing to his own children?"

"There be no tellin' what be in his heart an' mind but it be a tearful partin' when we left his children behind at the Workhus. They looked soo forlorn as we said goodbye. The matron had a stern countenance an' refused to let me stay to settle them in. When Dennis an' Aggie clung desperately to ma skirt she roughly pulled them away an' when Minnie cried incessantly she spoke to her in such a harsh tone. Carrie stood uncertainly, fightin' hard to keep back the tears, yet bravely tryin' to calm their fears. But she were sore afeard. Oh, George, it were pitiful."

"Such shockin' happ'nen's fer ow'n village! The Good Lord be their protector!" George walked across the room and placed his arms around Edith's shoulders. She leaned gratefully into the comfort of his embrace.

"Oh, George, oi juss can't put aside those doleful, accusin' eyes that looked at me so appealin'ly as oi left those li'tle uns." Her hands added a pair of liberty bodices to the small pile of clothing on the end of the bed, but as her foot caught the edge of Annie's former bed Edith's mind engaged with a number of possibilities as her tongue continued its tale of woe.

"Dennis is to be sent to work on the Union farm next to the Workhus. The bor can barely stand. He'll not survive the harsh elements an' at the mention o' cows his knees buckled. Carrie is to learn net makin' an' wool spinnin' an' arter they've bin to the schoolroom the other two are to help cultivate produce in the garden an' do hemp cardin'. Such unrealistic expectations o' youngsters in their condition. Maybe..."

George nodded knowingly.

As night began to fall similar conversations were taking place at the forge. "Ma, what be a'goin' to happen to Dennis an' his sisters?" Susan asked as the Castleton family sat around the supper table in the forge kitchen.

"They be gone to the Workhus to be looked after till such time as their Pa returns." Dora's cheerful tone did not echo the unease she felt in her heart for the plight of the Maddox children. They were so frail and fragile of limb and mind.

"But, Ma, Caleb say thass an awful place. How could the Squire taak them to such a horrid hus? Oi thought he be good an' kind. Oi shan't speak to him agin," said Bobby crossly.

"Yew saw how hungry an' sick they were. They needed to be safe an' cared for, with food, bed, warmth an' clothes, as wel..."

Animatedly Bobby jumped up. "But we hev those things here. Wi' Harold an' Millie now a'sleepin' at the farm their beds be empty."

"What will happen when they be hum on their days orf?"

"We'll manage. Dennis can share wi' me. He be m'friend." Dora caught Joseph's eye. He smiled and inclined his head.

"We'll see, m'bor, we'll see." Bobby had to be content with the non-committal response but knew that when he and his siblings were in bed his parents would fairly discuss his suggestion, because that's what they always did.

At Newton Westerby Manor Lady Marion left the Squire pacing in the drawing room. On his return to the Manor House he had updated her on the situation of the Maddox children.

"On their admittance to the House of Industry they were stripped, bathed and deloused then given Workhouse uniforms after which Doctor Cooper examined them. At this point the boy was separated from his sisters as males, no matter their age, are segregated. It was a heart wrenching scene to witness."

"Where was compassion?"

"My dear, I didn't find it an easy decision, but it was a question of leaving them in a deplorable mess or removing them to a place of safety until such time as their father can be located. It's my duty to ensure the protection of those children. That governed my decision not sentiment or sympathy, no matter how much I detested such action. My immediate objective was their wellbeing. The Blything House of Industry was my only option. We were able to get a quorum together to agree parish payment for them."

"What a dreadful predicament. Here we have all that we need, empty unused rooms and sufficient food, yet those poor children so close by had nothing and were left to die," Marion's voice broke as she contemplated their terrible suffering.

"My dear, you have such a tender heart but in life people have choices and there are consequences to the choices they make. However, we cannot take in every waif and stray when those choices present as such an appalling situation as the one we found at the Maddox cottage. That is why we have Houses of Industry to provide for those unfortunate enough to be in want through wrong choices they or others have made."

"I'm well aware what results from the consequences of someone else's misdirected choices. We've had to cope with the after-effects of that sort of behaviour in order to pull the estate through the crisis that was created following Quentin's conduct."

"My dear, I couldn't allow emotion to cloud my judgement. I had to determine what was in the best interests of the children."

"But, Ralph, these are innocent children. I'm sure Edith didn't approve your decision."

"Mrs Kemp was distraught. She felt they were too frail and sickly to be subjected to the harsh environment of the Workhouse."

"Knowing her tender and practical heart I can't see her letting this be the end of the matter for those children."

"Circumstances may change."

"I pray that will be so."

Tearfully Lady Marion departed from the drawing room and made her way up into the nursery to kiss goodnight to her little girl, Rosamund, her heart reeling as she recalled the precious little boy they had lost. She would have given anything to save his life. Momentarily her eyelids closed and in her mind's eye she saw Edmund's first tottering steps and heard his early lisping words. As she reached the nursery door she paused and quickly wiped the tears from her eyes.

Annie had bathed and prepared Rosamund for bed. She now handed the baby to her mother to settle for the night in her crib.

"She'll soon need the bigger cot, m'lady, she be a'growin' soo quickly."

Lady Marion held the precious child tightly to her before reluctantly laying her down into the crib and tucking her in, choking back a sob in her throat. Another child she almost lost, but for the persistence and care of Annie. How she thanked God for this caring young woman.

"How can a father deliberately inflict suffering on his own children? Suffering, so I understand, almost to the point of death. Depriving them of a mother who cared for them." She reached out and placed a hand gently on Rosamund's back. "Did he not cherish them? Children are such a precious gift. When you have little ones of your own, Annie, you will understand."

When Annie remained silent Lady Marion looked at her closely. "Annie, is all well between you and Fred?"

Annie pressed a hand across her chest hoping to quell the sick feeling that cavorted in its depths. Fred's officious attitude in his new role as under steward still rankled. His caring nature seemed to be obliterated by the weight of his new responsibilities on the estate.

"Oi hardly see him these days, m'lady, he be soo busy and when we do meet it be more loike strangers than friends, certainly not close friends." Annie's heart had not known peace for months as far as Fred was concerned. Involuntarily, she shook her shoulders as if to rid herself of the burden of frustration and disappointment she carried.

"At least oi know oi hev a Ma an' Pa who love me an' would nivver abandon or mistreat me. Oi can't think Ma would hev bin happy to leave the Maddox children at the Workhus," Annie said with tears in her eyes.

Marion looked directly at her nursery maid. "She won't,

will she?"

Annie shook her head. "Noo, I doan't believe Ma will leave them there. Ma will pray abaht it. She woan't let it rest. She will sort suthen out," she affirmed with confidence.

"Your mother is a wise woman and a good person to talk with about many things," Marion agreed, having been the beneficiary on many occasions of Edith's down to earth common sense, grounded in the Good Book.

Annie's confidence in her mother was not misplaced. Before the end of the week Edith had organized new homes for the Maddox children. No one had room to take them all but by the dawn of the New Year Carrie was lodging with Beatie, Dennis and Minnie were settled with the Castleton family, much to Bobby's delight, and Aggie was established in the loft home above the stables. In these homes the children were given love, warmth, care and food which enabled them to gradually heal, gain strength and begin to flourish. They were not plied with questions about events leading up to their horrendous ordeal but listening ears were available at such times as they wanted to voice worries about their experiences and what they witnessed happen to their mother. Edith insisted the police did not pester the children till they became much stronger believing that truth would emerge over time in natural conversation. For some while Minnie and Aggie had nightmares and both Dora and Edith spent many a night soothing the brows of troubled little girls with night-time cuddles.

However, although Edith ensured the children were comfortably housed, the police were less successful in their search for their father; nothing was heard of Albert or Archie although it was believed they must have made their way to Liverpool and somehow boarded one of the boats setting sail across the Atlantic Ocean.

Annie never spoke to Edith about her relationship with Fred as Lady Marion had hoped, but she did pray that God would guide her thoughts and actions with regard to her friendship with Fred. They no longer met up on Sundays after the morning service as Fred did not accompany his family to the Chapel services choosing instead to attend St Andrew's church along with most of the Manor household staff. But, in her free hour each day, following Rosamund's lunch, Annie intentionally watched out for Fred. She then endeavoured to ensure their paths crossed. In those snatched moments she listened with interest as Fred spoke animatedly about activities on the estate, her heart beating rapidly against her ribs at his nearness. However, their meetings were always brief as Fred always seemed anxious to be on the move.

"Fred, yew be allus in such a hurry these days."

He smiled at her as he scratched his head. "Well, oi do hev a lot of business across the estate to attend to," he explained as he started to move on. With a sinking heart Annie watched him stride away. She was beginning to wonder if his interest in her was waning especially after Ethel Capps had innocently let slip that she had seen Fred in conversation with her cousin Lizzie in the orchard.

Unaware of Annie's forebodings Fred reflected how glad he was of Annie's company. The brief encounter brought joy to his heart and a spring in his step. He was sorry he hadn't the time to linger in her presence. *We fit together like a comfortable pair o' ole boots,* he thought. He knew he could discuss anything with her, his concerns as well as his achievements, knowing Annie would not gossip but hold her own counsel. "It be difficult at toimes to correct someone oi hev known all my life or persuade them to perform a task in a different way wi'out them gettin' uppity," he confided.

"Ma would say it be best to talk to the Good Lord abaht ev'rythin'. He allus knows what be best an' will guide ow'n words an' decisions."

"Oi'll do m'best to remember that advice."

Still living at home with his Ma and the family Fred had yet to tell Annie of the offer of the cottage. Fearful she would be unwilling to relinquish her position at the Manor and might reject his offer of marriage he held off from declaring his heart to her.

"Ýew lost in'erest in Annie, Fred?" Jimmy asked him one morning. " Oi heard tell that bor Castleton be keen on her. Ye best be a'doin' suthen abaht it lessen yew want to lose her."

Fred was shocked by Jimmy's observation. "But he be much older than Annie!" It was true he had heard gossip amongst the servants that Harold Castleton was sweet on Annie and that one of the footmen also had his eye on her but pushed it to one side as idle talk. *Perhaps she returns the interest.* That thought startled Fred. It suddenly came to him that he had been remiss of late in his attention towards her. *In fact, maybe oi hev taaken her affection fer me fer granted. M'duties on the estate seem to taak up soo much o' m'toime an' energy these days. Oi'll put matters straight on her next arternoon out. She be the joy o' ma heart.*

So, at the earliest opportunity he arranged to meet Annie by the kitchen garden gate, their special trysting place. It was bitterly cold. An icy wind was blowing in from the sea. As he waited Fred tightened the muffler around his neck.

He stamped his feet, blew on his nails and thumped his arms across his chest to keep warm. When Annie approached a dimple danced in one cheek as she smiled up at him and her eyes sparkled. Fred sighed at the sight she presented and ran his fingers nervously through his dark unruly hair. *She looks pleased to see me. Perhaps m'fears be unfounded.* He would have happily spent the time walking round the estate, or along the riverbank just to be in her company, but it was far too cold, the frost and ice making it treacherous underfoot.

"Let's visit Beatie. She will hev a fire blazin' an' we'll be warm," he suggested enthusiastically.

"What a good idea," Annie agreed as she gathered her shawl closer to her.

They walked side by side where possible as Fred eagerly regaled her with different aspects of the estate he was gradually learning to deal with, his face lit up and his conversation animated.

As the path widened out Fred turned, held out his arm as he warmly smiled at her. Annie slipped her hand into the crook it formed, her breath tightening in her chest as she did so. Annie listened carefully to all Fred imparted, pleased to be in his company, hoping to rebuild the closeness they had once shared.

Neither mentioned the deep-seated emotion the presence of the other evoked in their hearts. They reached the end of the track that traversed between the ploughed corn field and the walled garden of the Manor, turned into the lane that went through the centre of the village passing Beatie's cottage on its way, when Jimmy, the garden boy, came tearing down behind them calling out Fred's name.

"Yew muss come quick, Fred, Mister Jenner needs yew

in the estate office at once."

Fred smiled apologetically at Annie. Reluctantly she withdrew her hand from his arm as he turned swiftly to retrace his steps, leaving Annie to walk up to Beatie's front door alone. In her imagination Annie could see the future she had hoped for with Fred gradually receding. *We nivver hev a moment to pass the time of day let alone discuss feelin's an' plans wi'out the affairs of the squire an' his estate intrudin'.*

PART TWO
CHAPTER TWENTY-NINE

Five Years Later

"...They hear..."

The sun of a late, summer daybreak continued to stream through the Manor morning room windows as the footman set out platters of food upon the sideboard. A myriad colours danced upon the silver lids placed over the dishes to keep food warm. Hanson, the butler, cast an eagle eye across the arrangements and gave a cursory glance to the table settings as he placed the daily papers beside his lordship's place at the table. His sharp eyes checked the fire in the grate blazed sufficiently to send warmth into the room. He gave a nod of approval to the young man. The large hand of the mantle clock ticked towards the hour. The grandfather clock in the hall commenced to chime when footsteps were heard descending the stairs. Hanson walked to open the door while the footman stood in readiness to the right of the sideboard.

"Good morning, my lord," Hanson greeted as Lord Ralph bounded into the room.

"Yes, it is a good morning, Hanson," his lordship responded in a light-hearted manner, a smile creasing his features. "Not only because the weather is fine and dry, and the sun is shining, but because my wife will be joining me shortly."

"That is good news, sir. I trust she is feeling well."

"Much better than of late."

"That is certainly encouraging." Hanson glanced towards the footman as he expertly seated his lordship.

The young man stepped forward. "Good morning, your lordship, would you prefer tea or coffee this morning?"

"Aah, Catchpole, how is it going?"

"Very well, thank you, sir."

"Good. I will take tea, please. I'm not sure which her ladyship will prefer. Ask when she arrives. What has Cook prepared to break our fast?"

Philip Catchpole proceeded to list the items that were on offer. Lord Ralph made his choice and as the young man served his lordship's meal Lady Marion quietly entered the room to join him.

Hanson greeted and seated her ladyship then discreetly withdrew from the breakfast room leaving the footman in charge of proceedings yet hovered close at hand should he be required. In keeping with the policy his lordship and Elias Jenner, the estate manager, had instigated some years previously the butler had selected young Philip Catchpole to be trained to one day succeed him. Not having the same affinity with the land that his father Abel had, Philip searched for some while to find his niche. Mrs Catchpole understandably did not want Philip to go to sea as his older brother, Arthur, had done then been tragically lost in the storm that had also taken other lives aboard the ill-fated Grayling.

When the senior footman chose to accept a place in a London hotel the other footmen were promoted and thus a staff position became vacant in the Newton Manor household. When Abel heard about it he informed Philip who was interviewed, offered and accepted the post.

It soon became apparent he was ideally suited for the position, both Elias Jenner and Hanson could see the lad's potential. He had a likeable, cheery personality yet was steady, smart and dependable. Catchpole also had a keen eye for detail which pleased Hanson. Over the years they kept a close watch on him and fastidiously nurtured his development. Whilst Hanson had no imminent plans to retire he thought it wise to share duties with the young man to give him a measure of responsibility. It also enabled the meticulous butler to ensure Catchpole learned from the start of his service to perform tasks correctly, according to protocol.

"Good morning, my lady. It is good to see you. What can I offer you?" Lady Marion made her choice known to him. Quietly and efficiently Catchpole served her then stood inconspicuously to one side until he should be needed.

Overjoyed to have his wife's company Lord Ralph refrained from opening the daily newspapers so thoughtfully placed by Hanson.

"I am so pleased you feel able to join me this morning, my dear. You look delightfully rested. Are you feeling well?"

Marion nodded and smiled up at her husband." All is very well," she confirmed, a bloom of contentment radiating from her.

They conversed about the progress and development of their daughters, Rosamund, Judith and Averil, their differing natures and tendencies, discussed various aspects of work on the estate and commented on the continuing success of ventures that had commenced during the crisis created by Quentin's recklessness five years previously.

"This is delicious," Marion took a bite of the recently produced Seville orange marmalade she spread on the toasted bread handmade by Peggy. Peggy Bemment was another product of the Newton Manor training programme and was currently assistant cook to Mrs Sands in the Manor kitchen.

"I agree. I am pleased that we still have opportunity to savour some of the goods we offer to the commercial market."

"Peggy Bemment has proved a great asset, hasn't she?"

"Most certainly. She has a light hand, almost as good as her sister, Beatrice. Her sweetmeats and pâtisserie confections prove very popular in the hotels."

"Some are delectable. Initially, Mrs Sands and her staff experimented with many varied receipts to gage what would be acceptable to us, as well as the establishments we were able to interest, but after all these years production has been refined to what is the most well-liked."

"Fortunately, the hard work of our loyal staff has enabled us to keep our heads above water and incredibly Quentin hasn't once defaulted on his side of the bargain. We still have a little way to go till the estate is entirely solvent, but we have made positive progress."

"That is encouraging news. Surprizingly, I find I haven't missed the endless round of social calls and dinner parties as I thought I might. But rather, I've thoroughly enjoyed the extra time I've been able to spend with our girls, my additional input to household affairs and participation in the reorganization of the gardens. Life has become more meaningful, and this little one will simply add more joy." A hand fluttered over her midriff; her face suffused with serenity.

"What plans do you have for this day?"

"I am interviewing Amy Peskett...I suppose I ought to refer to her as Mrs Bemment...with a view to her becoming the girl's governess, as we discussed."

"Do you want me to be present?"

"I don't think that will be necessary. I want to create a relaxed atmosphere rather than a formal space hoping to convince her to take the position."

"My dear, you are blessed with insight and a persuasive ability to see what is best in any given situation. I am positive Mrs Bemment is an ideal choice. An excellent idea of yours to give Bracewell's vacant cottage to Stan Bemment and Amy when they married. Look at the secure homelife they gave to the Maddox children following their ordeal."

"Yes, Carrie is now well settled and proving such an asset to Beatrice. She has a natural flair for fashioning the leather items at the cobblers and is able to watch Rebekah when Beatie has to attend a confinement. Dennis has taken to the work at the flour mill and being well cared for by Mrs Jenner after the loss of her boys. Aggie and Minnie are doing well at school under the guidance of the new schoolmaster. Their own baby, Jeremiah, is flourishing and could be looked after by Annie and Ethel along with Averil whilst Rosamund and Judith are in the schoolroom should Amy accept the position."

"You have it all worked out admirably, my dear. I just hope Mrs Bemment sees it in the same light. Married women are not supposed to take employment."

"But it seems such a waste of her skills and training."

"My mother would not approve of the way you step across the bounds of propriety." Ralph spoke sternly but Marion saw the twinkle in his eyes.

She returned his smile. "Nor would Quentin approve my 'fraternizing with the peasants' as he put it. But the more I get to know our people the more I find we have much to offer to one another. They have feelings and struggles which may differ to mine, but I learn much from them, particularly their unswerving belief in Almighty God. Why not utilize their accomplishments for our mutual benefit. I also enjoy their company."

"You have a tender heart, Marion. I hope it will not be mis..." Lord Ralph broke off in mid-sentence as Hanson entered the room quietly and unobtrusively.

"The early post, sir." The butler presented a silver salver in front of the squire. It held an envelope embossed with a Barbadian stamp and postmark. "I've placed the business correspondence on the study desk, but I thought you might wish to open this one, now."

As he uplifted the envelope Ralph observed it closely. "We don't often hear from Barbados, but I do not recognize the handwriting. It's not mother's or Quentin's." He took up the paperknife and carefully slit the missive open. Turning the page over he glanced at the signature. "It's from Quentin's wife, Delphine."

Silence hung over the room for some moments as Ralph read the contents of the letter. No sound could be heard from the rest of the house and stillness seemed to pervade the garden outside the window as a cloud momentarily obscured the rising sun.

A guttural gasp escaped the squire's lips, a gasp that sobbed with anguished sorrow and pain.

"What is it, Ralph?"

"Quentin has been killed."

Marion gulped, swallowed hard as a lump rose in her throat and tears flooded her eyes. "Oh my dear! I am so sorry. How?"

"Apparently there was a tropical hurricane storm some weeks ago. Quentin insisted on going out, against all advice, was caught in torrential rain and a freak wind coming in off the Atlantic Ocean uprooted a tree on the plantation. He was in its path, and it crashed down on him, killing him outright."

"Your brother has caused us much heartache, but I wouldn't wish this on him," Marion spoke softly. "This is a blow your mother will find hard to bear. What will happen to his wife and family?"

"My first inclination is to send Jenner to sort out the affairs of the plantation, but in all conscience I believe it behoves me to go and see for myself what the situation is. Speak with Delphine to see what she purposes for the future and escort mother back to England. With Quentin gone I can't think Barbados will hold anything to keep her living there."

"But winter will soon be upon us. Would it not be better to wait till spring to travel?"

"This is something that cannot be delayed. Already some weeks have passed since Quentin's accident and this communication sent. I feel compelled to go immediately."

"Whatever you think will be best," Marion reluctantly acquiesced, but in her heart she silently pleaded with the Almighty. *Dear God, be the sufficiency of those so recently bereaved and watch over my beloved husband as he sails those treacherous seas.*

"Hanson," Lord Ralph called in a loud voice. "Please, locate Mr Jenner and ask him to meet me in the study."

As the butler left to carry out the squire's wishes Lord Ralph turned back to his wife. "From this distance it would seem best to sell the plantation land and retain only the property. It could be deeded to Quentin's wife for her lifetime and subsequently pass to Quentin's son. But would that be the right course of action from their point of view?"

"I recall how excited and proud Quentin was when his son was born."

"Yes, he wrote home boasting that he had a son and heir, and I didn't."

"That was following Edmund's death and just prior to Judith's birth and was so hurtful."

"He had this notion that as the entailment had to pass through the male line his son would be in line to inherit the Newton Manor estate."

Although Quentin had never openly acknowledged Beatrice Bemment's child as his, he had continued to forward a monthly allowance for Rebekah. Some time after Quentin's departure to Barbados it was learned from correspondence with the estate lawyer that the cottage allocated to his daughter and her mother was completely paid for. Consequently on hearing of Quentin's untimely death Lord Ralph decided to send for Marcus Capps and instruct documents to be drawn up that stated the property was Rebekah's. "To be held in perpetuity for her, and her heirs, by Beatrice. That will give closure and provide security for them."

Colin Jenner had faithfully courted Beatie and just prior to Rebekah's birth the couple had quietly married in the de Vessey family chapel with Lady Marion in attendance.

Beatie's brother, Stan, and Edith Kemp were the only witnesses to the marriage. Within two years of their wedding Colin died succumbing to the lung disease that constant working with flour particles had caused. Beatie nursed the caring man she had grown to love who had proved a fine father figure for Rebekah.

As her grandfather Jonas aged Beatie took over more and more of the cobbling and leather work. For convenience, tools were gradually transferred to the end house and the outhouse attached to the former forge building was converted into a work room and part of the space in the redundant forge housed the larger implements and equipment. Beatie called in next door daily to attend to her grandfather's needs but as he grew frailer Jonas moved in to live with Beatie. In her cheerful, no-nonsense manner she absorbed his care into her ever-increasing workload.

CHAPTER THIRTY

"...the Shepherd dogs..."

Diverse happenings further afield had an impact on some families in the village community. Joe Jenner did not return from the Indian mutiny. He was killed in crossfire in a skirmish with the rebels. It was a considerable blow to Miller Jenner and his wife. However, Silent Pete Tuttle displayed a fascination in the workings of the mill and was taken on as an apprentice. Being deaf the noisy mechanisms of the mill did not bother him. He soon built up a rapport with Danny Jenner who patiently developed a method of communication with him. Pete proved a good little worker once he knew what was expected of him. He missed the companionship of Bobby Castleton, but Bobby, as had been expected, was eager to learn all the skills of a smithy and farrier and worked closely with his father in the forge.

The eldest Baldry boy came home injured in body and mind from the horrors he had experienced in India and was unable to assume his former responsibilities at Manor Farm. All be it, Harold Castleton continued working on the farm, began courting Violet Baldry and was proving a valuable asset to Farmer Baldry.

Dennis Maddox was sent to the farm with Harold, but his fear of horses also extended to cattle and sheep. The whistles and calls of the shepherd to the sheep dog to direct the movement of the sheep intrigued him but he stood petrified if they came anywhere near to him. He was given the opportunity to work in the smithy alongside Bobby but while he was comfortable standing on the sidelines watching his friend and his father fashion metal in the furnace and was captivated by the way they shod the horses with shoes he shied away from taking up any tools and engaging in the task himself. He was scared of the sparks and fierceness of the furnace.

Joseph and Dora Castleton racked their brains not knowing in which direction to channel the young lad who had been entrusted to their care, for, although provision was made to house the Maddox children together with Stan and Amy Bemment, Dennis insisted on staying at the Castleton's. He persisted in addressing them as Bobby's Ma and Pa, but never spoke of the day that led to his mother's death or the disappearance of his own Pa and elder brother, Archie.

Dora spoke over her concerns with Edith recalling the boy's childhood friendships, "Ow'n Bobby, along wi' Caleb an' Silent Pete did much together an' bor Dennis, although slightly younger, allus tagged along."

"Wi' Colin an' Joe gone oi wonder if working at the mill alongside Silent Pete would be an option fer Dennis."

"It be a possibility. The miller needs all the help he can get, he an' Mrs Jenner not be gettin' any younger."

"I understand Danny is proving competent an' will obviously assume more responsibility now his older brothers be a'gone. Oi guess he'll eventually taak uvver from his father, but he will require workers skilled in the workin's o' the mill."

"The only other option as oi see it would be fer Dennis to taak uvver from Jimmy as kitchen boy as Abel has promoted Jimmy to work in the glass houses."

"There aren't any other vacant places in the household, as far as oi know."

"Oi doan't think Dennis would be comfortable in any of the roles in that environment. Hezzie Kemp took him out fishing but the poor bor wuz so sick he thought he wuz a'goin' to die. He would shy away from another experience like that."

"Life can be soo hard at toimes!"

"The Good Lord muss surely hev a place fer the bor."

"We'll pray he foinds it."

Dora reiterated her conversation with Edith to Joseph that evening after the youngsters had ascended the stairs for bed resulting in Joseph having a quiet word with Danny Jenner after the Sunday morning chapel service. The following morning he walked with Dennis along the riverbank towards Jenner's Mill. At supper that evening Dennis was more animated than the Castleton's had ever seen him. He was full of his day's experience.

"You loike working at the Mill, then bor?"

"Ooh yus. It be moitey foine. Silent Pete be ma friend an' Mister Danny be pretty foine."

Joseph and Dora smiled at one another, a silent prayer of thanks ascending from both their hearts.

Fred Bemment flourished in his responsibilities under Elias Jenner's tutelage and was now well entrenched in his position as under steward on the Newton Westerby Manor Estate. So that their roles did not over-lap Fred was given sole charge for specific areas of estate management, particularly that involving horses. He was in his element when checking the animals and their stables, liaising with George and Stan about their needs and requirements. He conversed frequently with the stable lads about their concerns and ensured the new boys were well-versed in all equine matters across the farm. Fred thoroughly relished the time spent with his horse friends.

Fred was also in charge of boundary management working closely with Harold Castleton. He still enjoyed getting involved with the hedge-layering recalling the days he spent being instructed by ole Alf. Food production for the household as well as the commercial market was now his responsibility. Frequently he consulted with Abel Catchpole in the kitchen garden about what fruit and vegetables would be required for the Manor table and what was on offer for market. He also discussed with Lizzie Capps what was available for preserves and chutneys. Regularly he had conversations with Seth who ran the team organizing transportation of animals to Smithfield's meat market, as well as a variety of food produce to the different outlets locally and further afield. Once a week Fred worked closely with Elias Jenner on the books in the estate office.

Nannie Biddle had been pensioned off and given accommodation in the West Wing of the Manor House. Annie was promoted to the position of Nannie and training Ethel Capps as nursery maid. Ethel proved quite an asset in the nursery being blessed with an abundance of common sense. She was a gentle, quiet girl who had boundless patience with energetic Rosamund who despite her traumatic early start in life was now quite a robust, chatty, mischievous little girl. Her sister Judith was much slower and rather solemn with a more placid nature but anxious not to be left out of things was always keen to imitate her older sister. Eighteen months previously Averil had joined the nursery incumbents, a contented baby with a ready smile for everyone. Annie assisted Edith with both confinements as Beatie was at the time tied up with her other duties. The new arrival was anticipated with joy, Lady Marion hoping for a son and heir for Lord Ralph and prayed her husband would return from Barbados before the baby's arrival.

***

Ralph shifted on the hard bench. The heat was unbearable. He wiped his brow, took off his hat to waft it fan-like in an attempt to cool himself down. He had safely crossed the Atlantic Ocean despite days of unrelenting storms at sea on a ship that tossed and moaned as waves crested and fell mercilessly. Sickness had not stricken him as it had so many of his fellow passengers, but the extreme temperature seemed to swallow him almost beyond endurance the moment he landed on the shores of the island.

Having reached Barbados Lord Ralph negotiated transportation to the address he presented to his would-be carrier, but he appeared at the plantation house before the letter announcing his impending arrival had been delivered. The flustered servant who answered the clanging bell Ralph pulled assured him, "The mistress and Lady A'minta return shortly, and the overseer be back soon. He inspect work on the plantation." She had pointed to a bench to the side of the wooden porch and brought him a cold drink, refreshing with a taste Ralph could not identify, but did not invite him into the house where the shade it afforded would have been welcome.

Perspiration dripped down his face. He loosened his collar, pulled out a kerchief and wiped it around his neck. Across the earth packed courtyard he could see clumps of trees bearing fruit he did not recognize. Stripping off his outer garment Ralph strode towards them hoping to gain some respite under the canopy of their branches from the fierceness of the heat radiating from the sun. It was here that his mother found him wilting in the oppressiveness of a climate to which he was unused. Her greeting was less than cordial.

"If you hadn't banished him your brother would still be alive," Lady Araminta accused him.

"Quentin's preference was to come here rather than face the consequence of his actions in England," Ralph quietly reminded her.

Araminta sniffed, tossed her head, and stomped towards the house. As he followed his mother Ralph could hear loud voices emanating from the interior of the house. A female voice he assumed to be that of his sister-in-law was raised angrily, lashing into the maid who first greeted him.

"That man is Lord Ralph de Vessey the owner of this plantation. Your master, and mine, and you left him outside!" The enraged voice rang out. "How could you! We may both lose our jobs and homes because of your thoughtlessness!"

"Bu...u...t, I didn't know who he was," was the feeble rejoinder.

"Didn't you ask his name?"

"N...n...o. He just enquire after you."

"And you thought, what?"

"I...I..."

"Stop your snivelling, Jessie, and get on with the meal preparations. At least we can show him we are civilized and can offer a meal fit for a man in his position."

In his ensuing conversation with Quentin's widow Ralph

learned Delphine was a Bajun of mixed-race decent. She was not the socialite he had imagined but an intelligent woman with an astute head for business. He deduced Delphine was the real power behind the commercial success of the plantation. His brother had been nothing more than a figure head. It became evident she was also plantation manager having her finger on the pulse of all the workings of sugar production. Delphine was the one who kept the books, handled all financial matters including Quentin's repayments to the Newton Westerby Manor Estate. His sister-in-law was conversant with market trends, costings, transport and export requirements. The overseer was in charge of all aspects of sugar cane production and management of the plantation workers. Ralph found him to be a harsh man and brutal in his conduct towards the plantation workers, but he was truly knowledgeable about sugar and rum production, well versed in the necessary conditions required to produce good quality and quantity of both.

Lord Ralph went out on horseback with the overseer to view the plantation. He observed back-breaking work in scorching sun coupled with cruel treatment of both male and female workers. The Abolition Act of 1834 had granted freedom to slave workers, but Ralph witnessed that some workers were still enslaved by the way the apprenticeship scheme was being implemented. It had been designed to ease slaves into freedom but in reality it tied them into a way of life that was beyond physical endurance.

He was appalled to see children as young as 6 years working in the fields as well as being involved in the production of rum. Much to the displeasure of the overseer his lordship stopped to speak with apprenticed mothers and learned their babies had died from lack of nourishment.

"We expected to work too hard and too long. Not produce enough milk to feed them." Grandmothers were no longer available to look after children as they formerly did because they too had to work as apprentices. Both men and women worked long hours for their 'employers' then at the end of an exhausting day had to tend their own meagre plots in order to grow crops to feed their families. Ralph felt sick to the pit of his stomach, he was so horrified at the harsh conditions he encountered he wanted to do all that was within his power to rectify the appalling situation.

"Don't interfere, Ralph," his mother remonstrated. "This is how it is. It is not England."

"It is not right. They are people. The Abolition Act says they are free but from what I have observed they are more enslaved than they have ever been, and it is proving detrimental to their health and family life."

"You are naïve, Ralph. Leave well alone."

"I had no idea that our family were party to such barbaric practises."

"Stop harping on, Ralph. Things are done differently here."

"But some of the children are the age of Rosamund, or younger, and expected to carry out a day's work in this heat. It is stifling."

"What do you expect wearing thick English tweeds!"

Outraged by his mother's calm acceptance of the ruthless and inconsiderate treatment of those 'employed' by their family Ralph went in search of his sister-in-law.

Delphine was busy at a desk positioned under a window at the far end of the large living space. To her right a boy and girl were happily playing on the wooden floor.

She looked up as Ralph drew closer.

"Your children?"

"Yes, Alberto Edmund and Juanita Rose."

Ralph winced to hear his dead son's name, surprized that Quentin should have used the de Vessy family names for his children. Probably an indication of his conviction that his heir would one day inherit the English estate. As the children turned to acknowledge him with sheepish grins Ralph quickly turned his frown to a smile.

"I have the books ready for your inspection." Delphine indicated open ledgers set before her.

"Oh, I am sure everything is as it should be. My real reason for coming over from England was to work out with you the future of the plantation and learn what proposals you have for the property. Have you given thought to plans for your family?"

Sitting erect in her chair his sister-in-law looked Ralph directly in the eye. "I expect to continue living and working here. This is our home."

"Do you have a marriage certificate?"

Ralph's question completely threw her. Flustered, Delphine started to rummage frantically through the drawers of the desk.

"It's here somewhere," she declared as she tossed papers like confetti to the ground.

Surprised by her reaction Ralph assured her it was unimportant. However, Delphine rose abruptly and called to one of the servants to ready a horse and conveyance.

"We will go to St John's. There you will meet the vicar who married us and see the record in the marriage register," she commanded. After a pause she added softly, "That, too, is where Quentin is buried."

CHAPTER THIRTY-ONE

"...rounding call."

Lord Ralph mulled over the options before him. He recognized provision would have to be made for Quentin's widow and family but on the other hand income from the sale of plantation land would offset some of Quentin's debt still owing to the Newton Westerby Manor estate. Delphine made it clear that she expected to remain in the plantation house. It behoved him to ensure sufficient property was retained to give the household a viable income.

When opportunity presented itself he spoke with other plantation owners to ascertain who might be interested in purchasing de Vessy land, particularly those whose holdings were adjacent to the de Vessey plantation.

Lady Araminta had once again become used to living in a lavish style. Quentin had indulged her every whim, and she expected that to continue to enable her to retain the status she had acquired amongst the elite in Barbados society. She unrelentingly persisted to lay blame for Quentin's death on Ralph although it had been her younger son's own wilfulness and foolhardiness that had resulted in his death.

"I understand his overseer had warned him of the impending storm coming across the Atlantic Ocean which

Quentin blatantly chose to ignore. His wife also pleaded with him not to venture out."

It soon became clear to Lord Ralph that Delphine would not be easily swayed by his mother but was able to stand her ground. She was a strong woman, able to make her own decisions with regard to household and plantation affairs. If Lady Araminta wished to stay on in Barbados, as she had indicated, it would be on Delphine's terms, even though the property had formerly belonged to her late husband Lord Edmund de Vessy.

"However, the situation cannot remain as it is," Ralph intimated.

Despite the overseer's reluctance to accept the requirements of the Abolition Act and his continuance to exploit workers on the plantation Delphine was keen to implement it amongst her household staff giving them the option to stay on as freed persons or move on elsewhere.

"It will be necessary to cut back on staff," Ralph explained to her in company with his mother. "When land is sold there will be a considerable depletion in income and you will have to economize accordingly."

Delphine nodded in understanding, but his mother snapped, "Even in death you continue to act harshly towards your brother."

"No, Mater. You need to accept Quentin brought about his own demise by the choices he made. I am so sorry this has happened to my brother. But, please, don't remain blinkered to his actions. Had he not been so grasping and selfish this situation would have never arisen in the first place. If you choose to remain here it will be within the confines that a reduced income imposes, which will be under the control of your daughter-in law."

Lady Araminta tossed her head and snorted in a most unladylike fashion. Undeterred Ralph proceeded to explain the situation as he understood it. "What remains after the sale will be held by Delphine in perpetuity for Quentin's son till he reaches his majority..."

"Such a precious child," Araminta interrupted. "So like his father."

"I will instruct the estate lawyer, Marcus Capps, to draw up the necessary documentation, Delphine. Mater, you may return to England with me, if you so desire, there is still a home for you within the Manor."

"I will remain here," Lady Araminta replied haughtily. "Here, I am treated like a lady."

"That is your choice, Mater, but remember you will have to curtail the lavish lifestyle Quentin indulged you in."

Araminta glared at her eldest son. "I wonder how many other mothers suffer such harsh treatment from the hands of their sons!"

"Mater, much of what you claim to endure today is a result of behaviour and choices of the past. I have spent the last few years rescuing the Manor with the help of loyal servants following the despicable actions of Quentin." Tension laced his words as he strove to remain civil towards his mother and her selfish manner. "Father would have been devastated, as well as angry, at the lack of family loyalty blatantly displayed by his youngest son, whole heartedly supported by you!"

"Tssk!" Disdainfully, Lady Araminta got to her feet, head held high, nose pointing to the sky she swished the skirt of her elaborate gown and made a pointed exit from the room.

"I apologize for my mother's appalling manners."

Delphine gave him a knowing smile. "I soon got the measure of your mother and when I married your brother I laid down rules and gave her boundaries which she adhered to or else she moved out. I loved your brother despite his failings..." Her voice broke and for the first time Ralph witnessed a vulnerability in his sister-in-law.

"I am so sorry. It was not my intent to distress you."

Delphine shook her head and wiped the tears from her eyes. "Quentin was a charming, passionate man but I soon learned that his habitual wilfulness was fully endorsed by an indulgent parent. He found it difficult to break the habit of a lifetime. Following our marriage he agreed to attend church services with me. St John's vicar, the godly man you met so recently, befriended him and in recent months they met frequently for discussions on faith. Quentin's heart was changing..." Delphine's voice broke. She stifled a sob. "...and the morning of the storm he was under such conviction he was determined to get to St Johns to kneel at the altar, repent of his failings and surrender his life to God."

Ralph laid a hand upon her shoulder. "I am so sorry for your loss, Delphine, but glad Quentin finally recognized his need of salvation."

Delphine gave him a weak smile. "That is my greatest consolation. Araminta tries to indulge Alberto, but I am determined she will not shape him into a miniature Quentin with her spoiling."

"I will insist she return to England with me if that is what you would prefer."

Delphine shook her head. "I have engaged a tutor for my son. A fine young man whom I believe will not only educate Alberto's mind but also instil worthwhile ideals in his heart. Your mother's influence will have a minimal effect on my son. He will also be mixing with other boys of his age, sons of my friends who will be joining him in his studies. Of late Araminta spends a great deal of her time in the north of the island with cronies of her ilk whose company she craves so her sway will have less impact on Alberto."

Ralph could not cease to be amazed at Delphine's perception and grasp of his mother's manipulative wheedling yet remain unfazed by it. He bowed his head in acknowledgement.

"I will endeavour to sort out this mess to your best advantage," he assured her.

"Just don't take away my purpose for living," her dark set eyes pleaded.

In bed that night sleep eluded Ralph. Dawn would bring his return journey to England, and he had yet to reach a definite decision regarding the plantation's future. Night-time sounds encroached upon his troubled thoughts. Frogs and crickets engaged in their normal activities unhindered by human difficulties.

Delphine was so self-assured. He knew her dream was to retain all the property and pass it on to Quentin's son as a successful enterprize when he attained his majority. But how was that going to be possible with all the debt Quentin had accrued? Much had been repaid thanks to his sister-in-law's careful stewardship, but some still remained.

In his short acquaintance with her Ralph had ascertained that Delphine was a determined and driven lady. He had seen that it was this attribute that motivated her desire to see the plantation thrive and succeed, to support Quentin in this endeavour and ensure his debt was paid and prove the

Barbados land profitable. Failure was not in her vocabulary. Love prompted her actions. Her declaration of love for his brother surprised him. He sincerely hoped that love had been reciprocated.

Ralph tossed in his bed. The window was wide open, yet still it was so hot. How he longed for home. Clean, frosty air where he could breathe freely. He ached for Marion's presence; her calm, reassuring approach to dealing with problematic people and situations. Right now, home and Marion seemed as far away as eternity.

Eternity! What a reminder, Lord! Such a rounding call! Forgive my negligence to come to You with these issues. Hear my prayer, O Lord, to direct and control my thoughts and actions to deal with all these matters in accordance with Your will and design.

The following morning Ralph stood with his bags packed awaiting the carriage that was to convey him across the island to the harbour at Bridgetown. His sister-in-law came forward to wish him farewell and safe travel.

"Are you a praying man, Lord de Vessey?"

His lordship did not express the surprize the question evoked but a smile creased his features. "I asked you to call me Ralph," he teased. "The answer to your question is yes, I am."

"Do you think God hears our prayers? Does He really listen?"

"Absolutely."

"But..." Ralph held up his hand as Delphine was about to fire another question at him.

"However, I find He doesn't always give us what we ask for when we request it, nor in the manner we expect it. Otherwise, we would never learn to trust and depend upon

His wisdom to know what is best for us."

"But you and I may be praying for different things with regard to the issues we have been discussing this week."

Compassion filled Ralph's heart. The anguish she felt was reflected in Delphine's eyes. "The Bible tells us that the prayers of God's people are held up in bowls before the throne and affect the worship of heaven. The Almighty hears all our petitions. I assure you I will consider prayerfully all aspects of matters relating to the future of the plantation before reaching a final decision. I acknowledge your concern but believe our prayers really do make a difference and will ultimately result in a harmonious outcome rather than a discordant one."

***

Ralph glanced around his study. It was so good to be home. The memory of stifling heat and tossing waves did not sit well with him and he had no desire to repeat either experience. As he absorbed the ambience of the familiar surroundings thankfulness washed over him. The top of his desk was unusually tidy, no papers strewn across it. Unbidden the palm of his hand slid over the polished wooden surface.

"I am sure that is not an indication work hasn't continued in my absence." He knew how conscientious his staff were. Their reliability was impeccable.

He shivered as he glanced at the clock on the mantle shelf. It was ten minutes to seven o'clock. Soon he would be having breakfast with his wife. Winter was coming on apace and although a fire had been laid awaiting his return it had yet to be lit. No one had known the hour of his arrival, yet Hanson had been at the front door to greet him. *Soon the household will be aware of my presence.* A baby's cry pierced the morning silence.

He rushed out of the study and bounded up the stairs two at a time and pushed open the Nursery door. A scene of total serenity greeted his homesick eyes. Marion was seated nursing a baby. He saw a tiny suckling infant nestled in his mother's arms. His heart leapt. "My child!"

Marion turned as she heard the voice of her husband. A smile lit up the whole of her face.

"Oh, Ralph! You're home!"

In a moment she and the babe were enveloped in his arms. Tears of joy flowing down their cheeks.

"Thank God you're safe."

"I'm sorry it took so long but the storm delayed our arrival."

"You're here now."

Ralph tenderly held her face in his hands and silenced her voice as he kissed her lips then gently wiped away the cascade of tears. With his hands upon her shoulders he held Marion at arm's length as he gazed down at the baby in her arms.

"Ralph, meet your son."

"My son! He's perfect."

"John, this is your Papa."

"You called him John."

"John Edmund Ralph. That is what we agreed."

Ralph gazed in wonder. He could not take in enough of this precious child.

"Has he been christened?"

"No, I awaited your homecoming, but Parson Wisbey will arrange the ceremony whenever you desire."

Ralph's arm moved around her shoulders, and he held her close. How he had missed this precious woman. The love of his heart, the light of each day, the joy of his existence.

"I missed you." He kissed the top of her head, his free hand caressing her hair which was tumbling freely down her back. "I can't tell you how good it feels to be home."

Her eyes spoke volumes as she looked up at him and smiled.

"I'll get Annie to settle John, then I will be down to share breakfast with you." Marion, ever conscious of practical matters, called immediately for Nannie but Ralph knew it was his wife's way of saying I can't wait to be alone with you and make up for the time we have been apart.

"I'll take a peek at the girls before going down."

"Tread quietly or Rosamund will wake the household."

Subsequent squeals from the girls' nursery proved her certainty correct as a childish shriek broke the morning stillness, "Papa, ooh, my Papa."

As girlish arms were boisterously flung around his neck Ralph's eye caught the fleeting exit from the Nursery of the waif of a young woman. He did a double take. "Annie?"

CHAPTER THIRTY-TWO

"So, they leave their work..."

"Marion, what on earth is wrong with Annie? Is she ill? Has Doctor Cooper seen her?" Lord Ralph shared his concern over Annie's appearance when Marion joined him for breakfast.

"I suspect it is an affair of the heart."

"Young Fred Bemment, I suppose?"

Marion nodded.

"Having witnessed maltreatment of loyal people in our service in Barbados I am convinced that we have a responsibility to ensure the welfare of all in our employ."

Shocked by her husband's response Marion replied indignantly, "But I haven't mistreated Annie."

Ralph reached out a hand to her arm to calm his wife's agitation. "I'm not suggesting that you have, but just consider for a moment how those young people have for some while been wholeheartedly involved in their tasks for the de Vessey family which has left precious little time for them to conduct a proper courtship. I am anxious that we treat all our people with courtesy and care."

Slowly Marion nodded her head. "You're right. They are both conscientious in carrying out their duties."

Ralph placed down his coffee cup. "Caring for our children and affairs around the estate every waking moment leaves little time for themselves. I suggest they are given a holiday. Surely arrangements can be made to cover their obligations?"

"Mm...mm, I expect so," Marion murmured thoughtfully.

"I think time away from their responsibilities will hopefully allow them opportunity to resume their friendship." Ralph spoke decisively.

"I believe they were contemplating marriage when they were appointed to their new roles."

"But that was years ago. They've obviously become so emersed in their new responsibilities their personal desires have been set aside or abandoned."

"You're right. We have expected too much of them and encroached on their loyalty. It is time we readdressed this situation on their behalf. Is there an estate cottage currently available?"

Ralph got up, stood behind Marion's chair, put his hands upon her shoulders and planted a kiss upon the top of her head.

"How I've missed you, my dear; missed your practical approach to matters. However, Jenner is the authority on tenant property matters, not me."

Marion turned and smiled into his dearly loved face.

"Yet it took your absence to pick up on something I should have noted. Annie is so efficient and obliging I fear I have leaned on her, taken her dependability and availability for granted."

"She has filled Nannie Biddle's shoes admirably, hasn't she?"

"Yes, I can't fault her care of our children but sorr..."

Ralph silenced her with a kiss. "No more recriminations.

We'll do our best to encourage a satisfactory solution. I regret I must make a move to tend estate affairs. You speak with Annie, and I will talk to Fred."

"Yes dear."

Lord, I don't know what to do with this one. I guess I'll leave it in Your hands for the time being, as I should with all things, Ralph prayed as he prepared to take up the reins of estate affairs again and initiate the sale of the Barbados plantation.

However, Marion was perturbed that in so short a time away her husband had noted a deterioration in Annie's well-being and demeanour that she had missed. She determined to set in motion changes to the nursery routine in response to Ralph's suggestions that would hopefully benefit Annie.

Both Ralph and Marion hoped that time away from their duties would give Annie and Fred opportunity to resolve whatever has gone wrong in their relationship.

Lord Ralph reluctantly took his leave from Marion, withdrawing from the tranquillity of the breakfast room, to meet up with Marcus Reydon Capps and Elias Jenner in the estate office to discuss the disposition of the Barbados Plantation and his desire to have them travel out to the West Indies to carry out his wishes. He explained conversations he had held with his sister-in-law, the overseer and landowners adjoining the de Vessey property, such as the Codrington estate, who had expressed interest in some acreage.

"It will be quicker to travel from here by railway, rather than stagecoach, along the route Peto instigated from Lowestoft to get the freshly landed fish to Manchester by tea-time. Stephenson's line will then get you to Liverpool."

When the necessary arrangements were in place the men

left their work and set off for Liverpool to board the next ship sailing to Barbados. Lord Ralph ensured they had clear instructions on how to proceed in the matter of sale and drawing up of documents deeding the remaining property to Quentin's son on his maturity.

"Do speak with Delphine. She is the one who holds the reins of management. I no longer want the responsibility of the holding in Barbados so wish to relinquish all interest in the property. Quentin's widow seems a very capable woman, well able to maintain and administer what will remain to the best advantage, enabling us to offset the outstanding deficit Quentin owes to the Newton Westerby Estate from the funds the sale realizes."

Following their departure Lord Ralph sent for George Kemp to attend him in the estate office and discussed how Fred's responsibilities could be apportioned between Stan and Seth during Fred's absence. He then spoke with Fred about taking a holiday.

"Oh, sir, oi can't be doin' that," was Fred's immediate response.

"Why not?"

"'Cos Mr Jenner be away."

"And why is that a problem?"

His face suffused by shock Fred spluttered, "There be no one to manage the estate."

"Young man, you and Mr Jenner work admirably together to ensure that all aspects of Newton Manor run smoothly. All the cogs of the wheel of management are in place. Do you think they will suddenly cease working due to your absence for one week?"

Flabbergasted into silence Fred eyed the Squire as though he had taken leave of his senses.

"Stan and Seth will attend to essential day to day matters and, because of your meticulous oversight, all else will continue as usual." Fred remained quiet, ruminating how that could possibly work.

"The Good Book reminds us of the importance of taking rest from our labours. You have worked exceptionally hard for my family which is appreciated, but you need to take time now for yourself, your family, and your young lady." Ralph threw in that reference to Annie then waited a moment for it to sink in. Fred fidgeted, anxious to be getting on with the tasks for the day, particularly as his workload had now been increased, to allow for acquainting Stan and Seth with the duties they will be responsible for in his absence.

"Have you given thought to accepting the tenancy of the estate cottage that comes with your position as under-steward?"

His lordship really was throwing him unexpected surprizes this morning, bringing to the forefront of his mind a number of issues that he hadn't given serious thought to for some while.

Fred shook his head.

"Consider carefully all that I have spoken about, Mr Bemment. Your holiday will commence at the end of this week."

"Yus sir."

In the meantime Lady Marion walked into the nursery to have a word with Annie.

"Nannie, I want you to take time for a holiday. You have worked incredibly hard this year you deserve a break to recoup your energy. All will be well in the Nursery, I am sure, in your absence."

Annie nodded her head uncertainly in acknowledgement of her Ladyship's directive.

"Prepare Ethel for her responsibilities during your time off. It will be an opportunity to see your training put into practise. I am sure Louisa Kemp will come in each day to assist after George has gone to school."

"Yus, m'lady." Annie stood twisting her hands in front of her, but while the Mistress was issuing further instructions, her mind was running round in circles calculating all the plans she would need to put in place before taking days off.

Ethel was becoming an able assistant in the Nursery, but would she cope in her absence and keep abreast of all the girls' needs as well as tend to baby John. The nursery maid was good at dealing with the children one at a time, but would she remember to think and plan ahead for each of them at the same time. *She will look after Averil an' John well when Rosamund an' Judith be in the schoolroom with Miss Peskett , ur...m, Mrs Bemment. She be excellent with rumbunctious Rosamund on her own, but God only knows how she will manage the other three as well.*

Annie's thoughts continued to pile on top of each other and weighed down on her shoulders like boulders. *Ma would advise me to trust in You, God, to lead an' guide me, but You sometimes seem so far away, and I doan't want to mess this up for her ladyship.*

"...commence at the end of this week."

Annie gulped. *So soon!*

Over the next few days Lord Ralph strolled around his estate, conversed with his employees, asked after their families and checked work was going well. He pulled his muffler closer around his neck. Crisp, cold mornings so indicative of the changing weather patterns of English seasons seemed much more preferable to the stifling heat of Barbados. Moments on his own, whether on foot or horseback allowed for opportunity to mull over recent decisions he had made, his brother's untimely passing and, his mother's dismissive attitude towards him and his family and the Newton Manor Estate. Ralph looked forward to the evenings when he could spend time with his wife around the hearth of a blazing fire relating incidents, thoughts and feelings concerning his experience in Barbados, or precious moments at the beginning of a new day when he could share with Marion around the morning breakfast table about the joy of their newborn son.

"Marcus Capps recommended that rather than sell off part of the plantation we put the whole of the property into the hands of Quentin's widow and let Delphine pay a premium to the Newton Estate coffers until the debt is repaid in full. Then, when that is achieved reassess the situation. But having given serious consideration to Delphine's circumstances, and ours, I prefer to have done with any links to our forebears past. To enslave human beings in such a way seems to me barbaric and I wholly support the Abolition Act. I granted freedom to all the workers on the de Vessey Plantation which Delphine endorsed, and the overseer reluctantly agreed to. Some of the best workers have agreed to continue to work as freed men and women under Delphine's direction. I know that when they heard of my intent a number of the other plantation owners harshly criticised my action. However I have instructed Marcus to draw up papers to hand to each freed person to legalise their status.

"I warned the overseer that if this was not implemented

he would be out of a job and lose his tied home. It will be some time before Marcus Capps and Elias Jenner reach Barbados shores, so he will have a few weeks to prove he is a man of his word.

"Mother kept warning me to leave well alone as life is far different there to what it is in England. I could see that by the way blacks were treated by the whites. They are considered of no account apart from as working machines to be lorded over, machines without feelings. I fear if the overseer is not true to his word and has to be let go, Delphine, who is of mixed race, may struggle to hold her own in a dominant white male economy, now Quentin is gone. Her right-hand man is Jacob, a stalwart loyal servant, a fine African Christian who knows the business inside out but whose voice would not be heard in such a bigoted society.

"I am torn. On the one hand I desire to relinquish all involvement with affairs out there, but on the other I don't want to leave Quentin's widow in an impossible position. Whilst I was in Barbados it all seemed clear-cut but travelling home has given me time to rethink the situation and consider possible repercussions."

"Edith would tell us to pray about the situation," Marion spoke quietly.

Ralph smiled. "Yes, you're right. What would we do without her timely reminders. My mind is tangled and constantly goes round in circles. I can't find a clear focus."

Marion studied the strong face of the man sitting across from her. The Bajun sun had burnished his cheeks with a ruddy glow but worry lines creased his forehead. She could see the matter laid heavy upon her husband's mind. Ralph rose from the table and walked across the room. Tenderly he placed a hand upon Marion's shoulder.

"I am so pleased to be home, my dear. Sorry I was absent when John was born, but delighted we have a son. Thank you for your listening ear."

Marion turned and smiled up at him as she put her hand upon his and squeezed it affectionately.

"I'll go and sit in the chapel for a while. The calmness and coolness of that place frequently brings peace and clarity to my mind and heart."

CHAPTER THIRTY-THREE

"...and homeward bound..."

Within moments Ralph had covered the short distance between the morning room and the family chapel and was seated in a pew deep in thought and prayer. The rays of morning sunshine moved round and burst through the window depicting Jesus as the Good Shepherd. Unbidden Ralph's eye was drawn to it. The words of Psalm 23 darted into his mind, 'The Lord is my Shepherd, I shall not want...He leadeth me...'

Dear Lord, as You have guided me in decisions in the past lead me now to do the right thing with regard to the situation in Barbados.

He looked up again at the brightly lit stained glass window. 'I am the Good Shepherd' meandered into his thinking continuing with 'I know My sheep and My sheep know Me.'

You know those who follow You and lead them along the correct path.

Suddenly, Ralph had a burning desire to get out on the farm amongst the sheep and watch Duncan, the shepherd, at work, observe the interaction between him and the animals in his care.

Ralph strolled thoughtfully to the stables. He chatted with Stan and Caleb as they saddled his horse. When ready he mounted Prince and rode across the land of his estate feeling humbled that the soil beneath him had been tended by loyal servants for generations for the benefit of his forebears. *I wonder if those faithful people were treated as well as they treated our property or was harshness and brutality meted out to them as it has been to our workers in Barbados?* The maltreatment of those who worked on the de Vessey plantation and the cruelty they endured really concerned him. "Leave well alone." His mother's constant admonition darted like an arrow into his thoughts. But he couldn't leave it alone nor brush aside what he had witnessed in Barbados. *Continuously whipping weary and broken bodies in this day and age is barbaric. Yet my mother and others, including the overseer, consider it normal behaviour, and the workers seem to expect such treatment. But it is not right!* Words of Parson Wisbey from the previous Sunday's sermon leapt up into his mind, clear and plain. "We are all one in Christ Jesus, male and female, Jew or Gentile" Subconsciously Ralph added English or Bajun, black or white. As he sat aloft Prince and watched Duncan issue instructions to the sheepdog with calls and whistles Ralph marvelled at the response of the dog as he rounded up the sheep.

Father God, forgive me. I realize that I neglected to seek Your counsel with regard to the plantation situation whilst in Barbados. I made snap decisions and never truly listened to Your voice despite assuring Delphine I was a praying man. Like the admonition in Proverbs I stopped listening to instruction from You and strayed from the Word of Knowledge –'Cease to hear instruction, my son, and you will stray from the words of knowledge. I seek now to 'Trust in the You, Lord, with all my heart and lean not on my own understanding.'

It is clear to me that my sister-in-law needs the means to provide not only for her family but those in her employ, yet without all the land Delphine's economic means will be greatly reduced. She has godly people around her whom I have reason to believe will stand by her and continue to serve the plantation well. The only person I have misgivings about is the overseer who seems less than sincere in the correct implementation of the Abolition Act intent on continuing to mete out brutal treatment to those loyal workers.

Purposefully Ralph rode Prince back towards the stables. *I have watched Duncan lead sheep from one field to another pasture. It is incredible how the sheep dog acts upon his calls and the sheep respond to his movement. As Duncan opened the gate they followed his direction. Duncan does precisely what the job description of his roll states, he shepherds and leads those in his care.*

Ralph paused to process his feelings.

Forgive me, Lord God, for trying to craft the outcome of other people's lives. That is exhausting! I need to acknowledge You are in control of every aspect of life and I don't have to take charge of every situation, here or in Barbados.

I know now what I must do. Dear God, help me to practise what I profess and lead all those in my employ and care with honest diligence under Your direction.

On his return to his study in the Manor House the Squire sent for his under-steward.

"Mr Bemment, I want you to arrange for a telegraph to be sent to the Captain of the ship Marcus Capps and Mr Jenner are due to sail on to recall them back to Newton

Westerby Manor, immediately, prior to its leaving Liverpool docks for the West Indies."

"I'll attend to the matter straightaway, your lordship."

"Emphasize the urgency."

"Yus, sir."

"How are arrangements going for your days off?"

"Foine, sir. Juss foine."

After Fred left to fulfil his errand Lord Ralph dug out a battered box stuffed towards the back of the lowest shelf behind his desk marked Barbados Plantation. He blew dust from the top and raised the lid. One by one he carefully lifted out fragile, yellowed documents.

"I don't think these have seen the light of day for quite a while," he murmured to himself. "Some are barely decipherable." Painstakingly Ralph closely scrutinized every page. He was so engrossed he failed to hear Peters enter with the coffee tray.

He absorbed the historic information, intrigued, yet disgusted by the apparent involvement of his ancestors in the slave trade. Ralph rubbed a hand across his eyes. The strain of concentration, deciphering the almost ineligible script, was causing his head to throb. Then, one sheet caused him to sit up and gasp. He read the letter again and again. Troubled by its contents he rose and pulled the bell. Gazing contemplatively out of the window he stood silent and still. *This is staggering, appalling! My family were instigators of this atrocity! Oh, Lord, how can such injustice be made right?*

Ralph turned as the door creaked and the butler unobtrusively entered the study.

"Hanson, have Peters bring fresh coffee. I have neglected what she brought in previously which has gone cold. Would you also see if Lady Marion is free to join me?"

Hanson inclined his head. "Yes m'lord."

Lady Marion arrived at the study door as Peters was manoeuvring the coffee tray. Graciously she held open the door. His lordship smiled as his wife moved into the room.

"My dear, thank you for coming. Please read this." He waited while Marion perused the proffered paper.

"Oh, Ralph! It's happened before."

Silence hung between them for some moments before Ralph confirmed his wife's observation, a break in his voice.

***

Later that day receipt of the telegraph was acknowledged and the return of Marcus Capps and Elias Jenner confirmed. This news brought relief to Lord Ralph.

Over supper he shared the decisions he had come to with his wife. "I am relinquishing all ownership of the de Vessy holdings in the West Indies. We have come through the worst of the crisis Quentin created for the Newton Westerby Manor Estate, thanks to our hardworking staff. We don't need the income from the Plantation, but Delphine does. I intend to bequeath the entire property to Alberto under the administration of Delphine, for her lifetime, with the proviso that he is properly trained in the management of the estate when he is old enough, land, people, production, as well as financial matters.

"Although my mother has a strong inclination to spoil that grandson in the same manner she spoiled her youngest son I believe her daughter-in-law is strong enough to resist pressure from Mater and not allow Alberto to become a replica of his wastrel father. She has already put in place plans for his education."

Ralph felt a burden lift from his shoulders.

Lady Marion could see that having reached a decision worry lines that had creased her husband's brow since his return from Barbados were now erased. "That seems a wise decision."

"Whilst out there I was astounded to learn that Quentin had been in conversation with men in Barbados intent on building a rail track across the island from east to west, to get cut sugar cane to mills more quickly, then from there to the Bridgetown harbour, because once cut canes deteriorate very rapidly."

Marion shook her head sorrowfully, "It's hard to believe that Quentin once again was contemplating selling off de Vessy land without consultation. Leaving the plantation to his son means it will remain in the family but not be your responsibility."

"Yes, I feel as though I can now pause and enjoy the knowledge that God will sustain them and us."

On his return from Liverpool Marcus Capps drew up documents to that effect.

Elias Jenner also took on board Lord Ralph's suggestion that Seth and Stan become under stewards responsible for areas of estate management at Newton Westerby Manor that were their particular area of expertise. Mr Jenner was made to recognize that he had been shifting far too much onto Fred's youthful shoulders.

"The workload needs to be apportioned more fairly. There are but twenty-four hours in a day and everyone needs time to eat, sleep and recoup energy as well as work."

"I understand, my lord," the estate steward acquiesced.

Whilst agreeing to the terms set out in the documents forwarded to her by Marcus Capps Delphine felt it needful to send the current year's instalment of Quentin's repayment debt to the Newton Westerby Manor Estate. Lord Ralph was reluctant to accept it, but Delphine insisted.

"That will bring closure to our association."

Consequently, the Squire decided to reward the staff whose loyalty and hard work had enabled the Estate to recover from the unprecedented crisis.

"My word, what a surprize!" was a sentiment expressed by many of the recipients. The household staff voiced grateful thanks for the Squire's generosity but those workers who were struggling to make ends meet, astonished by such unexpected largesse, accepted the gift with tears pouring down their faces.

"We'll be able to pay the rent this month."

"Oi'll be able to buy some staples, come market day."

"Jimmy, yew'll hev new boots fer the winter."

Their joy knew no bounds and reverberated through the community. The unexpected gift would enable them to eke out their meagre income a little further through the winter months. "Oi'll ask Charlie to drop orf a sack o' coal."

Lord Ralph intimated to Mr Jenner that he had also decided to reinstate the staff Christmas ball. "This will give everyone something to look forward to and prepare for after enduring so much austerity." Not only had family hospitality and entertainment been stopped but estate staff celebrations such as harvest barn dances, May Day, Summer and Christmas balls curtailed. Immediately, Elias Jenner apportioned responsibility to his under stewards and delegated tasks to the senior household staff to ensure they had sufficient time to prepare for this momentous event. As word spread so excitement rose.

Alone, in the stillness of his study Ralph thoughtfully added duplicate copies of the latest plantation correspondence and documentation into the battered box containing the historic papers relating to the Barbados Plantation knowing the originals would be archived at the solicitors. *There is no way I can right the wrongful actions of a former banished ancestor involved in the slave trade, but I pray that the recent decisions I have made will benefit the current workers on the plantation.*

***

Annie had continued with her daily routine to the end of the week vague suggestions flitting in and out of her mind as to why the Mistress was insisting she take a holiday at this time. Gentle Ethel was competent under direction, but she had no experience with babies and Master John was so newly born and required careful handling. You needed eyes in the back of your head to keep abreast of Averil's explorative nature. Rosamund took all a bodies' concentration to keep up with her incessant questions and activities whilst Judith was content to stay put she demanded constant attention to redo her hair, put on her shoes or read aloud her book, or anything else she decided required immediate action.

Just thinking about the children's demands made Annie feel weary. *Perhaps that's why oi require a holiday. Maybe m'lady sees that oi need to slow down an' live life at a different pace for a while.*

A room in the West Wing had been offered to her but

Annie chose instead to return home to the loft house above the stables. Therefore, unbeknownst to her, Lady Marion had arranged with Edith for a spare mattress to be conveyed from the West Wing to their home where between them George and Edith adapted their living space to accommodate their returning daughter. No longer a little girl able to fit into a cot at the foot of their bed but a grown woman with responsibility for young ones in her care, they curtained off a space in the left-hand alcove beside the hearth.

"Oi believe it be fer the best that Annie hev a complete break from the Manor," George commented.

"Yus, if she hear that babe cry in the night she be wantin' to be up an' attendin' to him," Edith agreed.

Her parents determined to ensure Annie had opportunity for rest and relaxation in body, mind and spirit.

Having realized the wisdom of Lady Marion's instruction Annie began to look forward to returning home.

CHAPTER THIRTY-FOUR

"Kowing with God..."

The tang of late autumn had been replaced by the chill of winter, north easterlies carrying icy air from the Artic. Annie shivered. It was an inclement day darkened by a drizzling fog emanating from the sea. Not an ideal start to a holiday. However, her spirit was not dampened. As she opened the back door of Newton Manor the scent of damp grass rushed to meet her, mingling with the earthy odour of fallen leaves, the whiff of a wet yard and salty sea. Her valise was packed and rested by her booted feet. She clamped her hat tighter upon her head and pulled up her coat collar, picked up her valise and stepped down the backdoor step. Eagerly she set out towards the loft house.

She had quietly exited her room so as not to disturb the children. Last evening she had explained to them she was going to be away for a few days. There had been a few tears. Rosamund stamped her foot in protest. "I don't want you to go Nannie Annie."

"Now, yew be good fer Nannie Ethel," Annie admonished her. "Oi look forward to hearing about yow'n adventures this week, in the Nursery an' the schoolroom, an' oi'll share moine wi' yew when oi return."

Despite the dull, greyness of the morning Annie viewed her surroundings with a lightness of heart. "Obviously 'cos oi not be pressed down wi' the burden o' duties." Lady Marion's words echoed in her mind, "All will be well." *Oi'd best believe that* she whispered. She pushed back her shoulders and lifted her head knowing with God all would be well.

"Annie, Annie," a voice called after her. She halted her footsteps and turned. Through the foggy gloom Peggy came flying along the path.

"Slow down Peggs or yew'll be a'fallin' on the slippery path."

Breathlessly Peggy laughed and pushed a parcel into Annie's hand.

"Juss a morsel to see yew on yourn way."

"Oh, Peggs, oi'm sure Ma will feed me," Annie joined in her friend's mirth.

"M'gift to yew as yew commence yourn holiday. Fred also be hevin' days orf this week an' say he be a'callin' on yew."

Annie's eyes lit up at this news. "Oi'll look forward to seein' Fred. Now, git yew back, Peggy, afore yew catch a chill. Thanks fer m'treat."

Peggy waved and returned to her chores in the Manor kitchen. Annie held the packet carefully in her free hand. "Oi guess this be one o' Pegg's delicious pâtisserie confections." Pale sunlight wavered through the morning fog casting the sky in a luminous mist above the distant spire of St. Andrews church as she continued the journey towards home, her heart and mind churning at the thought of spending time with Fred.

She mulled over all she knew of him. *Such a committed young man which be why oi hev seen soo li'tle o' him.* She had loved Fred for as long as she could remember. Loved him for his imagination and humour, his kindness towards her, his thoughtfulness for the needs of others, his care of nature, particularly the horses, his knowledge and understanding of the countryside, his willingness to apply himself to new things. She enjoyed his company. She admired the way he had submitted to the tutelage of Elias Jenner and absorbed skills necessary for running so large an estate as the de Vessey land. Annie marvelled at Fred's zest for tackling each problem as it arose, methodically and in detail, whether to do with animals or land. Above all she admired his declared intention to honour God in all he said and did. "He hev saved me from my sins so oi will allus gi' Him thanks. The Good Lord hev blessed us wi' beauty an' bounty. It be ow'n responsibility to treat it carefully an' wi' respect."

However, at times, Fred's dedication to duty rankled. "His busyness with estate affairs gi' us li'tle time together."

Trees and buildings blurred in the fog, air was damp on her face, tears clouded her vision. Around her everything was still. Tiny droplets clung to her coat and the icy wind worked its way through the layers of clothing to chill her skin. Annie raised her pace to a brisk step taking care not to slip on ice glazed puddles. Activity warmed her, cloudy breaths came in quicker bursts.

As she reached the cobbles leading to the stables a watery sun was doing its utmost to push through the fog. The freezing drizzle had almost stopped. The cold made her eyes glisten. Annie plonked her valise on the bottom step of the stone staircase that led up to her parent's home and placed her confectionary delight with care on the top. She took time to quickly wipe the moisture from her face.

Voices and sounds of activity emanated from the stables.

Her feet were drawn to wander down this familiar haunt of her childhood. She peered through the open stable doors. Horses snickered and ambled towards her to nuzzle a friendly hand. "Sorry oi hev nuthen to offer yew, today." Faces of unfamiliar stable lads stared at her with suspicion till she reached a stable where Stan was working.

"Mornin' Annie. Be yew well? Yourn Pa be tending Blossom in stall six."

"Thanks, Stan. Oi be very well. Oi'll goo an' foind Pa. Be Blossom not soo good?"

"Touch o' arthritis."

"She muss be quoite an age. She wuz around when I wuz a li'tle gal."

Stan nodded. Annie moved along the stalls, captivated by the familiarity of a space that time had not altered, sharing greetings and pleasantries with the stable lads she knew.

She peered through the open top part of the stable door of stall six. "Mornin' Pa," she called softly.

George looked up from his position by the side of the suffering horse. In no time at all he was at the stable door, leant across with arms open wide, to embrace his beloved daughter.

"Oh, ma dear gal, oi be roite glad to see yew. Ma hev breakfast riddy fer us. Fred will goo wi' yew. Oi'll be along shortly." He turned his attention back to the horse.

Annie quickly straightened her hat that her father's exuberance had knocked askew. Her eyes had been all on her father and not lighted on Fred crouching in the dimness at the back of Blossom's stall. Fred stood up and looked directly at her, a depth of feeling in his warm brown eyes that caught Annie in the chest and sent a thrill down her arms.

"Hello, Annie." Something trembled between them, fragile yet precious. Annie held his gaze as he moved towards her. Fred drew a breath as if to say something more instead as he exited the stable door he reached to take her chilled hand in his. As they walked along the cobbles he drew her to his side to whisper into her ear.

"Fr...ed," a voice shouted out from one of the stables and broke the tender thread between them. Lowering Annie's hand Fred turned to respond to the calling voice.

Annie's shoulders slumped. *What had Fred been about to say? Were they nivver to hev moments to themselves?*

The icy breeze swirled across the stable yard. Annie stood shivering as Fred spoke with the stable lad. Disappointment pinged the pit of her stomach. Reluctantly her feet turned to make their way homeward, but Fred reached out and grabbed her arm. "...not available this week. Yew muss speak wi' Seth. He be a'dealin' wi' those estate matters."

Feeling Fred's gaze upon her Annie drew her attention back to the moment instead of lamenting past setbacks.

"Oi asked yourn Pa's permission to court yew," he blurted out drawing her closer to his side.

"Ye...w did?" Annie gulped. Her heart somersaulted. She smiled up at him with tears in her eyes. For once she was lost for words. Her free hand reached up to the crinkled lines radiating from the corners of his eyes, eyes that conveyed a message of love.

Just as Annie was impressed by Fred's determination to improve and apply himself to learning all there was to know about running such a vast estate Fred was attracted by Annie's resolve to stand by her beliefs, admired the way she informed her mind, yet did not take on airs and graces. She was still the opinionated friend of their childhood, open and honest. She still spoke her mind though it was not tinged with the sharp-tongued brusqueness of her mother but rather suffused with the gentleness of her father. Fred determined to allow nothing to create a wedge between him and Annie, ever again. He recognized in recent times he had shelved the precious closeness with Annie for what he felt was his duty. No more. He needed the sweetness of her presence, the constancy of her faith, love and trust. He believed she was of the same mind.

"By God's help we will make this work, Fred." The tender smile that accompanied Annie's words confirmed his thoughts.

"Yus, we will. Yew loikely know that oi hev toime orf this week."

Annie nodded. "Peggy told me as oi left this morning."

"Come, let's goo fer the breakfast yourn Ma hev riddy fer us. We'll maak plans in the warm." Hand in hand they hurried towards the steps that led up to the loft house eager to share their news with Edith.

"Race yew to the top," Fred teased as he grabbed the valise. Annie chuckled as in a flurry she swiftly reached out to salvage Peggy's gift as it sailed through the air.

Hearing the commotion Edith had the door open by the time they ascended the stone staircase and hustled them in.

"Quick! Quick! Doan't let the heat out," Edith pulled them across the threshold. "Where be George?'

"He be a'comen, Mrs Kemp."

As the wind blew her through the doorway Annie thought, "How li'tle the place hev changed since oi wuz a child."

The same comfortable warmth embraced her as the wholesome smell of breakfast cooking and bread baking mingled with wash-day odours. The same white scrubbed table stood squarely in front of the hearth with the same four chairs tucked underneath. The same spick-and-span-ness testament to her mother's common sense pervaded the space.

"Taak orf yourn sodden garments afore yew taak a chill." Edith's busy hands helped them off with their coats.

"Come yew on an' sit by the fire. Did yew see yourn Pa?"

"Yus, he be attendin' to Blossom an' will be a'comen' shortly."

Edith draped the wet coats across the clothes horse to dry, stirred the gruel, turned over the bacon and checked the bread oven."

"Why yew be washin' a'day, Ma?"

"Wanted to git ahead o' m'sel' but didn't anticipate this wet blustery change in the weather." She put butter and a jug of milk onto the table.

"Oh Ma, it do be winter," Annie laughed as she reached out to warm her hands near the glow of the fire in the stove.

"Ma, Fred hev asked Pa if he moite court me." She smiled shyly at Fred.

Edith raised her eyebrows. "Soo thass why yew be soo quiet, m'bor. Yew'll be a'wantin' all those pennies an' farthin's back now."

Sheepishly Fred grinned at her. Both of them remembering his childhood promise to put aside a little each week from his earnings so that by the time he and Annie wed he would hev sufficient to pay the rent on a cottage.

Thank You, Father, thank You. Edith's prayers flowed

freely as did the joy she passed on to Annie and Fred with a hug that made Fred wrap an arm around her waist and the other across Annie's shoulders. "The Good Lord bless yew wi' all joy, m'dears. May yew be as happy as yow'n Pa an' oi hev bin."

Tears glistened freely.

"Come, there be Pa's footsteps. Let's git breakfast on the table."

***

In the low light of a late afternoon in January snow began to dust the cottage roof tops. By 4 o'clock the wintry sun had slipped away leaving a pale orange glow in the sky and a thickening white blanket spread upon the ground.

"Light the lamp. It nearly be dark alriddy."

"Ma, Ma, look. It be a'snowin'," voices called out in glee as eager faces pressed against cold windowpanes to view the spectacle in a number of village homes. In others, nimble fingers sewed final stitches into new, borrowed or altered garments fashioned for the servants ball. Precious pennies had been saved to purchase material or adornments or reclaim suits from the pawnbrokers so as to be suitably attired for this special occasion.

Excitement rippled like an unseen thread throughout the community spilling over into intense activity at the Big House drawing everyone in a united bond of purpose. The ballroom locked up and unused for too many years was being transformed. Comings and goings tingled with anticipation.

Under instructions from the Squire Mr Jenner had sent out invitations to all the servants and tenants of the estate to attend the revived servants Christmas ball. At Newton

Westerby Manor it had traditionally been held on Twelfth Night following the family's Christmas festivities and given in acknowledgement of service rendered throughout the previous year.

The day finally arrived with a feverish intent. Whilst additional staff had been recruited from the surrounding area for the occasion Cook ensured the kitchen servants were frantically engaged beforehand in preparations for the sweetmeats and savouries that were to grace the buffet table. Beatrice was called in to assist Peggy. Together they worked flat out to produce the pastries and confections that were such a palatable delight.

Alice Housego directed the housemaids in thoroughly cleaning, not only the ballroom with its drapes and furnishings but ancillary rooms and closets, closed up for a number of years, that were now required for use again. The senior footman assigned some of the under footmen to assist with the removing of furniture, climb ladders where necessary to dust and clean out of reach places, take down and replace chandeliers and wall sconces.

Under the auspices of Hanson, Philip Catchpole with other footmen prepared crockery, glassware and supervised table settings on white damask cloths laundered, starched and ironed under Bertha Hanson's watchful eye.

Garden staff brought seasonal fruit and vegetables to the scullery door for Maggie and Cora to prepare prior to being created into soups, terrines and pies by Mrs Sands and her staff.

Her ladyship hovered when plants and fresh blooms were brought in from the glasshouses along with seasonal foliage cut from the garden to ensure they were strategically placed after being skilfully arranged.

Mrs Baldry sent Johnny from Home Farm with additional milk, butter, cheese and cream for the festive supper.

Hanson meticulously concocted punch, Lizzie assisting him when Cook could spare her from the kitchen.

At a given time the hired staff were allowed to assume their responsibilities for the evening as household servants were instructed to "Goo an' git riddy."

"I want to see the ladies in their pretty dresses," Rosamund determinedly stamped her foot. A ball was something out of her experience, one not being held in her lifetime.

"If you are good fer Nannie Biddle yew may peer over the landing balcony fer a short while," Annie promised. The retired Nannie was watching the Squire's children for the evening to enable both Annie and Ethel to attend the ball.

When the ensemble struck up the first notes of the opening dance all eyes were on the Squire to see whom he would choose as his partner to commence proceedings. No one was more surprised than Maggie Saunders, the scullery maid, when Lord Ralph bowed and offered her his hand.

Pressed by the other stable lads Caleb Bemment approached Lady Marion. "My, lady, may oi hev the pleasure o' this dance?"

Fred sidled up to Annie. "Miss Kemp, would yew care to share this dance wi' me?" Her face glowed with joy.

"Certainly, Mr Bemment," she rejoined with a chuckle.

As he drew her to his side Fred whispered, "Oi would loike yew to be by my side fer allus, Annie."

"Yew would?" Annie's eyes sparkled.

Her feet took her automatically through the remainder of the dance, her heart and mind engaged elsewhere.

At the conclusion of the dance Fred kept his hand upon her elbow and steered her towards the full-length window at the furthest side of the ballroom. The curtains had not yet been drawn to allow participants to enjoy the scene being painted in the darkness by the falling snow.

"Oi love yew, Annie. Would yew be my wife?"

"Yus Fred, fer allus."

"Next week?" he said with a twinkle in his eye.

In a flash Annie looked up at him eyes open wide in astonishment. Slowly her lips curved into a smile. "Easter Day," she said decidedly.

CHAPTER THIRTY-FIVE

"...all is safe and sound."

Winter rolled on but it seemed as if spring remained resolutely out of reach. Woodsmoke rose through the cold air. Daylight was early to bed and north easterlies coming in off the sea chilled to the bone. All too soon cockerel's crow pierced the dark stillness to announce dawn. Shivering early risers reluctantly stepped out of bed knowing tasks and animals needed attention that could not be neglected. Milking cows lowed and horses whinnied their morning greeting as milk maids and stable lads sleepily commenced their daily routine.

Frost was still very severe. Complaints abounded on Manor Farm and in the village homes.

"Eggs freeze even when covered closely."

"Oi found the taters froze a few yards from the fire."

"The milk be a block an' the beef be hard."

Yet, beauty abounded to the eye open to see it. As Fred stepped towards the estate office the tracery of a leafless tree as the winking sun sat low in the sky was an exquisite sight. Peach tones merged with steely blue as the delicate spectacle rose across the sea on the distant horizon waking the village to a new day. *Annie would love this vista.*

Although the hedges, trees and empty fields might seem lifeless to a passing stranger to Fred's eyes the delicate watery colour was a foretaste of a vibrancy on the verge of bursting into its spring display. As he walked daylight revealed intricate patterns formed by ice on seedheads, twigs and cobwebs. The turn of the season approached illuminated by gem-like blooms of hundreds of bulbs pushing through their dark wintry bed adjacent to a blanket of promising green shoots in neighbouring fields. Glint of emerging white snowdrops and purple cyclamen sparkled under golden willow wands along the riverbank. Gleaming heads of primroses lit the pathway as he walked towards the stables. *How Annie would delight in this display. I muss bring her along to enjoy this picture o' God's handiwork.*

He quickened his steps to commence a day's work giving thanks for God's goodness.

As the two walked together on their days out around the boundaries of the estate or tramped the footpaths across the Common or strolled along the seashore Fred took her to the spots that had caught his eye so that Annie might appreciate the wonder of nature with him. "God be soo good to us. When out here it seem as if Jesus Himself draws near to us." They also took time to share the stories of their day's activities, became more comfortable in one another's company and fell deeper in love.

Their inner peace and contentment was reflected in the manner they conducted their daily work.

There was an undeniable joy in their relationship. Lady Marion was delighted with the happiness that radiated from Annie whenever Fred was mentioned.

"What a blessing Annie is. She is a conscientious God-fearing young woman who despite the many tragedies and setbacks she has faced in life has by God's good grace come through with a positive attitude to life."

"That is true," her husband agreed. "Annie has proved as dependable in fulfilment of her duties to our family as her mother, Edith."

"How I shall miss her when she and Fred marry. She has truly blossomed since her weeks holiday and has such a pleasing influence on the girls, particularly Rosamund." Marion commented to Lord Ralph over breakfast. "Ethel is a gentle creature and is good with the children, but she lacks Annie's methodical mind and tends to get into muddles. The girls, especially Rosamund, take advantage of that."

"Surely, my dear, you can circumnavigate that issue. You have never been one to hold to convention." Ralph replied, a quirky smile accompanying the mischievous spark in his eyes.

Marion laughed.

"Mater and Quentin are no longer here to criticise your decisions and actions," he added, tongue in cheek.

"I wonder..." Marion bit into her slice of toast her mind engaged elsewhere.

***

The months of courtship quickly passed. Their wedding day approached and to Annie's joy all the preparations for its arrival were complete in good time.

On her afternoon's out Annie's nimble fingers fashioned a simple wedding gown assisted by Edith's experienced hand.

On their permitted courtship days out Fred and Annie worked together on the estate cottage allocated to them. It stood on the main street in the village opposite the market square tucked between Beatrice's home and the wheelwrights, an archway separating it from the latter with a room above that gave views across the village rooftops to the harbour mouth. It had been Jonas Bemment's cottage but stood empty for quite some while. Other hands eagerly assisted whenever they were available. Stan and Amy called in when free after work and Caleb was enticed to join in by the promise of food at Beatie's afterwards. When the family gathered to tackle all the chores next door Beatie prepared a meal while Carrie kept an eye on the children in between her cobbling tasks as Rebekah played with Jeremiah after she returned from school. When she heard the hilarity bursting through the open doors and windows Beatie chuckled and wondered how much work was actually being accomplished. But she knew her brothers well. "They hev a tendency to tease, an' oi can imagine them chasin' one another, throwin' things an' sloshing water everywhere, but oi know they are hard workers an' will tackle all tasks conscientiously even though mixed wi' fun." Peggy also accompanied Annie, when their afternoons off coincided, to lend a hand. She helped Edith take down and wash the curtains. When dry Annie and Edith repaired them while Peggy cleaned the windows and Fred helped to rehang them.

"Yew shouldn't be climbin', yew might fall," he scolded.

"How do yew think jobs git done when yew men are not around?" Edith pointed out.

Peggy and Annie laughed. "We not be helpess, yew know."

Sadly Hester refused to take part in the scrubbing and cleaning of her son's new home, nor acknowledge the upcoming nuptials.

"Why woan't yew come alon' wi' me?" Edith

challenged knowing Hester's refusal to help Fred was because of the cottage's proximity to Beatie's home. She had not seen or had any dealings with Beatie since the day Hester had thrown her daughter out of the family home on hearing she was with child.

"Yew be the one missin' out, m'friend."

Hester pursed her lips.

"Rebekah be a foine li'tle gal, such a joy," Edith continued. Hester ignored her.

Edith let out a sigh. "I pray the good Lord will heal yourn stubborn heart, Hester. Neither Beatie nor that li'tle gal deserve such bitter treatment from yew."

"She should a tho't o' that all those years ago," Hester spat out, "afore she indulged in sin."

"Oh m'dear friend, the Good Book say, 'Judge not' an' Jesus say, 'He that is without sin among you, let him first cast a stone at her.' Beatie wuz wrongly used, Hester."

"Then why did she hev a hole-in-the-corner weddin' if they weren't guilty?"

"Remember the actions o' Joseph to Mary recorded in the Good Book? Colin acted honourably towards Beatie in the same way. Wanted to shield her from disgrace. He loved her an' became a foine father to another man's child."

"Humph!" Hester grunted dismissively.

"Juss gi' tho't to what it say in the Good Book an' pray fer compassion an' understanding."

***

Neglect had left the garden at the cottage an unkempt tangle of weeds, brambles and overgrown plants. However, Annie was keen to clear the overrun plot so that they might grow vegetables and create a run for chickens. "Ma hev promised us some laying hens." Carefully she ventured into the wilderness. "Oh look, there be fruit an' hawthorn trees at the bottom." A robin sat on a branch unperturbed by her presence cocked its head and began to sing. "Ma say the berries from the hawthorn maak a good medicinal drink. Oi'll ask her fer the receipt in readiness fer harvest."

"Yew'll hev to remember to leave some fer the birds," Fred called out teasingly.

***

One afternoon when the de Vessey girls returned from the schoolroom Annie called to them, "Come sit down oi hev suthen to tell yew afore yew hev tea." Rosamund bounded towards her and flounced down beside her. Judith made her way more unhurriedly, Averil toddling close behind her. Annie drew them towards her setting Averil upon her lap.

"On Easter Day oi be gitting married to Fred and we be goin' to live in a different house," she explained quietly.

"Where?" Rosamund demanded.

"A li'tle cottage in the village."

Rosamund thought for a moment. "So we won't see you anymore."

"Oi will be here on Mondays, Wednesdays an' Fridays, so yew will see me then."

"Oh!"

Lady Marion had argued her case with Fred to allow Annie to reduce her working days gradually. "It will have less impact on the children and ease Ethel into her responsibilities. Louisa Kemp will continue to cover occasionally in the nursery after George has gone to school bringing young Kitty with her."

"Will you wear a pretty dress?" asked Judith who was still thinking about the wedding day.

"Yes."

"Can we see it?"

"Oi will come an' see yew arter the chapel service."

Many expected the pair to be married in St Andrew's Church as was the custom, but Annie didn't want the pomp and ceremony that entailed.

"Oi doan't want a lot o' fuss. Juss a simple service celebratin' ow'n commitment to each other afore God," she explained.

"An' the chapel do be ow'n place o' worship," Fred added when they spoke with Reverend Coleman, the chapel minister. He had chosen to return to the chapel services instead of attending St Andrews church with the household staff so that he could accompany Annie.

"You don't have to stick with tradition. Since the introduction of civil registration in 1837 you are no longer compelled to get married in the Parish Church," the minister clarified.

Annie's eyes lit up. "So, we can be legally married in the chapel?"

"Yes," he confirmed.

Annie and Fred's eyes locked.

"Then thass be what we be a'doin'," Fred spoke decisively.

"We'll celebrate our Lord's resurrection with the joy of your union," Reverend Coleman affirmed.

Annie wanted to walk to the chapel with her father, but George thought otherwise.

Quietly he passed on his instructions for Easter morning

to the lads. "Aforehand clean the chaise spick and span. My Edith be a'maakin' a red velvet cushion to goo acrorst the seat an' we'll tack a portion to match along the back. We'll brush Buttercup's coat till it shines. Only the best fer m'gal."

When he had completed his early morning chores in the stables George washed up and changed into his Sunday suit, then waited in the stable yard whilst Edith assisted Annie into her simple dress, affixed a short plain veil in her hair ornamented with marsh marigolds and sweet violets.

With a lump in her throat Edith surveyed her daughter. "M'precious gal, yew look a picture." She stepped back, then reached out a hand to tuck in a stray strand of Annie's hair.

"Will Fred think so?"

"Fred will be delighted wi' yew. He loves yew fer the boo'iful person yew are not how yew look in the clothes yew wear. Remember allus to talk things uvver wi' each other an' nivver let the sun goo down on angry feelin's. Read the Good Book together each evenin'. Fred be the man o' the hus, yew be the manager, but Christ be the head o' the hum.

"This be a reminder," Edith handed Annie a sampler she had worked displaying the words from Proverbs chapter 3 verse 5 :- 'Trust in the Lord with all thine heart and lean not on thine own understanding,' with their names entwined at the bottom.

Spontaneously Annie hugged her mother, "Oh, Ma, thank you. We'll hang it where we can allus see it."

"Oi'll goo maak m'way. Pa be a'waitin' fer yew in the yard."

"Thank you, Ma, fer ev'rything. Yew an' Pa hev allus set

me a foine example an' Fred an' oi plan to follow that pattern to trust the Good Lord fer the days that are set afore us."

"The Good Lord gi' us helpmeets to encourage an' support each other. Now, oi muss be away. Pa will be a' wonderin' what hev happened to yew."

Edith leaned forward and affectionately kissed Annie's cheek. "The Lord bless you, m'gal," she whispered then exited quickly through the door ensuring her daughter didn't see the tears welling in her eyes.

"She be a'comin'," Edith told George as she passed him in the yard. George aware of the glistening eyes caught her hand. "All will be well, m'gal"

Edith nodded. "Yus, by God's good grace. Fred be grown into a foine young man. He'll taak care o' ow'n gal."

They heard the loft house door open. George took in a sharp breath at the lovely sight their daughter made as she descended the stone steps. Edith lifted her skirt and stepped out along the cobbles to reach the chapel ahead of them.

"Oh, Pa! What hev yew done?" The sight of the carriage took Annie's breath away.

"Nuthen but the best fer ma best gal."

George carefully handed Annie up into the beautifully decked chaise and trotted Buttercup towards the chapel to give the wellbeing of his precious treasure into the hands of Fred Bemment, a boy he had known, trained and influenced all his life.

With eyes for only one another their voices rang out clear and true as Annie and Fred pledged their troth.

Not until Reverend Coleman had pronounced them man and wife and they prepared to leave the chapel hand in hand were the couple aware of the size of the congregation that had stayed to witness their nuptials following the Easter service. Smiling to those on the left and then to the right of the central aisle Annie and Fred made their way slowly towards the open door. Tucked in the corner of the back row, hoping she would go unnoticed by anyone, sat Hester.

"Annie, Annie," a shrill voice shouted out.

All heads turned as a figure ran towards the couple.

***

The de Vessey family coach drew up in the front drive. Hanson opened the front door and Philip Catchpole went to assist Lady Marion and the girls to alight following their attendance at the Easter morning service in St Andrews Church.

"Thank you, Catchpole. My husband has elected to walk with our lunch guests and will be along shortly," her ladyship descended onto the steps he had carefully placed. A commotion took place behind her.

"Don't push, Rosamund. Wait your turn."

"Yes, Mama."

Philip held out a hand to assist Judith.

"I can come down on my own," declared Rosamund, pushing away the proffered hand, determined to show off her independence.

Once inside the hall the girls were anxious to make their way to the kitchen knowing Cook would have sweetmeats and milk ready for them.

"Take off your coats, then you may go." Lady Marion instructed. By the time they reached the corridor the pace of their feet had increased three-fold.

"Good morning, Miss Rosamund, Miss Judith. Yew

come fer yourn 'levenses?" Lizzie asked.

Judith nodded.

"Yes please, Lizzie," Rosamund spoke impatiently.

"Had a good service?"

Again Judith nodded in between sips of milk.

"Tedious!" splurted out Rosamund. Cook and Lizzie exchanged a glance with raised eyebrows.

Rosamund drank her milk in one gulp.

"Slow down, Miss."

Rosamund grinned cheekily, the milky moustache adding to the comical look she presented.

She put down the empty receptacle. "I'll race you up, Judith," and off she dashed.

But Judith continued to sip and nibble more daintily, absorbing all the activity of kitchen staff making preparation for the special Easter Day lunch which the girls would be sharing with their parents and their guests in the dining room.

"Come yew on, Miss, hev yew nearly finished?" asked Cook anxious that Lizzie concentrate on her kitchen duties rather than acting as nursery maid.

"Yes, Mrs Sands. Thank you, Lizzie. I will go and find Mama." Demurely she left the busy kitchen at her own pace and somewhat later reached Lady Marion's drawing room. She pushed open the door, but shyness overcame her when she heard voices talking with her mother, changed her mind and wandered off to the nursery.

Ethel glanced up when Judith entered.

"Hello, little lady. Hev yew come to play wi' Averil?"

Judith nodded. Ethel settled the two together then checked on John.

"Where's Rosamund?"

Judith shrugged. “She ran ahead of me.”

Perturbed Ethel shook her head. “But she isn’t here.” She pulled the bell to summons a footman.

“Will yew check Miss Rosamund’s whereabouts. She left the kitchen some toime agoo.”

When he returned with a negative response panic set in.

“Doan’t alarm her ladyship but please set everyone to look for Miss Rosamund.”

“Yus, Nannie Ethel.”

***

“Pa, Pa, look at me.”

Lord Ralph stopped mid-sentence, turned and was astonished to see his daughter waving frantically at him from the wedding carriage, sitting between Fred and Annie.

“Whoa!” Fred pulled the horse to a standstill as they drew abreast with his lordship. Annie climbed down and quietly explained the fiasco of Rosamund’s unexpected appearance in the chapel.

“Oi am soo sorry, sir. Oi hev admonished her for not telling someone where she wuz a’goin’.”

“I wanted to see Annie in her pretty dress,” interrupted Rosamund anxious to express her reason for going to the chapel.

“Oi leave it to yew, sir, to suitably chastise her.”

“My dear Annie, it is I who should be apologising to you for my daughter’s misbehaviour and intrusion into your private celebration. Congratulations Fred. Now, be on your way with this new wife of yours and do cherish her. God bless you both.”

Fred grinned. “Thank yew, sir.” He took up the reins

with one hand and held Annie's hand with the other one as Buttercup trotted towards the loft house and the family repast Edith had prepared.

"Spunky little madam, eh, de Vessey?" commented one of Lord Ralph's companions as they continued their stroll towards the Manor House.

"Wilful and disobedient at times," his lordship responded as he firmly took hold of Rosamund's hand.

Hanson opened the door on their arrival at the Manor.

Rosamund swiftly ran into her mother's open arms. "My darling girl I was so worried."

"Papa is cross."

Marion raised her head. The look she shared with Ralph conveyed the message 'explanations later'.

"Thank God you are safe and sound."

"I'm sorry we are so very late, Hanson, but if it's convenient I believe we would all appreciate lunch."

"Yes, my lord."

Lord Ralph turned towards his errant daughter. "We will say no more about your escapade, Rosamund. A new day will begin at dawn when you can make a fresh start on manners and behaviour."

"But I needed to see Nannie Annie," she rejoined in an emphatic whisper.

POSTSCRIPT

"But oi promised. An' oi allus keep my promises, Mr Bemment."

"Roite, Mrs Bemment," Fred grinned at the company gathered in the loft house, "'Scuse us," and grabbed Annie's hand. "Let us goo."

They tripped down the stone staircase and along the cobbled stable yard to the waiting chaise. With not a little merriment they arrived breathless at the front door of Newton Manor House.

"Decorum, Mrs Bemment," Fred teased as he knocked upon the oak door quite unabashed they were not using the servants entrance.

Annie smoothed down her skirt, felt her veil was in place and her posy was the right way round. Fred kissed her cheek. "You look roite boo'iful, Mrs Bemment." Both blushed when the butler opened the door.

"Good afternoon, Hanson. Mr an' Mrs Bemment to see Lord an' Lady de Vessey an' the Misses de Vessey."

Hanson inclined his head, smiled and said "Congratulations."

"Thank yew, Hanson."

"May you both be very happy. Step into the hall. I will announce you."

The couple waited nervously.

Hanson knocked on the drawing room door and stepped

inside.

"My lord, my lady, you have visitors, special visitors."

Lady Marion looked up expectantly, his lordship raised his eyebrows quizzically.

"Mr and Mrs Bemment have called to present their compliments to you and the young ladies."

Lady Marion's face lit up with delight. "Annie has kept her word." She reached to pull the bell.

Lord Ralph turned to their guests, "If you will excuse us for a moment." He rose. "Hanson, we will receive them in the library."

A footman peeked round the door in response to the bell.

"Oh, Haggard, will you tell Nannie Ethel we need to see the girls, now. Please escort them down to the library."

"Yes, m'lady."

Hanson opened the link door between the drawing room and library for Marion and Ralph to slip through in preparation to greet the newlyweds; a young couple they held dearly in their hearts.

Hanson returned to the hall. "Please, follow me," he directed Fred and Annie.

The moment they crossed the threshold to the library Marion stepped forward with outstretched arms. "Annie, you look radiant," and kissed her children's Nannie as an equal.

Lord Ralph put out a hand to Fred's and shook it warmly. "Congratulations, young man. Slip this in your pocket," he said as he handed him an envelope." You have a fine woman in Annie. Love and cherish her every day of your life. You'll have no regrets."

Further conversation was curtailed as shrieks of excitement emanated from the hall. "Look, look! It's

Nannie Annie's wedding carriage," Rosamund's voice pierced the stillness of the hall as she caught a glimpse of the chaise waiting on the drive.

Hanson waited by the open library door as the girls peered at the carriage through the window adjacent to the front door. He cleared his throat. Rosamund responded by running into the library. Judith followed more slowly accompanied by Averil.

"Annie, you came."

"Oi said oi would," Annie bent to embrace her charges.

"You look like a princess."

"Thank you, Judith. Now yew be good fer Nannie Ethel an oi will see yew in a few days toime."

"You will come back won't you, Nannie Annie?" Anxiously Rosamund clung to Annie's arm.

"O' course."

Knowing the affectionate bond that developed between their eldest daughter and Annie following her traumatic birth Lady Marion reached out kindly but firmly with arms around Rosamund and spoke reassuringly,

"Annie always keeps her promises, doesn't she?" Rosamund nodded. "Let us see them to the chaise and wave them off on their wedding holiday." She released her daughter and smiled at the young couple. "We'll look forward to seeing you again in a few days' time."

The girls ran through the front door to the top of the steps and exuberantly shook their arms till the chaise disappeared into the distance.

Fred pulled up Buttercup in the stable yard. He put a hand into his inner pocket. "His lordship handed this to me." He placed the envelope into Annie's hands. "You open it."

"Oh, Fred!" Annie clapped a hand across her mouth in utter astonishment. "It's the deeds fer the cottage!"

"The deeds?" Fred uttered in disbelief.

"Such kindness!"

Fred peered across his wife's shoulder at the document she held. "How God hev blessed us wi' things beyond ow'n imaginin'"

"Yus," tears streamed down Annie's face. "The Good Book says He be able to do exceedin' abundantly above all we ask or think."

Fred put his arms around her. "We will begin each day we hev together thankin' Him fer all His goodness to us."

Printed in Great Britain
by Amazon

52924485R00189